THE BLACK FLOOD

E. A. Rappaport

Book Nine in Legends of the Four Races
Book Three in the Netherworld Trilogy
Book Three in the Necromancer Trilogy

To Victoria,
keep on reading!

Owl King Publishing, LLC
Orange, CT

The Black Flood
Book Nine in Legends of the Four Races
Book Three in the Netherworld Trilogy
Book Three in the Necromancer Trilogy

Copyright © 2017 E. A. Rappaport
All Rights Reserved. No part of this book may be reproduced in any form without permission in writing from the copyright holder, except for brief quotations in reviews or news articles.

Copyright # Pending

ISBN: 978-0-9789393-9-7 (Paperback)

Library of Congress Control Number: 2017905077

First Owl King Publishing Edition: June 2017

Acknowledgments

Cover painting by:
Kamui Ayami

Special thanks to:
Irma Rappaport

Please visit **http://www.owlking.com** for information about:
- The Netherworld Trilogy
- The Necromancer Trilogy
- Legends of the Four Races
- Interlocking Matrix

For My Daughter, Hannah

Contents

Chapter I	Strangers	1
Chapter II	Thoroughly Dead	13
Chapter III	Closing Doors	24
Chapter IV	The Missing Arboreal	34
Chapter V	On the Trail of an Arboreal	47
Chapter VI	The Price of Power	58
Chapter VII	Ruins	65
Chapter VIII	Back from the Dead	78
Chapter IX	Good Intentions	87
Chapter X	Return of the Dead	95
Chapter XI	Return to Hillswood	103
Chapter XII	Ancient Wisdom	114
Chapter XIII	Remains of the Dead	124
Chapter XIV	For the Greater Good	134
Chapter XV	Up in Flames	144
Chapter XVI	The Fall of Luceton	155
Chapter XVII	Netherworld Released	168
Chapter XVIII	On the Trail of Fracodians	179
Chapter XIX	The Siege of Kroflund	189
Chapter XX	Temptation	201

Chapter XXI	Rise of the Demons	212
Chapter XXII	The Black Flood	225
Chapter XXIII	Teruns vs Demons	236
Chapter XXIV	Betrayal	248
Chapter XXV	The Demon Prince	259
Chapter XXVI	Starting Anew	273

Chapter I

Strangers

Chara stared into the mirror as she held a razor to her blond hair, just below her ear. Her grandfather had loved her long locks and so did she, but it only augmented the differences between her and everyone else in town. As the last of the humans living among the warrior race of Ferfolk, Chara knew she'd never truly fit in. She pressed the razor against the closest strands of hair, relaxing her grip when she noticed a nick in the blade. A dull edge might snag against her hair and tug at her scalp, but the pain would only be temporary. A knock on the door distracted her from the dilemma.

She thrust her head out the window to see who had interrupted her grooming. Her neighbor, an old Ferfolk woman, stood at the doorstep holding a small basket.

"Good morning, Chara. I've brought over a few extra eggs."

"That's very kind of you," said Chara. "I'll be right there."

She tossed the razor onto her table and headed for the front door, tripping over a chair that always seemed to be in the way. Chara kicked the chair aside before opening the door.

"Do come in," she said as she took the basket from her neighbor.

The old woman wore a tan shirt and rugged pants that covered most of her leathery skin, and her short black hair barely made it down to her ears. Many years ago she'd lost all her children in the war against the Arboreals, the long-time enemies of the Ferfolk, yet Chara couldn't remember seeing her without a smile on her face.

"Are you eating enough?" she asked and wrapped her fingers around Chara's arm. "You look too thin."

"Too thin for what?" asked Chara. "I don't plan to join Aiax's army, even if they decided to accept me."

She couldn't recall any females and certainly no humans allowed into the elite ranks. The Ferfolk had always been a proud race of warriors, slow to change their ancient customs and unwilling to trust anyone different from themselves. Men fought the battles, and women tended to the equipment. Chara would never advocate violence, but she definitely didn't dream of being subservient to anyone. She brought the basket of eggs into her kitchen and fished around the cabinets for something to eat, finding only part of a stale loaf.

"Would you care for some bread?" she called out. "I'm afraid I don't have much more to offer."

"No, dear, I have many chores scheduled for today. Take care."

Chara rushed back to the door, stubbing her toe against the toppled chair. The old woman had already left, probably gone to make a batch of food to bring over tomorrow. She reminded Chara of her grandfather, always busy and always pushing her to eat more. A massive wave had carried him out to sea along with many Ferfolk from her former home of Luceton. She missed living on the shore but knew it would bring back too many sad memories if she ever returned.

After choking down a few bites of the stale bread, she returned to her bedroom mirror. She ran her fingers down the smooth skin of her face and through strands of hair that rested on her shoulder. Her reflection was the only human she'd ever see. Why bother changing herself to be more like the Ferfolk? They'd never fully accept her into their society. The thought of remaining isolated until she died sent a ripple of depression through her body, forcing her to look away.

Her stomach gurgled, angry at the scant morsels of old bread tumbling around. Chara needed something more substantial to eat but didn't want to bother her neighbor. She grabbed a pouch of coins and left the house.

The morning sun had long since broken the horizon, although thick white clouds hid it from view. As she strolled along the cobblestones, voices from the busy market nearby echoed throughout the streets. The solidly-built brick houses conveyed a sense of strength as opposed to the ramshackle fishing huts of Luceton. One could never mistake this town for anything other than the home of warriors. She stumbled on a loose stone, kicked it aside, and kept going.

Several blocks away, a young mother pulled her child to the far side of the street so as not to cross paths with the human. Chara was used to sneers and suspicious glances in her direction, but this behavior was a new low. She managed to smile at the pair, who ducked into a swordsmith's shop to escape any possibility of interaction.

The whispers between Ferfolk increased as Chara approached the center of town. She tried to ignore them but found it harder and harder to maintain her smile. Her cheek muscles ached from forcing her lips to curl upward. Resolved to end this discrimination, she marched toward a group of three men that kept glancing at her during their rounds of hushed words.

"What's with all the secrets today?" she asked, placing her hands on her hips. "I'm the same person who moved here a year ago, and I doubt you're planning a surprise party for me."

The men looked at one another. Ferfolk would never show fear, especially toward a human female, but they seemed ready to bolt at the slightest provocation. Their tough, wrinkled skin made it difficult to determine their age, but two of them had graying hair, old enough to have seen a few battles against the Arboreals.

"No parties," said the younger man. "We were just...discussing...a new deal with the Teruns."

The other two nodded, their artificial grins cloaking whatever emotions they tamped down.

Secret business with Teruns? Doubtful. The short gray Teruns lived beneath the Pensorean Mountains, forever expanding their precious mines. All the other races came to them for metal supplies ranging from gardening tools to weapons of the highest quality. Even the beast-like Fracodians traded with them, remaining civilized when in their presence. The Teruns knew they offered the best equipment and signed tough deals even against the most skilled negotiators. These three lunks would give away half the town if they ever tried to match wits with a Terun merchant.

"Well, best of luck to you," said Chara. "Have a good day."

She shot her hand up to wave at them, causing the men to jump backward.

"I knew it," she said. "You were speaking about me. You're scared of me for some reason, and I doubt it's because you think I'll wrestle you to the ground."

"We're not scared of anything," said one of the older men. "We just don't want to be turned into hideous creatures."

"That makes even less sense than a secret deal with the Teruns." Chara stepped closer to them. "What were you saying about me?"

"If we tell you, do you promise to go on your way and leave us alone?"

"Why wouldn't I?"

The two non-speakers took another step backward.

"After a funeral last week, the body came back to life at night," said the older Ferfolk. "Since nobody else in town could have performed such a despicable act, it had to have been you. We're not judging your motives. We just want to be left alone."

Only a wizard could have animated a dead body, but with an innate resistance to magic, no Ferfolk had the gift of wizardry. Neither had Chara.

"You think I'm a necromancer?" She chuckled as she walked away from the group. "Go back to your negotiations with the Teruns. I'm sure you'll do fine."

That put a smile back on her face. She'd never intimidated anything larger than a striped bass caught on her fishing line. More than being amusing, however, the story might have meant that her friend Jarlen had returned. Half human and half Arboreal, Jarlen was the only necromancer in the world. Chara hadn't seen him in a few years, but such an extended time might have meant nothing to him. The green-skinned race of Arboreals lived far longer than any of the other races. Years to anyone else might have felt like days to them. Still, he and the rest of the Arboreals celebrated life and nature. He'd never defile a grave or turn an innocent Ferfolk into a monster. Perhaps this story was nothing more than a rumor to further alienate her from everyone else in town.

Chara continued down the road, ignoring the secretive stares and hushed voices, until she reached a farm stand attended by a young couple. She assumed they'd be less likely to fall prey to superstitions than the older Ferfolk. A mix of root vegetables and several varieties of apples barely filled half their cart, which sported a broken handle in front. Chara peered over the side to peruse the selection, by far the most meager of the entire outdoor market.

"Are you looking for something in particular?" asked the wife.

The husband edged in front of her without taking his eyes

off Chara. He didn't seem enamored with their new customer. So much for being more tolerant.

"Anything that tastes good," said Chara, "without having to spend hours preparing it."

Around them, Ferfolk stood in short lines at each stand, waiting to purchase their produce. These two should be thanking her for even considering their goods, not wondering if she's going to cast a spell on them.

"Try this one," said the husband as he handed her a bright yellow apple. "You won't find anything sweeter outside of the Arboreal Forest."

"You've been there?" asked Chara.

As bitter rivals for the past couple centuries, the Arboreals and Ferfolk didn't generally intermingle. She took the fruit and brought it up to her nose, breathing in the faint scent of honey.

"I've tasted what my competition has to offer," said the husband, "and I've heard stories about the Arboreal gardeners. Go ahead, try it. If it's not the best you've ever had, I'll dump the rest of these fruits into the street for the rats to enjoy."

Chara bit into the fruit, receiving a blast of tartness that gave way to a mouthful of sweet juice. The apple, like this Ferfolk farmer, surprised her.

"I'll take a dozen," she said. "Do you have anything to carry them?"

"You may borrow one of our baskets," said the husband, "but please return it. We can't afford to buy a replacement."

"That's very trusting of you," said Chara, "especially since I'm human."

She handed a few coins to the wife in exchange for a wicker basket with so many loose strands it appeared ready to unravel at any moment. This couple had obviously put all their effort into their crops. Their home was probably in shambles, as well.

Chara had to do something for them, and she knew just what would help.

After piling the apples into the basket, she walked around the marketplace and handed out samples to the Ferfolk at the back of each line. Many refused to accept anything from her, probably thinking the fruit was cursed, but the few who took bites immediately headed for the young couple's cart. She still had a few apples left when several of the other farmers surrounded her.

"Stay away from our customers," said a Ferfolk with particularly leathery skin. "You have no right to sell anything here."

"I'm not selling the apples," said Chara. "I'm giving them away for free. Since when can't someone give food to the hungry."

"They're not hungry."

Chara tried to squeeze through the group of men, but they crowded together, cutting off any chance to escape. Another farmer knocked the basket out of her hands. He clearly intended to intimidate her, but she neither flinched nor struck back. She'd lived among the Ferfolk long enough to become used to their childish behavior. The apples rolled along the street until a flurry of angry feet stomped on them.

"I expect you to pay for those," said Chara.

The farmer laughed. "You said you were giving them away for free...so I took them. I'll take the basket, as well."

He latched onto the basket handle, but Chara didn't let go when he pulled. The wicker flew apart, sending out a spray of fine, wooden hairs.

"What's the problem here," came a familiar voice from outside the circle of farmers. "Step aside."

A hole opened up between two of the men, and a tall figure capped by raven hair squeezed through. Tyraz! She hadn't seen him in more than a year. Whiskers covered most of his cheeks and chin, and he'd upgraded his armor from well-worn leather to shiny chain links.

"Chara," said the young Ferfolk warrior. "I didn't expect you to be causing trouble."

"I'm not responsible for this mess," she said. "These...men...destroyed my basket and trampled my fruit."

She kicked a flattened apple at the feet of the farmers.

Tyraz pushed a couple of the men aside. He'd grown a few inches recently and added a lot more muscle, so when he told the farmers to return to their stands, they obeyed.

"What about my fruit?" asked Chara. "You're just going to let them get away with it?"

"It would be your word against theirs," said Tyraz as he opened his belt pouch and dug out a few gold coins. "Is this enough?"

"Keep your money. I don't need it."

Chara returned to the young couple, who now had a line of their own, and offered them a gold coin of her own for the basket. They refused, thanking her for sending them so much new business. She bumped into Tyraz when she turned around.

"This is new," he said as he fingered the fishhook attached to a thin chain around her neck.

"It reminds me of home. What are you doing here anyway?" she asked. "Isn't this too small a village for such an important member of the Ferfolk army?"

"I'm trying a more efficient patrolling route," said Tyraz.

He'd shaved his head to be as close-cropped as that of Aiax, the tough commander of the Ferfolk army. Tyraz and Aiax had differing opinions in the past, but he admired the old veteran. Unfortunately, he was no longer the same young man that Chara had befriended before they defeated the lyche, an evil spirit that had vowed to destroy all life. Instead of a cooper's son hoping for a future in the army, he was now a seasoned warrior.

A smile lit his face. "My men will cover more ground in less time," he said. "Everyone in town will be safer."

"Safe from what?" asked Chara. "There's peace between the Ferfolk and the Arboreals, and the lyche is gone. Don't you think it's time to put more effort into helping your citizens?"

She dragged him around the crowd of people to show him the young couple's broken cart.

"What about sending a few warriors to become carpenters' apprentices?" She dug her foot between two cobblestones until one of them loosened. "Or masons."

Tyraz pulled his sleeve from her grip and stepped away from the crowd.

"I'm thankful there's peace now," he said, "but you never know what the future will bring. We have to be prepared."

"So go prepare yourself."

Chara headed back toward her house. She'd lost her appetite.

"It was good seeing you again," Tyraz called out behind her, but she didn't turn around.

If he was unwilling to compromise on his dedication to violence and war, then why should she yield on her pursuit of peace. A flurry of footsteps approached her from behind, followed by a hand on her shoulder.

"Chara," said Tyraz.

Her heart fluttered, expecting an apology or at least an admission of guilt.

"Has Jarlen been in town recently?" he asked.

"Not that I know. Why do you ask?"

"Oh, it's nothing," said Tyraz. "Sorry to bother you."

He turned to leave, but Chara grabbed his arm and yanked him back.

"Why did you ask about Jarlen now, of all times?"

"There were rumors about a dead man coming back to life," said Tyraz. "I'm sure they were only exaggerations, probably someone close to death recovering from whatever had sickened him."

"I heard the same rumors, but it was after a funeral. Unless his family buried him alive, I doubt he recovered on his own and dug himself out of his grave."

Tyraz's cheeks went pale, but he shook off whatever had spooked him.

"I suppose this warrants further investigation," he said. "Many good thanks for your help."

"I'm coming with you," said Chara.

"This is none of your concern. Besides, you've made it clear how much you detest violence."

"Most of these citizens think I'm to blame for the body coming back to life," said Chara. "And if Jarlen has returned, I'm as much his friend as you are. Where do we start?"

The scowl on Tyraz's face faded when Chara showed no sign of yielding.

"We trace the rumors to their origin," he said.

Excited to be on another adventure, Chara ushered him to the group of men that had confronted her on the way to the market. The worried looks on their faces meant they thought she'd brought a warrior to rough them up. Humans might have shied away, but as proud Ferfolk, they held their ground with fists clenched.

"We only came to ask you a question," said Chara, bringing instant relief to the group. "Where did you hear the story about the corpse coming back to life?"

Neither Chara nor Tyraz recognized the name they offered, but one of the men agreed to introduce them to the person. Unfortunately, he'd heard the rumor from someone else, but after several hours of tracking down one gossiping Ferfolk after another, they met the farmer who'd started it all. An older man with callused hands and cracked nails, he swore he saw his neighbor walking through the fields a day after the funeral. Although there could have been many explanations, the tremble in his voice as he relayed the story had convinced Chara of its truth.

"He clearly saw someone who resembled his neighbor," said Tyraz. "I can't believe I wasted the day on this nonsense."

Chara glared at him. "So spending any time with me is a waste."

"That's not what I meant," said Tyraz. "Aiax will think my new patrolling plan was a failure. I should have continued my rounds and ignored this silly rumor."

"Well, we're here already. We should check out his story."

Chara turned to the farmer. "Where did you see this creature?"

He led them to a distant set of wheat fields, overgrown with weeds.

"I promised to help his family with the harvest," he said, "but I've been so busy with my own crops. I really should get to it before those weeds take over."

After a brief word of thanks, Chara and Tyraz sent the farmer home and entered the wheat field. The thick undergrowth made their progress difficult until Tyraz unsheathed his sword to clear a path. Aiax had given him the special weapon, primarily composed of vistrium, a metal harder and more durable than steel. The sharp blade effortlessly sliced through stems, allowing them to search a larger portion of the field and find their way out when they were done.

They'd gone a few score paces when the pliable wheat stalks turned brittle and the green weeds turned brown.

"Perhaps this part of the field hasn't received as much water," said Chara.

"That may be," said Tyraz as he knelt, "but this might be of importance."

Chara joined him beside the partially decomposed body of an old Ferfolk. She turned her head and held her hand in front of her nose.

"The neighbor?" she asked.

"No doubt."

Tyraz put his arm around her shoulder and ushered her out of the field.

"I'll have my men retrieve the body," he said, "but we have to find out how a dead body made its way here from the graveyard."

Chapter II

Thoroughly Dead

"You don't have to worry about those rumors anymore," said Tyraz as he righted a chair and moved it to the center of the room. "My soldiers and I will find out what happened to that body."

Chara scrambled to find something to use as a table, eventually settling on a half-empty barrel of potatoes. She rarely entertained guests other than her neighbor, who'd given her the barrel as a housewarming gift almost a year ago. A fine layer of dust covered the living area other than a narrow path between the front door and the kitchen. Chara hoped he didn't mention the state of her house. She certainly had enough time to clean in the past few months; she just didn't feel it was necessary.

"I wasn't worried," she said. "This is the most excitement I've had since we defeated the lyche. What else do I have to do with my life? Sit around watching vegetables grow?"

She dragged a stool in from the kitchen and placed a plate of boiled eggs on the barrel. Tyraz raised his eyebrows, indicating his concern about her hospitality. He'd argued that she shouldn't have moved so far from the center of town, but she ignored his pleas. At the time, she wanted to put as much distance between them as possible without moving all the way back to Luceton. The fewer people around her, the less she had to deal with their discrimination.

As she sat on the stool, she bent her leg out to the side, displaying a tattoo of a green vine on her calf. The artwork covered up a nasty scar that she'd received from a fishing accident when she was younger.

Tyraz glanced at her leg before turning his head as he cracked open an egg and bit off the top half.

"In any case," he said, "this is a matter for the army to resolve."

Chara kicked the barrel, sending the remaining eggs onto the floor to pick up a coating of dust.

"Everything comes down to violence with you," she said. "What if Jarlen has gotten back from his...wherever he went? I'm sure he would have a good reason for what he did–no need for swords or armies–just a peaceful discussion with our mutual friend."

"You're right," said Tyraz as he collected the eggs and returned them to the plate, rubbing them off as best he could. "But I'm responsible for the town's safety. I have to assume the worst."

"And what's the worst?"

"That we never actually defeated the lyche."

"But we both saw that demon drag it to the bottom of the sea. It couldn't have survived."

"What if it escaped? Or what if Jarlen never sent the demon back to the netherworld?"

"Maybe this time Aiax will listen to your warning," said Chara. "Maybe the demon and the lyche joined forces. Aiax will have to send the entire army against those fiends. Maybe we should get the Arboreals involved, as well, and the Teruns. Let's alert everyone before it's too late to get them armed and ready for glorious battle."

He returned her smile with a frown. It was only a little joke. He shouldn't have taken it so seriously.

"Fine," she said. "We'll wait until we learn a bit more before going to war."

"This was probably just an innocent prank some youngsters played on that farmer. If I leave here to finish my investigation, would you promise to stay out of it?"

He couldn't be serious. Maybe that was his playful response to her joke. Chara shook her head once to each side.

"Then come along," said Tyraz. "We'll speak to the groundskeeper next."

They reached the cemetery by late afternoon and had to wait for a funeral to complete before speaking with the groundskeeper, a man with skin as pale as a Terun's and clothing caked with soil. He led them into his house, a small hut near the border of the woods, and offered them mugs of spiced ale.

"How can I help the army?" he asked. "I'm not often visited by a soldier."

"One of the bodies that was recently buried here has been found in the middle of the wheat fields closer to town," said Tyraz. "Do you know anything about it?"

"Only that it's bad luck to disturb the dead. Who moved the body?" asked the groundskeeper. "And why?"

Chara took a sip of the ale and spit it back into the cup. She preferred her drinks without any added flavoring. Tyraz finished his in two swigs, yet another difference between them.

"Rumor has it that the body moved itself," he said, "but I think it must have been kids. The farmer swears he didn't see anyone else in the field."

The groundskeeper refilled Tyraz's mug.

"If it wasn't a person," he said, "then it's most likely an animal. Some hungry wolf must have dug it up and dragged it away before realizing it wouldn't make a good meal. I can understand how someone might have thought the body had moved by itself."

"A perfectly reasonable explanation," said Tyraz. "Many good thanks."

He pushed away from the table, but Chara remained seated.

"Have you seen anything out of the ordinary these past few weeks?" she asked. "Including any hungry wolves. I've never heard of any animals sniffing around a cemetery for food."

"Maybe a few strange sounds at night," said the groundskeeper, "but these woods hold many secrets, especially with the Arboreal Forest creeping closer every year. You're welcome to stay as long as you'd like, but I'll be retiring at dusk. I rise before the sun each morning."

Tyraz helped Chara up from the table.

"You're not thinking of spending the night here," he said. "This mystery has been solved."

"Then maybe I'll get to see a hungry wolf." She led him to the edge of the woods. "Feel free to return home. I can always call for the groundskeeper if I need protection from a dangerous animal."

"One night," said Tyraz. "And we put this incident behind us in the morning. The rumors will eventually die out on their own."

Chara weaved around the trees, brushing her fingers against the rough bark. Jarlen could have been hiding in the branches above their heads, and they wouldn't have known. The Arboreals coexisted with nature in a way that humans and Ferfolk could never comprehend. They turned invisible and silent when in the trees without the use of magic, blending perfectly into their surroundings. Being half human, Jarlen had always complained about fitting in with the Arboreals, but Chara wouldn't have been surprised if he dropped down from a branch this very moment.

"Don't bother looking for him," said Tyraz. "He's not

around."

"I know." Chara gave him a coy smile, wondering if his curt statement showed a hint of jealousy. "But what else are we going to do while we wait for the wolf to show up for his next meal?"

"I'll get some food, both for us and to make it more enticing for any animals that might be near." Tyraz headed toward the center of town. "I'll be back before dark."

After finishing a quick bite that Tyraz had picked up from the market before it closed, they laid out strips of dried meat one hundred paces away from the edge of the woods. If a hungry animal had caused the rumors, the free meal would definitely attract its attention.

Darkness brought an eerie gloom to the cemetery. Chara knew she had nothing to fear, but her mind replayed visions of their battle against the lyche. With the ability to combine living creatures with the dead, the lyche's army often haunted her nightmares. She hoped the wolf would show up early, giving them closure to this little adventure.

"You can go to sleep when you're tired," said Tyraz. "I'll take the first watch."

"Only if you promise to wake me when it's my turn."

He hesitated before nodding, belying his intention to remain awake until dawn.

"Nah," said Chara. "I don't like being woken up from a good dream. You sleep first–I insist."

She returned his gaze with an unflinching stare, indicating her unwillingness to negotiate. With a sigh, he laid his sword on the ground and closed his eyes. Chara sat against a trunk across from him, thinking about how their relationship would have progressed if they'd resolved their differences. Maybe she was just as discriminating as the Ferfolk.

"I can't fall asleep when you're staring at me," said Tyraz.

"I'm not," said Chara while she shifted her body around the trunk to face the woods.

A warm breeze rustled the leaves before caressing her skin on its way through the cemetery. Chara slumped back against the oak and enjoyed the serene night. An owl hooted nearby, while a chorus of crickets chirped continuously. If nothing else, this quest reminded her to spend more time outdoors. Although she preferred rocking atop the waves in a sturdy boat, anywhere in nature was more inviting than stuck within the confines of a city.

Chara wasn't sure if she'd dozed off, but a loud clawing or scratching noise startled her. She crawled over to Tyraz and tapped his arm.

"Time for us to switch already?" he asked with a yawn.

"I heard something," said Chara. "Towards the center of the graveyard."

Tyraz grabbed his sword and jumped up.

"Stay here," he said.

"And miss the fun? Never."

"I don't want to worry about you if there's any danger."

"Then hand over that dagger of yours."

Tyraz put his hand over the hilt of his dagger, sheathed against his belt opposite his sword.

"I've filleted enough fish to know how to handle an oversized knife," said Chara, holding out her hand.

"Just keep your voice down." Tyraz flipped the dagger over in his grip and handed it to her hilt first. "And stay three paces behind me—I need enough room to swing my sword."

They tiptoed past the strips of meat, untouched by any animals, on their way into the cemetery. Silvery rays from the moon reflected off the headstones, providing enough light to see without the need for a torch. A single pass around the graves yielded nothing. No hungry animals digging for food, no more strange sounds, and even the crickets had gone to bed.

"You probably fell asleep and heard the noises in your dreams," said Tyraz. "Go ahead and get some rest. I'll stay up until morning."

On their way back to the campsite, Chara noticed that the owl had joined the crickets in silence. She tugged on Tyraz's sleeve to stop him. No sounds came from anywhere around them.

"Something's not right," said Chara. "It's too quiet."

She strained to hear the faintest squeak or chirp and was rewarded by a few more scratches nearby. Tyraz must have heard the sounds, as well, and rushed toward the freshly dug grave from the previous day's funeral. He unsheathed his sword. Something was moving below ground, disturbing the loosely packed soil.

Chara's heart raced as she clenched the dagger. It was no wolf that had moved the other body. She gazed around the cemetery, expecting to see Jarlen, but they were alone. Another round of scratching ended with a pale hand breaking through the topsoil of the grave.

"I don't believe it," said Tyraz. "The rumors were true."

"But how is it possible? Is there another necromancer around here? I thought only Jarlen could summon creatures from the netherworld."

The hand jerked back and forth, opening a small hole to allow its counterpart into the night air. All ten fingernails came to sharp points, and a row of bumps traveled from the back of the hands down the arms. Eventually the body pulled itself up from the grave. Either it wasn't a Ferfolk or it had been transformed somehow. Bright red eyes glowed from the center of a triangular face, spikes tore through its clothing at each joint, and its leathery skin had shrunk to the point of barely fitting around its bones.

Tyraz didn't wait for the creature to attack. He swung the sword at its neck. The creature raised its hand to block the heavy swing and let out an infernal howl when the blade sliced through its fingers. Chara stepped backward to give Tyraz more room. Normally, she opposed violence, but it seemed appropriate against this vile being. A few well-placed blows from Tyraz removed the creature's legs and arms, and a final swing took off its head. He retreated next to Chara and planted his sword blade down in the grass, keeping his eyes fixed on the dismembered corpse.

Chara wanted to look away but found her eyes drawn to the remains. For more than an hour they watched for any signs of movement, but the body finally appeared to be at rest. Tyraz approached the grave, fell to his knees, and dug through the soil with his hands. When he'd opened a hole large enough to fit the remains, he buried the creature and quickly covered it up.

"There's no point feeding into these rumors," he said as he wiped his hands on the grass.

Chara handed back his dagger and gave him a stern glance, conveying her feelings without a single word. She wouldn't listen to him if he intended to send her home. This was no longer an innocent little adventure for the two of them, and she was unwilling to give up without answers.

"Come on then," he said. "If we leave now, we'll reach the complex by sunup."

The hike through the outskirts of Krofhaven, the largest city in Ferfolk lands, brought them to a path along the Sinewan River. From its source in the northern Pensorean Mountains, the river turned east when it hit the hills of Krofhaven and flowed through the Arboreal Forest, eventually emptying into the Great Ocean. Many fishing shacks lined the riverbank, making Chara long for the days when she and her grandfather would head offshore in their little boat. She didn't even realize she'd slowed down until Tyraz had disappeared up the trail.

"Wait for me," she called out and trotted toward him.

The morning sun brightened the eastern sky as they entered the city proper. After a few clusters of merchant shops, they came to the fortified wall separating the military compound from the rest of the civilians. The army grounds easily took up half the city with guards posted along the wall at all times. The two soldiers watching the front gate didn't seem happy to see Tyraz, but they greeted him with a respectful salute. Inside the compound, teams of men repeated sets of calisthenics on the few patches of grass, while their superiors barked out orders. Chara cringed at the strict regimen, happy to be free of such rigid structure.

Tyraz led her to the command center, a stark gray building with few windows and an extra set of guards outside the front door. Although the rest of the city had probably not eaten breakfast yet, Aiax was sure to be busy at work, always finding something to occupy his army. By the time they reached his room, they'd collected a following of six soldiers. Tyraz asked that they remain outside while he spoke with the commander.

Chara followed him into the room and closed the door behind her. Aiax looked as imposing as ever. Taller and more muscular than Tyraz, he wore a full suit of hardened leather armor that blended with his skin. His left hand was missing two fingers, and the terrible scar ran up his arm until it disappeared into his sleeve. The back of Chara's leg itched, but she resisted the urge to scratch.

"Greetings, Chara," said Aiax in a gruff voice. "It's always a pleasure to see you."

He swept a few scrolls aside and strolled forward.

"I expected you back yesterday, Tyraz. The last time the two of you showed up unexpectedly, you didn't bear good news. I suppose now is no different–so let's get on with it."

"You've heard the rumors about a dead body coming to life?" asked Tyraz, matching the commander's stance with feet spread apart and hands crossed in front of his body.

He clearly looked up to Aiax more than his own father, a talented woodworker with a popular shop in the merchant district.

"I have," said Aiax. "What about them?"

"They're not just rumors," said Tyraz. "Chara and I came straight from a cemetery outside of town where a recently interred body dug itself out of the grave and attacked us."

"Is this true, Chara?" asked Aiax. "Not the result of an evening of drinking after your reunion."

Chara felt blood rush to her cheeks, surely turning her face red. She looked away before the other two noticed.

"It wasn't much of a reunion," she said. "Tyraz stopped a group of disgruntled farmers from intimidating me. Then we investigated the rumor together. Everything happened as he told you."

Aiax brought his three fingers up to his chin and stroked his stubble. Chara hoped Tyraz didn't copy that move. The scratching noise irritated her.

"I can think of only one expert in these matters," said Aiax.

"Jarlen," said Chara. "We thought it might have been him, but we didn't see him anywhere."

"Whether he animated the body or not," said Aiax, "we should consult him. Given our strained relations with the Arboreals, you two would make the best emissaries. Do you accept–"

"Absolutely," said Chara. "When do we start?"

Tyraz put his hands together in the formal gesture to accept an order, prompting Aiax to return to his desk and fish for a blank scroll. He wrote a few words, rolled it up, and handed it to Tyraz.

"Please extend this invitation to Jarlen," he said, "but if he's unable to return with you, get as many answers from him as you can. I trust you'll keep this information from the general populace until we know more?"

"We will," said Tyraz, "and we'll be back with Jarlen within the fortnight. He'll know what's going on."

Chapter III

Closing Doors

Jarlen couldn't determine if he was awake or dreaming. Darkness surrounded his body, and he felt nothing. No warmth or chills, no breezes, and no sensations of rising or falling touched him. He fluttered his eyelids, but everything looked the same whether they were opened or closed. A moment of panic overtook his mind. What if he'd accidentally killed himself? He'd followed the incantations precisely, and he clearly had moved from his original location. He reached outward, feeling for anything around his body–a page from the book, a leaf, even a simple pebble would have given him hope, but his fingers encountered nothing but emptiness.

"Hello," he called out. "Can anybody hear me?"

His voice sounded muted, as if he were shouting through five layers of cloth. Maybe he shouldn't have tried this spell on his own, but he didn't want to put any other lives at risk. He had to succeed. Placing his hands on his knees, he closed his eyes and took deep breaths. If he were dead, why would he need to breathe? Then again, if he'd left his body behind, he wouldn't need a single puff of air to fill his lungs. He sealed his mouth shut, forced himself to stop breathing, and waited.

He knew something had changed when a flush of warmth brushed against his cheek and a spot of light prompted his eyes to open. Around him, fountains of lava burst upward from between hexagonal islands of hardened rock. A bright red tinge dominated the sky, fading to dull gray where dim mountains shot up from the horizon. He'd successfully sent his spirit to the netherworld without having died.

When he attempted to move from his current spot, however, his feet met no resistance from the ground and left him stationary. His legs pivoted back and forth, but his body didn't budge. When he stretched his hand downward, his fingers ignored the hardened lava yet stopped at his shoe. Was there nothing in the netherworld that he could interact with? He reached out toward the edge of his island and waited for a fountain of lava to spew from the ground. The liquid rock sailed through his hand, bringing with it an intense blast of heat. Jarlen yanked his hand back and flexed his fingers in front of his face. The lava hadn't left a mark, making him wonder if he imagined the burning sensation. He reached out once more, repeating in his mind that the lava couldn't affect him, but it again bubbled up through his hand and brought severe pain. Once he learned how to move, he still had to avoid anything that would harm his body.

As frustration set in, Jarlen flailed his limbs in a swimming motion and rolled his body both sideways and head over heels, but everything he tried left him in the same spot on the island. It wouldn't help that he'd breached the gap between worlds if he wasn't able to move around. He might as well have remained in his own world.

If he could only figure out how to get to the next island, he'd be happy. It didn't matter how fast he moved, as long as he didn't remain trapped where he was. He focused his gaze on the center of the adjacent island, willing himself closer. His eyes burned as he forced his eyelids to remain open until the ground shifted below him. He did it! Excited, he kept concentrating and eventually drifted from one island to the next. He could finally begin his quest to permanently seal his world off from evil spirits.

As time went by, Jarlen's mobility improved. He coordinated his crossings between islands to occur just after a burst of lava, allowing him to escape any contact with the scalding liquid. Unfortunately, he didn't know where to go, so he started by examining the closest islands and circling outward. He wasn't even sure he'd be able to recognize a portal from this side until he landed on an island somewhat different from the others.

The air around his body shimmered, casting off rays of blue, green, and purple in addition to the ever present red tinge. This had to be a portal, but he didn't know if it led back to his world or someplace else. It didn't matter. He'd close it anyway. Any other world connected to the netherworld had to be at risk, as well. Gathering his thoughts, he closed his eyes, spread his arms, and began the incantation. He repeated the mystical phrases several times before checking his results. The shimmering had disappeared, leaving the island no different from its neighbors. Jarlen smiled. His months of research and practice had paid off. He'd discovered a way to seal the rifts between worlds.

He circled through the islands until he noticed a small group of creatures coming towards him. Three of them rode reptilian beasts so large that the distance from their heads to their tails spanned two islands. The mounts trotted forward with an awkward gait from four legs of different lengths. Behind them strode a half dozen frog shaped demons with glowing red eyes and glistening bodies.

Jarlen thought he could outrun the newcomers but didn't feel like losing his place on the islands. He'd read stories about how the netherworld landscape was always changing and worried that he might not return to the same spot. The creatures couldn't touch him, so he had no reason to fear them. He folded his arms across his chest and waited for them to arrive.

A triangular head with spikes at each corner topped the

gaunt body of the lead rider, while icy crystals covered the other two riders. The mounted demons took up positions on the surrounding islands, interspersed with the frog shaped demons, which leered at Jarlen as they licked their lips with long tongues.

"Leave me to my business," said Jarlen, wondering if they could even hear him. "I have no quarrels with you."

One of the reptilian mounts stretched its head across the gap between islands, ignoring any splatters of lava that touched its skin. It sniffed the air a few times, grunted, and lowered its neck, allowing the triangular headed demon to slide down to the ground. The rider carried a two-pronged pole arm, which it thrust into Jarlen's midsection. The metal tip slipped into his body as if it had been swung through the air.

"I'm not really here," said Jarlen with a smile. "You can't harm me."

"We're not here to fight," said the lead rider. His circular mouth didn't move when the words came out. "We're here to escort you back to the city."

Jarlen glanced over the demon's shoulder.

"What city?"

As soon as the lead rider pointed the pole arm backwards, the dim outline of buildings appeared. Jarlen rubbed his eyes. He was certain the city wasn't there a moment ago.

"Will you come with us?" asked the rider.

"And if I don't?"

"Then our master will come to you," said the rider, "but he won't be pleased."

Jarlen stared at the city. A dark wall surrounded a collection of oddly shaped buildings, which rose from the ground at strange angles toward the sky. It seemed as if his work was going to be delayed no matter if he followed the demons or not.

"Will you show me this same spot when I'm done speaking with your master?" he asked.

The lead demon jammed the tip of the pole arm into the ground, leaving the weapon to guide Jarlen back.

"Fine," he said. "I have much to complete before I return home, so let's get this meeting done with. Lead the way."

With the icy riders behind him, the frog demons to his sides, and the triangular headed demon in front, Jarlen floated from one island to the next toward the netherworld city. They'd covered half the distance when the reptilian demon in front reared, forcing the rest of the group to stop. The demon rider attempted to calm the beast, but soon the other two mounts joined the first one clawing at the ground and snorting heavily.

With all efforts focused on the mounts, none of the demons noticed a dark speck in the sky approaching rapidly.

"Something's coming," said Jarlen but nobody listened to him.

He stared at the dark speck as it plummeted downward. An obsidian-skinned humanoid with arms outstretched flew directly toward the lead rider, knocking him off his mount. The two crashed into the lava between islands but only the black demon rose from the ground. Sharp teeth filled his evil grin as he plunged his clawed fingers into the chest of the nearest frog demon. The other frog demons and the icy riders fled the scene.

"You didn't think I'd notice if you returned here?" said the black demon.

It surprised Jarlen that he didn't recognize the creature, which stood more than a head taller than him. The demon washed his hands in the lava, flicking off pieces of rock as they hardened. Short spikes dotted his spine from the base of his back up to his neck.

"Do I know you?" asked Jarlen.

"I'm the one who will take your life and torture your spirit for the rest of eternity. You will never again know peace."

The demon clearly wanted revenge for something, but Jarlen wasn't worried. His body lay safe in his own world.

"I'm done with these distractions," said Jarlen. "If you have nothing else to say, then leave me to my work."

The demon took a swipe at him, raking him across his abdomen. As Jarlen expected, the attack caused no damage. He spun around with his arms outstretched and grinned at his attacker.

"So you're not as naïve as I expected," said the black demon, "but that doesn't mean you're safe from me. One must protect one's mind, as well."

The demon's confidence worried Jarlen. He willed himself to the next island, but once again his body wouldn't move. A sharp pain ran from his head down to his feet.

"What have you done?" he called out.

"Let's just say we're matching wits," said the demon, "and I'm winning."

Jarlen bent forward and clutched at his skull as what felt like a thousand shards of glass pierced his brain, until he could take no more and screamed. Beside him, the black demon's smirk spread even wider.

"Obidicut," shouted a nearby voice. "Release him at once."

Several islands away, a bloated gold lizard crawled toward them. Its belly dragged against the ground, while its tongue tasted the air every few steps.

"And what if I don't?" asked Obidicut. "What if I tear his mind apart? You can't punish me any more than what I've already gone through."

"Maybe I don't feel like punishing you," said the gold lizard. "Maybe I feel like destroying you."

Obidicut faced his opponent, freeing Jarlen in the process.

"You wouldn't dare break our ancient pact," he said. "The other princes would come after you–all of you."

"Would they?" The gold lizard stepped onto the same island as Obidicut and reared up. "Or would they assume this was part of our previous encounter? Are you willing to risk your one remaining body? Go now and you might still win my favor one day. Do you want a place in my new realm or not?"

Obidicut grumbled as he glared at Jarlen. Eventually he leaped into the sky, soaring over several islands before disappearing into the distance.

"I was afraid he might go after you," said the gold lizard. "I shouldn't have sent my guards to fetch you. I should have come myself."

"You seem familiar," said Jarlen, "but I don't recall meeting any golden lizards."

"You called for my aid against Obidicut in your world, but I left my body behind."

"You must be Mammon." Jarlen circled the demon but still didn't recognize him. "And Obidicut was the lyche."

"He and a wizard's spirit together," said Mammon, "but they've since been separated."

"Many good thanks for the protection," said Jarlen, "but are you here to stop me from my task?"

"Far from it." The gold lizard wrapped its tail around the frog demon that Obidicut had killed. "Do what you must, but beware of Obidicut. I doubt he'll attack you again, but he's been more unpredictable since his return to the netherworld."

Jarlen loathed asking for assistance from the demon, but he couldn't risk becoming trapped by Obidicut or any other adversary.

"How can I protect myself from him in the future?"

Mammon chuckled, sending waves of fat rolling along his

belly.

"You can return home before he immobilizes you, unless you'd agree to an escort while you're here."

"Your guards were ineffective at best," said Jarlen, "but even if you offered yourself, I'd prefer to work alone."

Mammon raised the body of the frog demon into the air, gave a quick frown, and plunged it into the bubbling lava.

"I'm not surprised." He turned back toward the city. "Good luck with your quest, but do not overstay your welcome."

Jarlen watched him retreat. For a demon, he seemed quite hospitable. Mammon must have had a plan, but he'd kept his motives secret. Perhaps if an archfiend wanted him to continue this quest, he should give up immediately and return home. Without more information, Jarlen could only do what he thought best, what he'd studied the past few months. He'd seal the rifts, forever denying demons access to his world.

In all the time Jarlen had spent in the netherworld, he never grew tired or hungry. He knew he should probably rest, but he'd made so much progress closing portals between worlds that he wanted to keep going. Rifts existed in every realm he'd passed through, from the islands in the sea of lava to the snowy mountains to the plains covered by sandy dunes. Each gateway he closed filled him with more confidence. His actions would protect more than just his world.

The horizon had become difficult to see, obscured by an increasing haze, and soon Jarlen was floating through a dense fog, which obstructed any attempt to see past the end of his limbs. The barely visible ground appeared soft and squishy, but his feet never touched anything. He stretched downward with his fingers, but they didn't quite reach the ground. It didn't matter. He wouldn't have been able to feel it anyway. Leaving his body behind had its drawbacks. Without his sense of touch, he couldn't interact with the environment. He was an intruder in the netherworld.

Dull gray surrounded him, draining his will to continue the quest. Perhaps he'd closed enough portals to ensure everyone's safety back home. He stopped moving and allowed himself to drift about aimlessly with his arms and legs outstretched. Any light that had been noticeable in the past was gone, but it didn't matter. There was nothing to look at, nothing to worry about. The stress of completing his quest had dissipated long ago, and he felt as comfortable as he'd ever been. He had difficulty thinking of any reason to return home.

A faint moan disturbed his moment of silence.

"Who's there?" he called out.

His voice sounded harsh and dissonant, jarring him awake. Although a thick cloud still enveloped him, hints of blue and green broke through from the distance. The colors, despite being muted, intrigued him. They shouldn't have been there. Without them, there was a perfect lack of sensation, but now Jarlen could do nothing else but focus on the beautiful hues. The more he stared, the more vivid the colors became until he could just make out a landscape of rolling hills. He urged himself forward, soon distancing himself from the numbing fog.

The grass below his feet appeared so inviting that he wished he could feel each blade brushing against his skin. High above, the pale blue sky stretched from one end of the horizon to the other without a single cloud marring its beauty. Unfortunately, more moaning disrupted the idyllic scene. Jarlen wasn't alone in this paradise.

He continued deeper into the hills until he encountered the first shade. The translucent spirit trudged up a steep slope with its eyes pointed at the ground. Unlike the ones from the Realm of Torture he'd passed through recently, this one didn't gouge out pieces of its own flesh. Jarlen floated to its side.

"Were you moaning just a moment ago?" he asked.

The spirit surprised him by lifting its head and staring at him before continuing its trek through the terrain. A distant screech followed by more groaning meant that more shades roamed this area. As Jarlen proceeded down to the next valley, another dozen spirits joined the first one. Most of them appeared to be human, but a couple could have been Ferfolk. All the shades ignored him except for one that ambled closer and closer with its eyes focused straight ahead.

"You're not one of them," said the shade in an eerie voice, each word causing Jarlen to shiver.

"One of whom?" asked Jarlen.

"The broga masters." The shade looked around. "Return home before it's too late."

Jarlen trembled at the words. Although very little could affect him in the netherworld, this creature's warning seemed to go beyond physical danger to his body or mind.

"Too late for what?" he asked. "You don't even know why I'm here."

"It doesn't matter."

Chapter IV

The Missing Arboreal

Chara and Tyraz left Krofhaven that same afternoon. They barely had time to take a quick nap and pack a day's worth of rations. Both of them had been to Jarlen's hamlet before, but no paths existed in the deep forest. They'd need a guide once they passed into Arboreal territory, but Chara didn't worry about finding someone to help them. The Arboreals were unlikely to let a pair of foreigners wander through their forest for very long before investigating. First, however, they had to reach the border.

They'd made good progress by evening, passing far beyond the southernmost farms, but they hadn't yet reached the Arboreal Forest. Chara searched her sack for a bite to eat, but Tyraz put his hand on her arm and shook his head.

"We should hunt for dinner," he said, "and save this food for later. The Arboreals will never let us take any animals from their forest, and their meals aren't the most appetizing."

Chara knew what he meant. The Arboreals ate only what they could collect from plants and trees, never cooking any of it. Chara enjoyed snacking on a sweet fruit occasionally but preferred a more substantial dinner most days. After setting up camp and lighting a small fire, they sneaked into the woods, making as little noise as possible.

Early evening sounds surrounded them. Deer dined on tender greens; birds settled in for the night, yielding the dark skies to the owls and bats; and frogs croaked in the distance.

Confident their hunt would be successful, Chara tiptoed around trees with Tyraz's dagger in hand. She didn't expect to catch an animal, only to scare it toward her companion, whose walking stick doubled as a spear. Unfortunately, she didn't spy a single creature.

They headed deeper into the forest until the light from the campfire had completely faded, yet they still found no animals.

"They're out here somewhere," said Tyraz, "but they seem to know we're coming for them."

"Maybe we're too noisy."

"I don't think so." Tyraz held her shoulder until she stopped moving. "I've gone on hunts before, and there's always one or two animals either too brave or too ignorant to flee."

They stood for a moment, barely breathing as they listened for a potential target. A soft munching came from nearby, as if a large animal supped on young leaves only a few paces away. Tyraz took one step toward the sound and immediately the crunching noise went silent.

"The animals are extremely skittish today," he said. "I wonder what spooked them."

"Well we won't go hungry," said Chara. "There's always our rations for today and Arboreal food for tomorrow."

A yawn interrupted Tyraz's weak grin.

"Then let's make this trip as short as possible," he said as he headed back to camp. "I can only tolerate their food for a meal or two. Tomorrow will be a long day of hiking. We leave early."

True to his word, Tyraz woke Chara while it was still dark. He smothered the fire, gathered their gear, and hiked southward before the sun showed itself. Every few steps scared dozens of birds out of the trees in all directions, indicating that whatever had spooked the nocturnal animals was still present. When a twig snapped underneath Tyraz's foot, Chara jumped sideways.

"You too?" asked Tyraz.

"Something has to be wrong," said Chara. "Why else would all the animals act so strangely?"

"Add it to the list of questions to ask Jarlen when we reach Hillswood."

Tyraz forged ahead, increasing his pace whenever the underbrush thinned out. Chara darted after him, ignoring any noises she didn't recognize. They stopped only twice, once to finish their rations and once to gather some water from a stream. By mid-afternoon, Chara's muscles ached and she'd picked up a layer of burrs on her pant legs. She was thankful when the underbrush was too thick to pass, giving her a chance to rest while Tyraz cut through it with his sword.

"We're getting close," he said. "Once we pass into the Arboreal Forest, it would be best not to use my blade."

"How do you expect to get through this jumble of weeds?"

"I doubt we'll have to go far on our own." He swung through a thick vine. "The Arboreals are sure to patrol their borders, especially on the northern edge of their territory. Although relations with the Ferfolk have improved these past few years, we're still wary of each other."

He was right about the patrols, but he should have put his sword away earlier. A pair of green skinned Arboreals dropped down from a tree and blocked his weapon with slim swords of their own.

"Why do you cut down our woods?" asked the taller one.

Both Arboreals were slender with long green hair in a single braid. They wore simple outfits that appeared to be cloth but had probably been made from leaves or wood like the rest of their belongings. Their clothing sported no clips, pins, or buttons. Of all the Arboreal's belongings, only their blades were metal, forged in the Pensorean Mountains by the Teruns.

"I didn't realize we had crossed into your territory," said Tyraz as he sheathed his sword.

The Arboreals eyed him suspiciously but shot Chara a quick smile. She recognized the look they gave Tyraz, the same way Ferfolk regarded her. Although she didn't want any trouble between Tyraz and the Arboreals, it felt good to be accepted for who she was.

"Where's the border?" asked Chara. "If you're so protective of your land, perhaps it should have been marked more clearly."

At first, the two Arboreals looked at each other with concern, but their smiles returned as they burst into laughter. Chara shrugged her shoulders at Tyraz, who also seemed confused by their behavior. Their merriment died down when they realized it wasn't shared with the newcomers.

"You're serious," said the taller Arboreal. "I apologize. I thought you were joking with us. We marked our border with a row of ironwoods. You cannot enter our territory without passing through this fence."

"But this forest is full of ironwoods," said Chara. "There's one yonder if I'm not mistaken. How can you–"

Tyraz tapped her on the arm and shook his head.

"It was our oversight," he said. "We promise to be more observant in the future, but we did come with good reason. We're on our way to Hillswood to speak with Jarlen."

"Then you must be Tyraz," said the tall Arboreal with his arm outstretched. "Well met."

Tyraz grasped arms with him and held back, but the Arboreal pulled him close and gave him a firm slap on the back.

"And you must be Chara," said the other Arboreal, extending her a similar welcome. "We've heard the tales about you three. You must come back to our hamlet. Everyone would be so excited to meet you."

"I'm afraid we don't have the time," said Tyraz. "We must get to Hillswood as soon as we can."

The tall Arboreal's lips turned up slightly. "Another one of your jokes?"

Chara stepped between him and Tyraz.

"Yes, we'd love to visit your hamlet," she said. "Tyraz didn't want to admit it, but we're not sure exactly how to reach Hillswood. Perhaps someone in town would be willing to show us the way."

"Many would be honored for the opportunity," said the tall Arboreal, "but I, Nerthelsar, shall be your guide. Come this way."

With a single glance at his companion, the other Arboreal leaped into the branches and disappeared. Arboreals shared a silent form of communication based upon facial movements, body positioning, and hand gestures. Jarlen had told her that he never mastered the silent Arboreal language, but he seemed to fit in perfectly whenever Chara saw him around his people.

Chara expected Nerthelsar to climb into the tree, but instead he led them across the ground. Vines and underbrush retreated after a single wave of his arm, only to grow back even thicker once Chara and Tyraz had passed through. The Arboreal Forest was more densely packed than the woods outside Krofhaven, so much so that it would have been impossible to reach Hillswood without assistance, even if they knew exactly which direction to go. Chara stopped briefly to listen to a pair of songbirds calling to each other. Whatever gloom had scared the animals on the Ferfolk side of the border hadn't taken hold in the Arboreal Forest, and she hoped it never would.

Their trek ended in a spot identical to every other part of the Arboreal Forest. Trees battled one another to reach the distant sunlight, dense undergrowth filled the gaps in the hopes that a few rays would filter down through the canopy, and thick vines crawled up unsuspecting trunks.

"Wait here," said Nerthelsar, "while I announce your arrival."

Chara had been around Arboreals enough to know all the activity occurred in the treetops. She gazed upward but couldn't see anything other than branches and leaves. Before long, several Arboreals had dropped to the forest floor from nearby tree limbs. Much like what had happened in Hillswood, they gathered around her to see the rare human. A few even showed interest in Tyraz, despite having recently been at war with the Ferfolk. Although they were long-lived, many of these Arboreals probably had never seen a Ferfolk, especially if they hadn't been part of the army.

Tyraz made his way through the crowd toward Chara.

"We should look for Nerthelsar," he said, pushing a few curious hands away from his arms. "I don't want to spend any more time here than necessary."

"We're doing exactly what we promised," said Chara as she waved a few of the Arboreals closer. "I'm sure he'll be ready to guide us tomorrow morning. With his help, we'll reach Hillswood far sooner than on our own. Until then, just enjoy the attention."

"No, thank you." He put his hands up and backed away, trying to interact as little as possible with their hosts. "Have fun with the Arboreals but be ready before dawn. I want to be on our way when the sun breaks the horizon."

"That'll be noon judging by the heights of these trees."

She smiled at him, but he'd already disappeared behind a growing mass of bodies.

Chara spent hours answering questions, the most common of which was, "Are there any more of your kind?" Eventually, the Arboreals ushered her up a particularly large trunk with special footholds to make the climb easier. She stepped into an opening between the branches that appeared to be a meeting room. Smaller branches rose from the floor to form a set of chairs around a long table. Nerthelsar guided her to the far end.

"Everyone wanted to join us for the feast," he said, "but this is our largest space. It was difficult determining who received the honor."

"We could have eaten down there," said Chara, motioning toward the forest floor. "Then nobody would have been left out."

His look of confusion meant that was never a possibility. He stuck his head through the leaves on the wall.

"Where's Tyraz?" he asked. "Isn't he hungry?"

"He may or may not be hungry," said Chara, "but he didn't feel comfortable around so many...people."

"I'm sure many of us would feel the same in his home. This means one more seat is now available. I'll deliver the good news."

Arboreals filtered through the wall of leaves, each one spending several minutes introducing him- or herself, and by the time Nerthelsar had returned, the room was packed. Chara savored every moment of the positive attention almost as much as she enjoyed the surprisingly delectable food. She ate until her stomach refused to accept another morsel, her favorite being a nutty spread atop root vegetables sliced so thinly they were translucent. The celebration ended abruptly a few minutes before midnight, a time when the Arboreals returned to their homes for meditation. They claimed not to sleep like humans or Ferfolk, but Chara suspected this time of relaxation wasn't much different between the races.

Nerthelsar brought her to the neighboring tree, where a small room containing a single bed made from the branches awaited her. A blanket of fresh leaves covered the bed. Although it didn't feel as comfortable as her furniture back home, Chara lay down and closed her eyes. She could easily spend the rest of her life here, appreciated for who she was, but she had a quest to complete, a quest that might end in answers she didn't want to hear.

The red tinge in the water reminded Chara of the day when thousands of fish washed ashore near her home. They'd all died mysteriously, bringing with them a dreadful odor that spread from the shoreline all the way into the mountains. It took the village of Luceton an entire week to clean the mess, but the smell lingered for months. No carcasses tainted this water, however. Small waves lapped at the edge of the beach, staining the sand red wherever it touched. Chara had to form a barrier before it tainted the rest of the land.

She pushed sand toward the ocean, piling it up into a wall as high as her shoulders. Although the wall held together as if it were a single block of stone, the water easily tore a hole in the center to resume its encroachment of the beach.

Chara quickly scooped up a handful of sand and shoved it into the hole. The sand merged with the rest of the wall, sealing the leak. Unfortunately, the pounding waves opened two more cracks. Chara set to work filling the new holes, but more kept opening until she was spending her entire time shoving handfuls of sand into the wall. In frustration, she kicked a hole through the center of the structure, allowing the fury of the ocean access to a single part of the beach. Satisfied, she strolled along the dunes until she found a dry spot to lie upon and gaze at the dark sky.

"Chara."

A firm hand touched her arm, but she didn't want to wake up yet. She rolled over in her leaf bed, ignoring the branches poking into her side.

"The sun will be up soon, and Tyraz insists we get started."

She opened her eyes to Nerthelsar holding a glowing leaf lantern, probably lit by luminescent lichens or fungus. The Arboreals never used fire, whether for light, heat, or warfare.

"I'm ready," she said, "but can we find some food from last night? I'm sure even Tyraz wouldn't turn down those delights."

Nerthelsar handed her a heavy sack.

"I noticed how much you enjoyed yourself at the celebration," he said. "You're always welcome to our hospitality."

Chara didn't wait to bring the food to Tyraz. She stuck her hand into the sack and munched on a few treats on their way down to the forest floor, where Tyraz stood with his arms folded.

"You look tired," said the young Ferfolk. "Perhaps you should have gotten more sleep instead of celebrating. We do have a quest to complete."

"And you look hungry." Chara handed him the sack. "Try anything in there, and if you don't love the food, I'll promise never to attend a party again."

Tyraz pushed the sack back to her.

"I'm sure it's delicious," he said, "but I've already eaten. Let's get started."

With a wave of his hand, Nerthelsar separated a pair of overgrown bushes and hiked deeper into the forest. Tyraz took up the rear after Chara followed the Arboreal.

"You didn't have to be so antisocial," she called out. "We still would have left the hamlet before dawn."

"I'll make it up after we speak with Jarlen," said Tyraz. "Until then I have to focus on my mission."

"Sounding like a true Ferfolk. Good now, let's see if our guide can go any faster."

Chara sped up until she trailed Nerthelsar by only two steps. The Arboreal must have heard their conversation and increased his pace until she was jogging through the woods. She took deep breaths. This was going to be an exhausting journey.

Hillswood didn't look any different from either the forest or Nerthelsar's hamlet. Lush vegetation surrounded densely packed trees, covering every spot that had a chance to receive sunlight, while carpets of moss and mushrooms dominated any perpetually dark locations. Chara was thankful they had a guide, because it would have been impossible to find their way here otherwise. Unlike Nerthelsar's home, only one Arboreal greeted them when they arrived.

Cassor, one of the Arboreal elders, dropped down from a nearby branch and exchanged glances with Nerthelsar. At first, the guide seemed excited to see Cassor, but a serious expression overtook his face. The elder nodded toward Chara and Tyraz while raising his eyebrow.

"I should have sent word ahead," said Nerthelsar. "Now that I've brought you here, my work is done. Please do return to my hamlet one day."

"Many good thanks," said Tyraz as Nerthelsar leaped into the nearest tree.

Chara stepped closer to Cassor.

"That's no way to treat him," she said. "He was only helping us. We still would have come here without any prior announcement. It just would have taken us longer."

Cassor pulled her in for a hug. She resisted at first but soon yielded to his insistence.

"I extended him my sincere gratitude for his help," he said, "but he didn't give us time to prepare for your arrival. Besides, we just finished a ceremonial for a dear friend. This is not the best time for a visit from outsiders."

"We don't require any special treatment," said Tyraz. "We've only come to speak with Jarlen. Nothing else."

Cassor's jovial expression turned somber.

"Jarlen hasn't been in Hillswood for a while," he said, "but perhaps I can help you."

"Where is he?" asked Tyraz. "How long has he been gone?"

"He left a few springs ago but didn't tell us his destination."

"Jarlen's been gone for years, and you didn't think it important to let us know?" Tyraz threw his hands into the air. "What if he's lost? What if he needs our help? It might be too late by now."

"There's nothing to worry about," said Cassor. "I've gone on walks that lasted longer. Come. Aquila, Eslinor, and I were about to discuss new methods for training the tenderlings. I'm sure they'd be thrilled to see you."

Aquila and Eslinor were the other two Arboreal elders. Normally it would have taken weeks or more to schedule a meeting with them, but saving everyone in the land must have given Chara and Tyraz special privileges. She followed Cassor to a tree larger than most Ferfolk houses. Its branches spread more than one hundred paces from the trunk in huge arcs that ended buried in the ground. This Gathering Tree served as a space for important discussions and town functions, with much of the population spending their days within its broad reach.

Cassor led them up the trunk, through a veil of leaves, and into the main room, where Aquila and Eslinor sat at a branch table. Neither appeared any older or younger than most other Arboreals, and both exuded auras of tranquility. Only a few strands of Aquila's long green hair escaped her tightly wound bun and flowed down the front of her brown dress. Her dark green skin contrasted with Eslinor's pale features and delicate beauty. Eslinor let her olive hair brush against the leaves of the floor as her gaze drew Tyraz's attention. Chara grabbed his arm and helped him to the table so he wouldn't trip accidentally.

"Tyraz. Chara," said Eslinor. "I'm sorry you came all this way to find Jarlen away from home."

At first, Chara wondered how she knew about their plans but then remembered the Arboreal silent communication. Cassor must have relayed all the details to them already.

"Why don't you tell us what this visit is about," said Aquila. "If we don't have the answers you seek, then we might be able to help you find Jarlen."

Chara took a seat between Tyraz and Eslinor, while Cassor perched himself at the head of the table.

"You don't appear to have come for a social visit," he said. "So you must have wanted his advice as a wizard."

"Not just any type of wizard," said Tyraz. "As a necromancer."

"That is a subject best left to history," said Aquila. "No good will come of communicating with the dead. We've spoken with Jarlen about necromancy many times. If you keep your friends and loved ones in mind, they'll never truly die."

"We're not trying to contact anyone that died," said Chara. "Dead bodies have come back to life in Krofhaven, and we want to know why."

"You must be mistaken," said Eslinor. "Even the most powerful wizards could never bring someone back from the netherworld. Are you sure they didn't just recover from a terrible illness?"

"You don't think we know the difference between sickness and death?" Tyraz pulled a few leaves off the side of his chair. "This is why only Jarlen can help us. Chara and I watched a corpse dig itself out of its own grave. Another body had done the same a few days earlier. If you have no advice for us, then just show us which way he went. We'll find him on our own."

"That might be more difficult than you expect," said Cassor, "but I'll help you track him once we conclude our discussions."

Tyraz jumped out of his seat. "That could take days or more. We're leaving now. Come, Chara."

The Arboreals exchanged a few upturned lips and wrinkled brows.

"Aquila and Eslinor have agreed to postpone this meeting," said Cassor. "Shall we have our evening meal and head out in the morning?"

"Now would be better," said Tyraz.

"Now it is." Cassor opened a hole in the wall with a simple gesture. "Let's get some answers for you. Hopefully, Jarlen didn't try to hide himself from us."

Chapter V

On the Trail of an Arboreal

For a people known to take their time with every decision, the Arboreals didn't delay once they made up their minds. Immediately after the meeting with the elders had ended, Cassor left the hamlet on a course he claimed was due east. It surprised Chara that he didn't require any preparations for the journey. Tyraz would have spent a half day gathering supplies and planning his route. Their exit from Kroflund to get here had been comparatively hasty yet still took twice as long.

"Do you know where Jarlen went?" asked Chara as they glided through the undergrowth.

Cassor effortlessly controlled the vegetation, barely making any gestures to clear a path.

"I only have suspicions," he said. "Certainly not enough to set a course yet."

"Then why did you choose this direction?" asked Tyraz from the rear.

Behind him, branches and vines returned to their original position within seconds of his passing. It gave Chara a sense of importance to have the plants yield to their every step. She would have enjoyed wielding such power over the people of Krofhaven, forcing them to accept her as she was instead of starting nasty rumors.

"With the swamp to the south and Ferfolk territory to the north," said Cassor, "this seemed a good start."

He turned with a quick smile.

"Besides, the few people that saw him leave Hillswood told me he took this corridor."

"What corridor?" asked Tyraz. "These woods are as overgrown as anything I've seen."

"Above us," said Cassor. "Arboreals don't usually travel along the ground like this. Our paths connect through the canopy, but I doubted you'd find it easier to climb from tree to tree."

Chara looked up at the mass of leaves. Somewhere hidden behind the web of green were the Arboreals' streets, composed of branches instead of cobblestones. She would have asked to explore the treetops if they had time, but Tyraz wouldn't have allowed it. Maybe Jarlen would give them a tour of the treetops once they found him–perhaps on their way back to Krofhaven.

The speedy start to the trek had improved Tyraz's mood, but they'd brought no extra food. By mid-day, Chara's stomach reminded her why it was beneficial to be prepared. She called the group to a halt and reminded them that they'd travel faster with renewed energy from a filling meal.

"I'll find some food for us," said Cassor.

"I'm not interested in gnawing on a bunch of dry twigs," said Tyraz. "I'll hunt for something more palatable, and don't tell me it's not allowed. I wouldn't be doing anything different from any other forest predator."

"Forest predators have no choice," said Cassor. "You do."

"And I choose to–"

"Perhaps Tyraz would feel better if he had more involvement in procuring the meal," said Chara. "I know I would."

"I'd be happy to show you a few edible plants. At home we have experts who dedicate their lives to locating the most delectable treats, but I've learned a few of their secrets." Cassor hopped between a pair of trees. "Come along."

"You two go," said Tyraz. "I'll set up the campsite here."

He clearly wanted something more than a few bites of meat for dinner. Cassor had taken over the mission, and Tyraz probably envied the elder's role as leader. Speaking about it further would only make things worse. With the strained relations between Arboreals and Ferfolk, even Tyraz couldn't avoid feeling demeaned when following Cassor's orders. Once they succeeded in bringing Jarlen back to Krofhaven, Aiax might give Tyraz new orders, possibly under his rival Septu. Chara sympathized with her friend and promised herself to do what she could to keep this quest under his command.

She hurried after Cassor, who led her to a round bush covered with clusters of small, dark berries.

"If you find purple ones," he said, "they're some of the tastiest in the forest."

He reached into the bush and pulled out a single berry for her to try. A burst of sweetness flooded her mouth as soon as she bit down.

"Don't harvest any if they're green or black," said Cassor. "They're both bitter and poisonous. I'll find a few nuts to supplement the berries. They're higher in the trees and more difficult to gather."

Chara didn't watch when he left and instead focused on picking out every purple berry from the bush. Unfortunately, only a handful were ripe enough to eat. She popped them into her mouth and wandered deeper into the forest in search of another bush. Tyraz had to taste those amazing fruits, but she hadn't saved any for him.

Without Cassor leading the way, vegetation impeded her movement at every step. She ducked under low-hanging vines only to get caught in prickly outgrowths, and thick tree trunks always seemed to block any partial path she found. Worried that she might get lost, Chara circled the makeshift campsite, keeping track of every trunk wider than her body. She still hadn't found another purple berry bush after passing two score trunks, but she did come across a tall chestnut tree with several branches low enough for her to reach. The nuts weren't as tasty as the berries, but at least she'd bring something palatable back to Tyraz.

She held the bottom of her shirt like a pouch and filled it with chestnuts.

"Tyraz," she called out. "Where are you?"

A faint voice answered from nearby. She trotted in his direction, aided by a few more shouts, and soon found him sitting on a small boulder in a clearing.

"Cassor showed me a bush with the most delicious berries," she said as she dumped the chestnuts on the ground, "but I ate them all. We can start with these while we wait for him to return. He should be back with more food soon."

"Are you sure these are chestnuts?" he asked and proceeded to crack one open with his dagger after Chara nodded. "They seem rounder than the ones back home."

"I thought so when I picked them," said Chara, "but maybe we should wait to ask Cassor about them. He'll know if they're edible."

Tyraz nibbled the exposed meat and scrunched his face.

"It tastes bitter. Perhaps I'm just not used to them."

He opened a few more and offered some to Chara. When she hesitated, he tossed them all into his mouth.

"You see," he said as he rubbed his eyes. "It wasn't difficult to find food on your own."

He grabbed another nut but dropped it in a fit of coughing.

"Did you happen to see," he said, "any streams nearby? I could use a drink. Throat itchy."

"Not since this morning," said Chara. "I'll go look for one."

She was about to leave the campsite when Tyraz fell over, gasping for breath.

"Tyraz," she shouted and rushed to his side. "Cassor, something happened to Tyraz. Come quick!"

She held his head on her lap and loosened his collar. Her pulse pounded in her ears, terrified of what might happen to him. He needed water but she couldn't leave him in this state. Thankfully, Cassor soon appeared. The Arboreal examined one of the unopened nuts before tossing it into the woods.

"Did he eat any of those?"

A wave of guilt overcame Chara. She never should have brought them back to camp, not without approval from Cassor.

"They're not chestnuts?" she asked.

"We call them squirrel apples," said Cassor as he brought a leaf canteen up to Tyraz's lips. "Good for the animals but not for Arboreals. Apparently Ferfolk have the same reaction to them as we do."

"Will he recover?" Chara took the canteen from Cassor and poured another sip through Tyraz's puffy lips. "Is there anything else you can do?"

"The Ferfolk are a sturdy race," said Cassor. "Give him some time to rest, and he should be fine."

He discarded the remaining squirrel apples and replaced them with a pair of nuts the size of Chara's hand. Although curious about the strange food, Chara didn't feel like eating. Cassor must have understood her frustration and retreated into the treetops.

Throughout the night, Chara remained beside Tyraz, offering sips of water whenever he seemed thirsty. If he didn't recover, she'd never forgive herself for poisoning him. He started the quest so excited to have been given his own mission, and now he lay fighting for his life because of her. Each cough brought another bout of anguish to Chara, but his breathing became steadier by dawn. When Tyraz finally opened his eyes, Chara's heart fluttered as joy spread throughout her body.

"I didn't know if you'd ever wake up," she said. "Are you feeling better?"

Tyraz sat up and finished the rest of the water in a single gulp.

"What happened?" he asked.

"I seem to have poisoned you by accident," said Chara. "Next time we'll only eat what Cassor suggests."

"Are these for us?" Tyraz reached for one of the large nuts. "I'm hungry."

Chara kicked it closer to him and helped crack open the outer shell. She took the other one for herself. The meat inside was chewy and bland but satisfied her appetite. Cassor returned to the campsite as they finished the meal.

"Where were you last night?" asked Chara. "Didn't you care what happened to Tyraz? I could have used some help."

"I returned to Hillswood to speak with the healers," said Cassor. "They gave me medicine in case he didn't recover, but I'm glad we don't have to use it. Are you ready to continue our search?"

Tyraz stood on his own and pushed through the undergrowth at the edge of the clearing. This setback couldn't have been good for his ego, but he forged ahead like a true soldier.

"I'm sure we'll pick up Jarlen's trail soon," said Chara. "And we should cover a lot of ground with this perfect weather."

Cassor took the lead to open a path through the forest and kept a quick pace until early afternoon when the soil grew soggier. Puddles of water lay scattered about the trees, and thick moss mats surrounded most trunks.

"This swamp has grown since I was here last," he said. "It's been a wet season but not enough to cause this much change."

Chara's feet sunk into the muck whenever she stopped moving. She edged closer to a tall linden tree and stood on one of the roots that poked out from the soil.

"Should we try another direction?" she asked.

Cassor climbed into the branches and disappeared into the foliage. He moved up and down trees as easily as Chara could walk across a field. Jarlen possessed the same ability as the rest of the Arboreals but focused his efforts on necromancy, a human school of magic. The Arboreal community never approved his choice and probably isolated him from the rest of society. No wonder he left. Chara felt a closer kinship with him than when they were on their previous adventure together.

"This area seems familiar." Tyraz joined Chara on the root, causing a flush of warmth when he brushed against her side. "This might be the swamp where I first met Jarlen. Maybe he went back to the Forbidden Wood."

"I thought he said there was nothing there anymore."

"There isn't," said Cassor from a large branch above her head. "But Tyraz might be right about Jarlen. Why don't you two return to Hillswood, while I continue onward. I found a few branches out of place up here. He might have used them as a bed on his way eastward. If he's in the Forbidden Wood, I promise to bring him straight back to Hillswood."

"We're not going anywhere without him," said Tyraz. "We'll find our own way if you don't want to guide us anymore."

"I want to help," said Cassor. "It's just–"

"You don't want a human to see the Forbidden Wood." Tyraz took Chara's hand and led her into the swamp. "She already knows about your secrets."

Cassor darted ahead of them.

"Should we at least stay dry?" he asked. "We can go around the swamp or over it."

"We've been through worse," said Tyraz. "You can traverse

the treetops if you prefer."

He stepped to the side, but Cassor held out his arm to block the way. A low-pitched song and a circular motion of his other arm brought several roots up from the ground. They clumped together to form a bridge across the mud. Tyraz stepped onto the closest root, holding his hands out to the side for balance.

"It's a little slippery," he said. "Take care where you place your feet."

Chara followed behind him with Cassor in the back. Every few paces, the Arboreal repeated his chant, causing more roots to appear ahead of them. The muddy ground soon gave way to extended ponds and eventually deep water. Unlike the clean, crisp water of the ocean, the murky pond prohibited prying eyes from viewing more than an inch down. Reflections of the trees appeared darker and more sinister, and the tiniest ripples sent chills throughout Chara's body. She regretted not taking Cassor's suggestion and skirting the swamp.

On her next step, her toe caught hold of a kink in the root, sending her tumbling into the chilly water with a splash. Although she knew how to swim, it comforted her when her feet touched the bottom. Nothing too large could live in the shallows. With the water just reaching her neck, she slogged across the slimy bottom of the pond toward the root bridge. Tyraz held out his hand to help her up, but before she reached his fingers, another root snagged her back leg. She jiggled her foot but only seemed to become more tangled.

"I'm stuck," she said and pulled at her leg. "I can't get free."

"I'll help you," said Tyraz as he took out his dagger and dove into the water.

Cassor wouldn't approve of cutting through plants, but Chara agreed with Tyraz's method. She wanted to punish the roots for scaring her. Besides, the Arboreal wouldn't see what happened at the bottom of the pond.

Something brushed against her other leg. At first, she thought it was Tyraz, but the object felt cold and hard. Shivers ran through her body, interrupted only when a sharp tug yanked her under. She gulped one breath of air before water covered her head. Her arms flailed at her sides until her fingers touched another body. She opened her eyes, expecting to see Tyraz cutting through her bonds, but the face of a familiar Arboreal grinned at her before disappearing into the murk. Even though he sported brown skin instead of green, Chara recognized Yasnol, Jarlen's Arboreal rival who'd sacrificed himself to save others against an infernal creature a few years ago. How could he have been alive at the bottom of this swamp, and why would he attack his friends?

As the last bits of air in her lungs dissipated, Chara struggled against the roots. She wouldn't last much longer and worried not only for herself but also for Tyraz, who was probably caught in the same situation. Just when she was about to take in a mouthful of water, the roots that had held her back lifted her straight up out of the pond. She gasped, choking on a combination of water droplets and fresh air. Beside her, a mass of roots had wrapped around Tyraz, obscuring every part of his body except his hands and feet. The young Ferfolk coughed uncontrollably from within the tangle, but he was alive, setting Chara's mind at ease.

Nearby, a frustrated Cassor raised and lowered his arms while directing his chant at the bonds. Eventually the roots released Tyraz, who staggered next to Chara, took her by the waist, and brought her to the Arboreal.

"Why did those plants attack us?" he asked. "I thought you were in control of everything in this forest."

Cassor's song didn't pause for a moment, but his gestures turned from the swamp to the trees. Branches shifted lower and several vines snaked downward toward the group. Tyraz pushed Chara away from the green tendrils.

"Why don't you say anything?" he asked. "Are those from you?"

The water seemed to have become two shades darker as clouds blotted out the sun far above the treetops. Cassor hopped onto the nearest vine without a break in his song.

"I think he wants us to come with him," said Chara with a tug on Tyraz's sleeve.

"Do you trust him?" asked Tyraz.

She answered by climbing onto a vine and holding out her hand. Tyraz joined her, and the vine lifted them high into the canopy, where the Arboreal elder sat on a branch with a stern look on his face.

"I saw Yasnol in the water," said Chara as she tried to find a comfortable position in the tree. "Did you see him, too?"

"There was nothing down there except mud and plants," said Tyraz. "Certainly not a dead Arboreal."

"This attack disturbs me," said Cassor. "Only another Arboreal could have wrested control of those roots, but we're too far from the southern mountains for it to have been our cousins."

"I told you," said Chara. "It was Yasnol. He's come back from the dead just like the farmer in Krofhaven."

Cassor leaned backward, holding onto the branch with his legs, and peered down at the swamp. He returned to an upright position looking as concerned as ever.

"Yasnol wouldn't have attacked us," he said, "and he wouldn't have remained underwater for so long. Arboreals aren't as comfortable in water as humans or Ferfolk."

"Do you have a better explanation?" asked Chara.

Cassor stared at her, probably wondering if he should release another Arboreal secret.

"Just tell us," said Chara. "You'll neither surprise nor scare us."

Tyraz gave her a quick grin of agreement.

"When I was a tenderling long ago," said Cassor, "I heard stories about a dangerous swamp creature. It appeared as an old Arboreal with withered skin and fed on anyone who entered its territory, using ancient magic to overpower its prey. I always assumed the tale was told to keep young tenderlings away from the water. Now I'm not so sure. Either way, I think we should keep to the treetops until we clear the swamp."

"How can anything in the forest hide from the Arboreals?" asked Tyraz. "I thought you were connected to the trees."

"We may share a special bond with plants," said Cassor, "but countless creatures call this forest home. We should respect their environment and take our leave of the swamp."

"Anything to help us reach Jarlen faster," said Chara. "With the dead rising, I'm worried this situation is only going to get worse the longer we delay."

Chapter VI

The Price of Power

The shade put its head down, made a quarter turn, and wandered off. Jarlen chased after it, but the enigmatic spirit refused to acknowledge him. The quicker he moved, the faster it retreated. Behind them, another creature seemed to have taken notice of the interaction. With the torso and arms of a bear attached to the body and tail of a fox, the demon trotted forward holding a coiled whip in its claws. Spikes ran from the top of its snout, over its ursine head, and down its back, growing longer as they approached the bushy tail.

Jarlen didn't think this newcomer could affect him, but he didn't want to take the chance. He forced himself to float away from both the shade and the demon as fast as possible. Unfortunately the fox demon moved at twice his speed and soon overtook him. One fling of the whip answered his question. The leathery tip snapped inside his translucent body, but he felt nothing. The fox demon growled and charged toward the shade that had given Jarlen the warning. It lashed out at the spirit, tearing off a chunk of its shoulder. The spirit wailed and fell to the ground amid a flurry of heavy strokes from the whip.

"Enough," shouted Jarlen as he floated toward the altercation. "Leave that spirit alone. He's done nothing wrong."

The demon roared at him, forcing him to come to a halt. Jarlen wasn't sure what had stopped his motion, his thoughts or the demon's voice. Either way, he wanted to leave this realm as soon as possible, but he refused to allow this spirit to suffer because of him. He floated toward the demon, staring into its fiery eyes.

"Leave now before you anger me further," he said as he threw his shoulders back and raised his chin. "Or I'll summon Mammon to deal with you."

Nearby, the shade's gouged shoulder had regrown, and the other lash marks had mostly healed. The spirit cast its eyes downward and shuffled off to join its peers. Jarlen felt a connection to it—perhaps it had been a fellow wizard in a former life. The demon pulled the whip into a coil, gave a single snort, and headed in the direction from which it had arrived. At first Jarlen thought the snort was the creature's annoyance at being bested by an intruder, but when he turned to go, another demon was approaching, probably the fox demon's master.

An enormous crab-shaped demon stood for a moment on the adjacent hill, surveying the landscape. A bony exoskeleton encased its oval body and spindly legs, while its bulbous eyes rested upon long stalks. It scuttled down the slope, closing the distance within seconds. Jarlen knew it would be pointless to flee. This demon clearly could move much faster if it chose to do so.

"I'd heard rumors," said the demon, "but I didn't think they were true."

It circled Jarlen, examining him closely. The two eyes moved independently of each other, making it difficult for Jarlen to focus on either of them. Jarlen had never seen this demon before, but he knew it was another archfiend.

"You're neither dead nor alive," said the demon. "I haven't seen anything like this in millennia, but there's more. You're not human, yet you must be a wizard to have separated mind from body."

"I'm half Arboreal," said Jarlen. "Does it matter."

"Not necessarily," said the demon. "I have a proposition for you, but I don't feel comfortable speaking out here in the open. Would you come with me?"

"I'm not interested in anything you have to offer."

Jarlen turned away, but the demon sidled in front of him.

"You shouldn't trust Mammon," said the demon. "He's the prince of lies."

"And you are..."

"I am Dis, the fallen prince. Mammon stole my realm and my followers ages ago, and I have yet to fully recover."

"That doesn't concern me," said Jarlen. "I'm here to close the portals to my world and nothing else."

"If you close all the portals, you'll remain trapped in the netherworld forever."

"So be it. I only want to ensure that the people of my world are safe. What happens to me is but a small price to pay."

He tried to float around Dis, but again his body refused to obey.

"Release me," he said. "We have nothing further to discuss."

"If you're going to remain trapped here, wouldn't you prefer to be more than a disembodied spirit?" asked Dis. "Promise to send me to your world before you close the final portal, and I can ensure that you rule at least one realm in the netherworld."

"How can you promise that? Didn't you just tell me Mammon stole everything from you?"

"So you might be interested?"

"I was only making a point." Jarlen focused his mind, trying to break free of Dis's hold. "I'd never send an evil fiend into my world."

Dis let out a hiss before looking upward. A single black spot marred the otherwise perfect expanse of blue.

"When we meet again," said Dis as he darted away, "I won't

be as cordial."

In control of his body, Jarlen floated across the hills. He hadn't sensed any portals in this realm. Perhaps he was nearing the end of his quest. Although he didn't trust Dis, the demon prince had made one true statement. If Jarlen sealed all the gateways between worlds, he'd strand himself here. He'd certainly miss his friends back home, but ensuring their safety was a worthy sacrifice. Still, he would have preferred to send them a final message if it were possible.

The hilly terrain seemed to go on forever, but eventually uniform gray replaced the blue sky as the air grew damp. Jarlen couldn't feel the moisture on his skin, but he could see the tiny droplets falling from above. The light mist gradually became heavy rain as Jarlen continued onward, and the sporadic appearance of shades became commonplace. These spirits, however, seemed more oblivious to their surroundings than the ones that wandered through the hills in the mild weather. Not one shade acknowledged his presence.

Jarlen had read about this area of the netherworld in an ancient text. Nearby should be the Realm of Darkness followed by the Unending Walls and finally the Realm of Lost Spirits, wherein he would find the largest of the openings between worlds. If that were the last of the portals, his quest would be complete, and his mind would be stuck in the netherworld forever.

Back home, many of the people he cared about were gone. An evil spirit had killed his teacher Zehuti, many of the tenderlings he grew up with including Yasnol had died fighting the lyche, and the Arboreal elder Kuril had returned to the forest. He missed them all dearly, but he still had a few close friends who might not understand why he sacrificed himself. The Arboreal elder Eslinor had raised him for many years, but she knew the risks of magic and would support his decision. Tyraz and Chara might not. They'd urge him to find another solution and might even offer to join him in the netherworld.

Jarlen considered returning home to give them a proper farewell, but he was so near his goal. He couldn't risk returning to the netherworld at some later time and having the demon princes unite against him. And what if he became hopelessly lost the next time he sent his mind between worlds. He'd be in the same position as now except for having failed his quest. As much as he wanted to see his friends again, he had an important mission to complete.

He floated through a heavy downpour, passing scores of translucent shades. For once he was glad he couldn't feel anything. The creatures stuck in the cold, damp weather looked miserable, groaning every few steps as if the raindrops burned their nebulous flesh. In the distance, the horizon ended abruptly at a wall of solid black, looking like the edge of the netherworld. Jarlen knew the darkness was only the transition into the next realm, but he felt like he was heading toward oblivion.

Huge demon dogs pounced out of the darkness and attacked any shade that wandered too close to the dark border. Thankfully the guardians ignored Jarlen as he approached the black wall. He didn't want to learn if they were powerful enough to affect him, and he certainly didn't want to encounter their master. He hoped only to pass through their realm without incident. Sealing the final portal would do much to ease his mind.

Jarlen stopped next to the dark wall and reached out, sending the lower half of his arm into the inky blackness. It felt no different from being in any other realm of the netherworld. He retracted his arm and flexed his fingers. They appeared unaffected by the darkness. With nothing to fear, he drifted between the two realms, stopping when he was halfway through. One arm and one leg remained in the light, while the others had disappeared. What if he could enter the final portal and close it on his way between worlds? Then he wouldn't be trapped in the netherworld, and all the links would be severed. And if he became stuck within the portal, it couldn't be any worse than living out the rest of his years running from the archfiends. He'd accept either outcome, but the thought of being reunited with his friends filled him with excitement. Only two more realms between him and his return home. He plunged into the darkness full of confidence.

Without any frame of reference to judge his relative motion, Jarlen wondered if he was even moving. Sight and hearing had been the only senses feeding him information about his surroundings, and the Realm of Darkness lacked both visions and sounds. If Jarlen couldn't determine in which direction he traveled, he might easily become stuck going in circles, never to reach the next realm. Thoughts of Tyraz and Chara waiting back home spurred him to keep going. He urged his body forward, hoping he was heading toward the border.

Every so often a feeling of uneasiness overwhelmed him. He probably wasn't alone in the darkness, but most demons couldn't touch him, so he had little to worry about. An archfiend could halt his motion and cause him pain, but both Mammon and Dis let him go for some reason. Perhaps they weren't allowed to harm him, but he thought it more likely they had plans for him. In any case, once he sealed the final portal, they could do what they wanted. He'd never reopen the link between worlds.

Barely visible shapes danced in front of him, probably figments of his imagination. A few minutes later, however, something moved to the side of him. He turned his head and detected the dim outline of a doorway.

Jarlen sighed in relief. He must have reached the Realm of Unending Walls. The darkness receded, bringing intermittent images to his eyes, but after a few minutes, the doorway appeared to be as far from him as before. He tried floating forward but couldn't move.

A pale figure came into view a few steps away. His body looked human, but a pair of curved horns rose from the top of his head. He grinned at Jarlen as he sauntered forward.

"My offer still stands," said the demon. "My freedom from this world in exchange for influence in the netherworld."

"Is that you, Dis?" Jarlen struggled to escape the archfiend's trap. "You changed your body."

"Not exactly," said Dis. "You shouldn't have traveled so far from Mammon's base of power. It's unlikely any of his spies will find us here."

"It does you no good to delay me," said Jarlen. "I was already committed to trapping myself in the netherworld."

"I'll do more than delay you." Dis flung his arms forward, sending a blast of pain throughout Jarlen's body. "I'll fill the rest of your life with agony and then torture your everlasting spirit."

Jarlen closed his eyes as another searing pain ran from his head to his feet. He wasn't sure how much more he could endure.

Chapter VII

Ruins

After hiking for several days, Cassor stopped at a wall of thorns that ran as far as Chara could see in either direction. Spiky vines weaved in and out of tree trunks lined up so close together that a chipmunk would have had difficulty squeezing through. Chara knew the Arboreals had created this barrier to keep out humans and Ferfolk. Beyond it must lie the Forbidden Wood. Although excited to have finally arrived here, she dreaded what she might find on the other side–the secret Arboreals didn't want anyone else to learn.

"Why don't the two of you stay here, while I search for Jarlen?" asked Cassor. "I'll cover ground much more quickly on my own."

"Are you sure that's the only reason you want to leave me behind?" asked Chara. "Nothing on the other side of this barrier will surprise me. I've already heard all about the ruins of that old human city."

Cassor's shoulders drooped as he said, "Come along then. I'll open a hole between the trees."

He turned to the thorny wall, raised his arms, and returned them to his side. Either he'd changed his mind about letting them through or something had gone wrong. He inched closer to the barrier, focusing on a curious patch of brown vines that marred the mural of greens.

"These vines shouldn't be dead," he said. "New growth should have replaced any dead matter within a day, but these clearly have been drying out for weeks."

"That means Jarlen must have been through here," said Tyraz. "I've seen his magic turn plants brown."

"Perhaps," said Cassor as he reached forward, "but these still should have returned to the soil long ago, allowing new sprouts to thrive–unless he's nearby."

Chara called out for Jarlen and was about to search the area when the brown vine lurched at Cassor, wrapped around his arm, and pulled him toward the trees. Another vine grabbed his free arm, cutting into his flesh with its sharp thorns.

Tyraz drew his sword and charged at the vines, while Cassor chanted a trill at the neighboring trees. Tyraz's sword hewed downward through one of Cassor's bonds. Although the blade severed the vine, the portion attached to Cassor's arm didn't loosen. Instead it squeezed tighter, forcing the Arboreal to scream in pain as drops of blood pooled up around each thorn. The other half of the vine retracted into the branches, turned around, and slithered down. The long brown tendrils weren't vines. They were snakes. Cassor would have known the difference between an animal and a plant, so these snakes must have been neither. They weren't alive.

"Jarlen might not have left these creatures behind," said Chara as she snatched Tyraz's dagger and made her way closer to the battle. "They might have come back to life like the dead farmer. How do we stop them if their tails can function without their heads?"

"Help me free Cassor of these vile things first," said Tyraz. "We'll deal with the rest later."

The undead snake hissed at him, showing a mouthful of sharp teeth. None were as long as a viper's fangs, so perhaps they didn't have to worry about venom. Chara focused on the tail around Cassor's arm and sliced deeply into the spiked appendage. The tough scales slowed the dagger, but she cut through a small section and tore it away from his arm.

"You need something to cover those wounds," she said.

"Keep going," said Cassor. "I can almost move my hand again."

Chara hacked away a few more sections of the tail before turning her attention to his other arm. Nearby, Tyraz had severed the snake's head and was continuing his attack against the rest of its body. They only way to defeat the creature was to hack it into scores of small pieces. Chara joined him and cut into the second snake, immediately drawing the head's wrath. It came at her from a low branch and sunk its teeth into her shoulder, forcing her to drop the dagger in agony.

"Chara," shouted Tyraz as he rushed to her side, grabbed the snake, and tore it away from her body.

The teeth left a painful gash in her shoulder, but she could still move her arm. She recovered the dagger, intending to finish off the snake but instead fell backward in a fit of dizziness. Cassor freed his arm and completed his song, summoning his own set of green vines to help immobilize their opponents. Tyraz finished the work by carving the snakes into a heap of flesh and spikes.

Although his arm dripped blood, Cassor covered Chara's shoulder with a set of large leaves and chanted a lilting tune. She could have listened to the song for hours, but it ended when the Arboreal helped her to the ground. The leaves tightened around her wound, at first causing discomfort before numbing the entire area. Chara tried to flex her fingers, but her arm and hand wouldn't obey her commands. She opened her mouth to ask what had happened but instead fell unconscious.

Chara only had to fill one more barrel of fish and she'd be done working for the day. Evening couldn't come soon enough. Tired and hungry, she wanted to return home, eat a good meal, and sleep for the next two weeks. She tugged on the wooden lid, but it wouldn't budge. How was she supposed to finish her work if she couldn't open the barrel? She searched for another way to store the catch, but not a single hole graced the slatted sides.

"What do you want me to do with the rest of the catch?" she called out but nobody responded.

With no tools to pry open the lid, she only had one option left. She grabbed a fish from the net and placed it atop the barrel. The next few fish went beside the first one before Chara had to stack them in a second layer. Within minutes, she'd created a tower of fish so tall she could barely reach the top. Whoever came for the next shift could worry about transporting the barrel. Her work was done.

A whining creak came from beneath the fish tower. Before Chara could escape, the wood shattered, sending splinters everywhere. A sharp piece flew at her and embedded itself in her shoulder.

Chara awoke suddenly with a piercing pain in her arm. Tyraz and Cassor stood over her.

"If you wanted to sleep for the night," said Tyraz, grinning at her, "you could have asked us to make camp first."

He held out his hand to help her up.

"How long was I out?" she asked.

"Long enough for Cassor to treat his wounds and forage for a barely edible meal."

Leaf bandages, similar to the one on Chara's shoulder, covered Cassor's arm all the way down to his wrist. Behind him, the wall of thorns looked as impenetrable as ever. If Jarlen had summoned the undead snake as a sentry, why didn't he want anyone finding him? If not, how many more people and animals would return from the dead to harass the living?

"How do we get through the barrier?" asked Chara.

Cassor strolled past a few of the thorn-encrusted vines, settled on a spot in front of rich green foliage, and tried his song once more. This time, the tree branches separated, opening a hole large enough to grant easy access.

Tyraz went through first, followed by Chara. When Cassor reached the other side, the branches returned to their original positions, sealing the barrier.

"Jarlen's been here," he said as he picked up a cracked shell from the forest floor.

"Hundreds of forest creatures eat nuts," said Tyraz. "How can you be sure this was Jarlen's meal?"

"Look closely." Cassor held the shell out on his open palm. "What do you see?"

Chara and Tyraz crowded around him to examine the evidence. The shell looked similar to the pseudo-chestnuts that she'd fed to Tyraz. Jarlen wouldn't have made the same mistake.

"It's no different from any number of shells opened by squirrels or chipmunks," said Tyraz. "Just tell us what's different so we can be on our way."

"This was crushed by a heavy object," said Cassor. "Howlers never venture this far east, so it must have been an Arboreal, and only three of us have breached this barrier in the past hundred springs."

"So why are we standing around here?" asked Chara, excited to be on the correct path. "Let's go find him."

She marched away from the wall, thinking about how to chastise Jarlen for putting their lives in danger.

Their trek brought them across grassy fields that must have once been farmlands, across streams that had provided water for the crops, and over stone walls that marked the boundaries between neighbors. None of these locations were worth hiding from anyone, but when they approached the first building, Chara fell to her knees.

The remains of an old farmhouse stood in the center of an overgrown pasture. Stalks of wheat or another tall grass obscured a full view of the structure, but the architecture was clearly human. Arboreals lived in houses hidden within the branches of tall trees, Teruns carved their abodes directly into the stone of a mountain, Ferfolk built minimal buildings to satisfy their needs, but humans constructed luxurious homes. Even the small farmhouse was a mansion compared to Chara's current house in Krofhaven.

"I told you it would have been better for me to do this alone," said Cassor.

"I'll be fine," said Chara as she pushed herself up and approached the building. "Give me a few minutes."

Poor farmers might have lived here at one time, but the house reflected their love of life. A row of horseshoes lined the door frame, although half of them had long since fallen to the ground, and each room sported a darkened hearth. Chara imagined herself sitting by a crackling fire, reading stories to her children.

Tyraz walked in and put his hand on her good shoulder.

"This doesn't seem much different from the houses back in town," he said. "What do you see in here that I don't?"

She gave him a weak smile and said, "Nothing. It's just a house."

After one more glance at each room, she led Tyraz back outside.

"There will be many more buildings once we reach the city proper," said Cassor. "Are you–"

"Yes, I'm sure," said Chara as she continued eastward. "Let's get our answers now."

The crumbling towers of the tallest structures peeked above the treetops as the group drew closer to the coastline. Even from a distance, Chara could tell this city had once dwarfed Krofhaven. There would be many places to search for Jarlen, too many for a single person to cover in a reasonable time. Cassor might have been extremely fast in the trees, but a Terun would have been more appropriate here. Both the structures and the streets were made of stone, and nothing had escaped the ravages of time.

Patches of weeds thrust themselves up between the cobblestones, roofs had caved in, and holes pockmarked every wall in sight. Every one of these buildings could collapse at any moment, but the potential danger didn't scare Chara. A few days of poking around didn't compare to the hundreds of years they'd already withstood.

"We should split up," said Tyraz. "We'll cover more ground that way."

"These ruins aren't safe," said Cassor, evoking a frown from Tyraz.

"The whole point of us coming to the Forbidden Wood was to find Jarlen," said Chara. "If we're just tagging along behind you, we might as well have stayed in Hillswood."

"That was my initial suggestion," said Cassor.

Tyraz pointed to the north.

"Cassor, you search the streets up that way," he said. "I'll go south, and Chara will take east. We'll meet back here at sunset to discuss the strategy for tomorrow."

"Unless we find him today," said Chara as she left the group, hopeful of her chances.

They could have made the search into a game to see who found Jarlen first. He had to be in one of these buildings, probably poring through some old books. She glanced over her shoulder. The others had gone off in their respective directions, prompting her to move faster in and out of each building that lined the street. After the first dozen empty rooms, Chara reduced her hunt to the most likely targets. The buildings along the street had once been storefronts with living quarters in the back, but none had been inhabited recently. Jarlen might have taken up residence in any one of them, but Chara guessed that he'd avoid the shakiest structures.

For the rest of the day she focused her efforts on the buildings that exhibited the least damage. Unfortunately, they all came up empty, but many more possibilities lay ahead of her. Instead of returning to the meeting place as the sun set, she continued deeper into the ruins. Tyraz and Cassor could wait for her a few more hours.

In the dimming light, Chara tripped on a pile of stones, almost falling into a rut that ran the length of the street. Something had torn apart the cobblestones and dug several feet into the ground. She knelt at the edge and peered down a particularly dark hole. It had to have been more than several feet deep. She couldn't even see the bottom.

"Jarlen?" she called out. "Are you down there?"

The distant echo of her voice answered, followed by a low rumble. If Jarlen had gotten stuck underground, he wouldn't have survived this long. The noise must have come from something else living in the burrow. The hairs on Chara's arms and neck stood on end. She preferred not to meet the resident and tiptoed away from the ditch toward a set of buildings that had taken more damage than most others in town.

From the amount of rubble scattered about, some of these structures must have risen two or more stories. Chara had to be approaching the center of town. Farther down the road, the remains of another stone wall separated the lower city from a hill populated by gated properties and what probably had been a castle. One improvement the Ferfolk had made to living arrangements was that none of them required preferential treatment based on birthrights. Aiax lived on a street along with leather workers and fish peddlers alike.

Another rumble shook the ground, sending up a cloud of dust from the nearby debris. Chara covered her face until the air cleared. When she removed her arm, an enormous creature stood several paces away. Slick gray fur covered its massive body, and its paws ended in a set of curved claws. It squinted at her through small, beady eyes, while a circle of pink tentacles wriggled around its nose.

Chara put her hand on the hilt of the dagger, glad she hadn't returned it to Tyraz, as she backed away. Perhaps she'd disturbed its nest and only needed to put some distance between her and its offspring. The creature took two steps forward and charged. Chara turned and ran, but the creature bounded ahead and cut off her retreat.

"Stay back," she said, forcing the words through her dry throat. Sweat beaded on her forehead as she waved her dagger. "I don't want to hurt you."

Not surprisingly, the creature didn't heed her warning. It moved toward her, sniffing the air as it went. No wonder the dagger didn't scare it. The creature was blind.

"Chara," shouted Tyraz as he rushed toward her with his sword out. "Are you hurt?"

He inserted himself between her and the creature, pointing the tip of his blade at its head.

"It didn't touch me," said Chara, "and when it had the chance to pounce on me, it only blocked my escape."

"Perhaps it's just playing with its meal." Tyraz eased his sword back into its sheath and held both hands in front of his body. "Or perhaps this is the beast Jarlen told me about."

He edged closer to the creature, one foot at a time until he stood a single pace from its head.

"Are you Jarlen's friend?" he asked and reached forward. "So am I. Have you seen him around here?"

The creature sniffed around him, not showing any signs of aggression. Tyraz stroked the fur on its cheek, but the creature pulled backward and darted around him. It bounded several paces toward the destroyed building before coming to a halt and turning the front half of its body around.

"Are we supposed to follow it?" asked Chara.

"I think so," said Tyraz as he chased after the beast. "Come along."

"What about Cassor?" Chara called out. "Won't he wonder where we went?"

"I would have," said Cassor from down the street, "if you hadn't been making so much noise. Your voices echo off these empty buildings. I could have heard you from the other side of the city."

The three of them followed the creature toward a tall mound of stone blocks. Chara's heart raced. Was Jarlen buried beneath all this destruction? Had they come all this way only to uncover his broken body? Ahead of her, Tyraz had sped up. He probably felt the same as she did and wanted a quick answer. Chara rushed to his side and stopped in front of an opening between two portions of a collapsed wall. A set of crumbling stairs led down into the darkness. The giant creature remained a few paces away, its tentacles grasping at invisible objects in the air.

"Jarlen might be down there," said Tyraz. "Don't expect me to wait until the sun returns to give us more light. I'm going in."

Chara knew he directed his statement at Cassor. Arboreals disliked burning wood, even long dead branches, but she agreed with Tyraz. This couldn't wait until morning. She hunted around the ruins until she found a dried branch thick enough to carry a flame yet not so heavy it would burden her. Tyraz hacked it into two pieces, lit one end of each, and handed her a torch. The branches wouldn't remain aflame for long, but it was enough to let them see what awaited below ground.

They descended a long flight of stairs into a single chamber lined with shelves of books. A lone figure sat cross-legged on the floor in the center of the room. A surge of joy washed over her when she recognized the familiar face.

"Jarlen," shouted Chara, but he didn't respond.

A circle of black powder surrounded the young Arboreal, and a few open tomes lay scattered nearby. Jarlen's eyes were closed, and his chest expanded and contracted every few minutes with a deep breath.

"He's alive," said Cassor as he examined the circle of powder, "but he's in some type of trance."

"Can you wake him?" asked Tyraz.

"Those branches will burn out soon," said Cassor. "Now that we know Jarlen's safe, we can return when it's light."

"You go." Tyraz snuffed out the flame on the floor. "I'll spend the night down here."

Cassor didn't move.

"I promise I won't do anything until you return."

"Me, too," said Chara as she put out her torch. "See you in the morning."

It seemed as if Cassor had just left the room when the first rays of sunlight streamed down the stairs. Tyraz sat against a bookshelf, staring at Jarlen.

"He hasn't moved all night."

"I'm not surprised," said Chara. "Look at him."

A fine layer of dust covered his head, shoulders, and legs.

He'd become part of the ruins. Tyraz approached the circle of powder, reached over, and tapped him on the arm.

"His skin feels cold," he said. "We have to warm him up."

"You promised to wait for me," said Cassor as he delivered an oilsack filled with water and a pouch of berries for breakfast.

"And we have." Tyraz gulped down a handful and passed the pouch to Chara.

"We can't leave him like this," she said, nibbling a few of the sour berries and taking a sip of water. "He's been here too long already. Should we remove him from that circle?"

Cassor paced around the room, running his fingers along the shelves, opening several books, and eyeing Jarlen from every angle.

"It's too risky," he said. "That mystic circle might be the only thing keeping him alive. We don't know how he got into this state. Perhaps someone else–"

"Don't tell me there are any other Arboreals who might know the answer," said Tyraz. "Jarlen resurrected this type of human magic. Nobody else can help. I'm taking him out."

Cassor blocked him, but Chara moved between them before any violence erupted.

"I agree with Tyraz," she said. "Let's do what we can to wake him. Even if we didn't need his help, we couldn't leave him like this for the next fifty years."

She moved aside, breathing easier when Cassor followed her. He clearly cared for Jarlen and didn't want to make this situation any worse.

Tyraz stood outside the circle and stared at the black powder before stepping across. Chara gave him a quick nod when he looked back at her. Whatever they did couldn't be worse than allowing Jarlen's body to rot away beneath the ruins of an ancient city. How much longer could he survive without food or water. Tyraz grabbed him under the arms, hoisted him into the air, and carried him to the base of the stairs, depositing him in the sunlight. Jarlen didn't move—not even to fall over. Chara emptied the sack of water onto his head, but the act did nothing except clear away the dust.

"Do you have any other ideas?" she asked.

"It's true that Arboreals aren't versed in human magic," said Cassor, "but our healers know much more about the body and mind than the three of us combined. Shall we bring him back to Hillswood?"

Neither Tyraz nor Chara could think of a better solution. Cassor tied a dozen branches together and secured Jarlen's body to the makeshift sledge with vines. It would be a long haul back to the hamlet, and Chara wasn't convinced the Arboreal healers would be of any help. At least they'd found their friend.

Chapter VIII

Back from the Dead

They'd only just passed the wall of thorns when Tyraz stopped amid a cluster of old trees. Sunlight filtered through the branches, sending out patches of warmth during an otherwise chilly morning. Chara checked Jarlen, but the young Arboreal hadn't moved from his original position. His breathing continued infrequently but steadily.

"Krofhaven is closer than Hillswood," said Tyraz. "We should bring Jarlen there for help."

"Ferfolk have always been better at killing than healing," said Cassor. "Why do you think that would be any better for him?"

"He's half human." Tyraz put Jarlen down and stretched his fingers. "Your healers are more familiar with the Arboreal body."

"As yours are with Ferfolk anatomy." Cassor moved closer to the sledge, possibly intending to take over the task of dragging it through the forest. "I don't see any difference."

Chara edged between him and Tyraz. She didn't know if Jarlen could hear or sense what was going on around him, but she felt it had to be better if there were less tension. They'd managed to find Jarlen without any fighting. Now wasn't the time to start.

"Ferfolk and humans have lived side by side for centuries," she said, "while Arboreals kept to themselves. The Ferfolk healers are sure to know more."

"Only about his human half," said Cassor. "I fail to see any advantage in the Ferfolk's knowledge, but I agree Krofhaven is much closer. Bring him there while I fetch one of our healers—unless you don't think we'd be welcome in town."

"It doesn't matter if the entire population was against your assistance," said Tyraz. "Until Jarlen recovers, you'll be allowed to help with whomever you bring. I'll make sure of it."

Cassor clasped arms with Tyraz and Chara before disappearing into the branches. Knowing the speed at which Arboreals traveled through the forest, she wouldn't have been surprised if he and the healer were waiting for them outside of Krofhaven.

"Do you know which way to go?" she asked.

"South to the Sinewan," said Tyraz as he lifted the handles of the sledge, "and follow the river west to Krofhaven."

By evening, the weight of dragging the sledge along the riverbank had drained Tyraz's energy, but he refused to let Chara take over. She clearly wasn't as strong as him, but she could have carried the burden for an hour or so. Instead, Tyraz trudged across the terrain, complaining whenever they crossed outcroppings of rocks or overgrown roots.

"We've gone far enough for today," said Chara as she held out her hand to stop him.

He pushed against her. Even exhausted he was stronger than her, but she didn't budge.

"A few more hours," he said. "Until dark."

"And then what? Collapse without dinner?"

Tyraz lowered the end of the sledge to the ground, careful not to disturb his passenger. Chara secretly wanted him to drop the handles, hoping to jar their friend awake. She cupped her hands in the river, took a sip of the cool water, and tossed the rest on Jarlen's face. Nothing happened.

"You already tried that," said Tyraz, leaning against a small tree.

"It could have had a different effect this far from the Forbidden Wood." Chara took out her dagger. "I'll go hunt for some food."

Tyraz jumped up and took her by the arms.

"No, you wait here with Jarlen. I'll find something for us to eat."

He didn't seem ready to back down and arguing would only have tired him more before he prevailed. Chara sheathed the dagger, knelt beside Jarlen, and wiped the excess water from his face with her sleeve.

"Don't take long," she said. "I'm hungry."

"Find a few dry sticks," said Tyraz as he tossed her his tinderbox, "and make a fire. It's been too long since we had a decent meal."

He headed into the woods with a spring to his step. Chara couldn't tell if it pleased him more to be in charge of his own food or free of the extra weight. She followed him a few paces and veered off to look for kindling, always keeping within sight of the sledge. After gathering an armful of twigs and leaves, she picked up a thin branch with a long vine attached to the end. She brought her collection back to the campsite and dropped everything except the thin branch.

"This reminds me of my old fishing rod," she said, knowing Jarlen couldn't hear her. "It's been a long time since I caught any fish. You don't mind. I'm sure you'd prefer this to my starting a fire next to you."

She took the fishhook off her necklace, tied it onto the end of the vine, and dug into the ground. A few inches down she uncovered a juicy worm. Her grandfather had taught her how to bait a hook and cast a line. She never found the process disgusting, but the other girls in town had never wanted to hear her talk about her new skills. All her childhood friends were now gone, along with the rest of the humans, probably still searching the world for a home if their boats hadn't already sunk.

Chara sighed as she sent the vine into the water. She missed her grandfather and their simple life in Luceton. They lived amid hundreds of Ferfolk, but they had each other–the last two humans in the land. She glanced at Jarlen's green skin, paler than the other Arboreals but distinctly different from hers. Although he claimed to be young and inexperienced, he'd lived more years than she and Tyraz combined. Perhaps they should have listened to Cassor and brought him straight to Hillswood.

She felt a tug on the vine and yanked the branch upward, snagging some type of freshwater fish. She could name every creature in the salty waters around Luceton, from sea stars to black cod, but this was just a silvery fish with an appetite for worms.

"Now we won't go hungry if Tyraz doesn't catch anything," she said and sent the line back into the river. "One more and I'll stop."

Jarlen didn't move. How could he have survived for so long without food? Chara's mood would drop precipitously if she missed a single meal.

The fish next to her flopped toward the riverbank.

"Oh no you don't," she said as she shoved the end of the branch into the ground and pulled out her dagger.

She should have filleted the fish as soon as she'd caught it, but it wasn't too late. The fish kept moving around, trying to escape its doom. Its eyes had become cloudy, and its scales seemed to have projected outward from its body, forming an armor of spikes. Between its erratic motion and the sharp scales, the fish would surely take out a chunk of her skin if she tried to grab it. Instead, she plunged the knife into its head, but the fish kept flopping about.

Chara fell backward in surprise. This couldn't have been a trait of freshwater fish. She would have heard about it from someone already. The fish shook the knife loose, gave her a cold stare, and wriggled into the water. A sense of dread washed over her as she kicked the branch rod into the river and watched it float downstream.

"There's no way that creature survived a knife through the brain." She crawled next to Jarlen. "I don't even think it was a fish that escaped me."

Tyraz returned more than an hour later, and Chara still hadn't moved from her spot beside Jarlen.

"I thought you'd build a fire," he said and deposited the body of a raccoon next to the kindling. "What have you been doing this whole time?"

Chara lunged forward, snatched the raccoon, and hurled it into the river. The carcass floated downstream, bobbing up and down as it went.

"Why did you do that?" Tyraz grabbed her by the shoulders. "Chara, what's wrong?"

His fingers dug into her arms in frustration, while his eyes searched her face for answers. A shiver ran through her body as she thought about the raccoon coming back to life as they tore into its flesh for dinner. She pulled away from Tyraz and collapsed beside Jarlen.

"I'm not hungry," she said and turned her head from the river.

"Something must have happened when I was away." Tyraz sat next to her. "And your necklace is gone. Are you hurt? Were you attacked by Fracodians?"

"I tried fishing," she said and took his arm. "I caught one, but it came back to life."

"Are you sure about that? Some fish can survive a long time out of water."

Chara pointed at the dagger on the ground a few paces away.

"Can they survive a metal object piercing their skull?" She pulled him closer. "It looked at me with its dead eyes. It knew I'd killed it. And then it hopped into the water as if nothing had happened."

Tyraz placed his hand in his belt pouch and pulled out a handful of nuts.

"I found these in case you didn't like the taste of raccoon." He placed them on the ground. "If your appetite returns."

Chara handed him the tinderbox, and he lit the kindling. Soon a crackling fire brightened the night sky, bathing them in warmth. She glanced at Tyraz, wondering if he were as concerned as she was. Maybe he didn't even believe her about the fish. Maybe she imagined everything. She exchanged Jarlen's side for his and watched the dancing flames until sleep took over.

Their trek continued more than a week, following the Sinewan's northern bank. The river water rushing by overwhelmed Chara's senses. Its motion never ended, unlike the ebb and flow of the ocean's waves. One constantly bombarded her with incessant noise, while the other's rhythmic tones calmed her nerves.

"Can we move inland?" she asked, cutting through reeds with Tyraz's sword.

"Actually, we'll have to ford the river soon," said Tyraz, dragging the sledge behind her. "It branches to the north up ahead, blocking our progress. This is as good a place as any to get wet."

He released the sledge and wiped a bead of sweat off his forehead.

"Not much farther to Kroflund," he said. "But I know a few people living close to here. We could get a proper meal and some rest before finishing the trip."

Chara's stomach twinged at the thought of food. They hadn't eaten much of anything the past few days, and although the dead fish's eerie stare still haunted her, she wouldn't have turned down a plate of cooked meat. She'd even gobble down a loaf of week-old, stale bread.

"How deep is the water?" she asked.

"Deep enough that we'll have to swim," said Tyraz. "You take the back of the sledge. I'll take the front. The current will push us downstream a bit, but don't bother fighting it. We'll make up the distance once we get to the other side."

He dragged the sledge down the riverbank and into the water. Chara followed him in, stopping when she was shin deep. The chilly water numbed her skin but didn't compare to the frigid depths of the Cold Ocean. Unless the sun shone hot enough to burn the skin, more than a few moments in the waters by Luceton would be deadly. She still would have preferred to be there.

Chara grabbed the end of the sledge and waded deeper into the river. A vision of the dead fish coming back to claim vengeance caused her to pause. Tyraz tugged the front of the sledge.

"Keep going," he said. "Think about the hot meal and soft beds waiting for us."

The water flowed through the branches of the sledge, pushing against Jarlen, but the sturdy vines held him in place. As the river grew deeper, Chara submerged her body, allowed her legs to rise to the surface, and started kicking. They'd gone halfway to the other side when a moan came from ahead of her.

"Is something wrong?" she asked.

"Nothing," said Tyraz, taking strong strokes with his free arm. "Why?"

"You moaned."

"No, I didn't."

He kept swimming, but Chara stopped, allowing Tyraz pull her along. Atop the sledge, Jarlen's head tilted to the side. The river water pushing against him might have forced his head to move, but another moan proved otherwise.

"He's waking up," she shouted and kicked harder than before. "Get him onto the riverbank."

The current picked up near the center of the river, sweeping them all downstream. Chara wanted to fight back and make up the lost distance, but Tyraz kept them moving straight across. They soon reached the far riverbank and dragged the sledge onto dry ground.

"Jarlen," said Tyraz. "Can you hear me?"

Chara's hands trembled, but she steadied them and shook the young Arboreal's shoulder gently. Jarlen moaned once more and opened his eyes. Chara looked away at first, worried they'd be cloudy, but deep green orbs stared back at her.

"Am I dead?" he asked.

"I should hope not," said Chara as she gave a chuckle of relief. "You're here with Tyraz and me, just outside of Kroflund."

Jarlen tried to sit up, but his muscles must have been weak from lack of use. He fell back onto the sledge.

"I'm hungry," he said.

"Aren't we all." Tyraz lifted him up and placed him at the base of a tree a few paces from the river. "I'll see if I can find something to eat around here."

Jarlen grabbed his hand.

"Not yet," he said. "I just want to be around familiar faces for a while longer. I never thought I'd make it back alive."

"Back from where?" asked Chara. "You were in the Forbidden Wood the whole time until we came for you."

"I was in the netherworld," he said.

This couldn't have been a coincidence. Jarlen spending time in the netherworld had to be related to the dead coming back to life, but why would he bring such a curse upon the land? Perhaps a demon had influenced his judgment. There must have been good reasons why necromancy was a forbidden school of magic. Tyraz frowned, echoing Chara's unsettled thoughts. What had Jarlen done?

Chapter IX

Good Intentions

Jarlen kept eating as long as Tyraz and Chara brought him food. The more he consumed, the hungrier he became, but eventually they tired of scouring the surrounding area and took a seat next to him under a young elm tree. As exhausted as his friends looked, Jarlen didn't think he'd ever walk again. His muscles barely responded to him, angry about their inactivity for the past several months.

"I never thought I'd make it back," he said, munching on a few tart berries, "but I'm glad I did."

"What were you doing in the netherworld with the demons?" asked Tyraz.

"I sealed the links between our world and theirs." Jarlen tried to sit up but his arms couldn't support the weight of his body, even for a moment. "No more evil from the netherworld. Think of how many people would still be alive if the lyche and Oengus's spirit couldn't reach this world."

Tyraz reached over to help, but Jarlen waved him away. He pushed against the ground, edging slightly closer to the trunk. Chara, however, put a heavy hand on his shoulder and kept him from moving any farther.

"So you decided to travel to the netherworld on your own," she said, "risking your life to protect this world without giving us any indication of your plan?"

She stood up, straddled him, and grabbed his other shoulder. Her firm grip dug into his skin. Jarlen winced at the pain but couldn't escape.

"Don't ever do anything so foolish again." She pulled him close for a hug before releasing him. "I wouldn't have forgiven you if you didn't come back to us."

This time it was easier for Jarlen to push himself up. With his back against the trunk, he wiggled his toes and rolled his feet from side to side. As feeling returned to his lower limbs, he grew more relieved. For a while, he wasn't sure he'd ever walk again, but now he was positive he'd be back in the treetops soon enough. He stared at the green leaves fluttering in the breeze, waving at him to join them high above the ground.

"I'm not convinced what you did was a good idea," said Tyraz. "A few people and animals have come back from the dead recently, and some of them have attacked the living. The only way to stop those creatures was to carve them into little pieces–gruesome work, but necessary."

"And you think these events were related to my closing the portals?" Jarlen pulled his legs closer to his body and straightened them out again. "Maybe it was a few spirits slipping through before I closed the last of the portals."

A pang of remorse grew in his mind. What if there were side effects from sealing the two worlds apart? He didn't know everything about necromancy, certainly not more than the wizards who preceded him, but how could it be bad to protect this world from evil spirits?

"It shouldn't happen anymore," he said. "I think."

His legs ached as blood rushed down to his feet, but he was determined to stand up. He pushed against the tree, holding the trunk firmly as his body inched upward. Both Tyraz and Chara moved closer to help.

"I can do it," he said.

His friends grabbed him by each arm and lifted him to his feet.

"I know," said Tyraz, "but you can do it easier with some assistance. We'll have you walking again by sunset."

Jarlen hoped he was right, but when they let him go, he wobbled and fell backward against the tree. He held his hands up to keep them away. They'd done enough to get him started. It was his turn to stand on his own. He took one step away from the trunk and gave them a broad grin, but his second step brought him straight back to the ground.

"One more try," he said. "This time on my own. I promise to let you know if I need help."

Tyraz and Chara respected his wishes but remained within reach in case he collapsed again. He shifted onto his knees and pushed himself up. He might not have been able to leap from branch to branch yet, but satisfaction with his progress filled his body, giving him as much energy as all the food he'd eaten.

Tyraz held out his hand.

"Shall we try a few steps?" he asked.

Jarlen accepted the offer, pulled Chara to his other side, and put one foot in front of the other. He'd made it back from the dead.

It took several hours before Jarlen could walk without assistance. He spent much of the time sitting against a tree trunk to recover his strength. Tyraz and Chara remained by his side, asking about his time in the netherworld, but he preferred to put those events behind him. He deflected the conversation to focus on the events of the past several months. Although the activities in and around Kroflund interested him, he couldn't wait to see Cassor and Eslinor again.

"Can you make it past that next hill?" asked Tyraz. "The old fisherman lives up there."

Jarlen remembered the place. Tyraz had borrowed a boat from the fisherman without asking and returned it with a hole in the bottom. They should have repaired the damage but instead rushed off to speak with Aiax about a potential war between the Arboreals and Ferfolk.

"Are you sure the old man wants to see us again?" asked Jarlen. "As I recall, you destroyed his property."

"I'm sure he'll welcome us as long as we don't borrow any more of his belongings." Tyraz smiled at him. "And don't worry about the boat. I sent a few men to fix it long ago. I'm sure it's in better shape than before we touched it."

Jarlen fought off his exhaustion and stood up.

"Let's make it a quick hike," he said. "I've had enough walking for the day. Chara, you should have a lot in common with that fisherman."

"I doubt it," she said as she placed his arm over her shoulder for support. "There's a big difference between freshwater and saltwater, but I'm hungry enough to suppress thoughts of the bizarre fish that got away from me. Let's see what he has for dinner."

With his friends' help, Jarlen made it to the fishing cabin just after the sun had set. No lights shone from within the house, and only the din of crickets' chirps rose over the whoosh of the river flowing past the decrepit structure. Tyraz rapped on the door.

"Is anybody home?" he called out. "It's me, Tyraz."

When nobody answered, he pushed the door open to find the main room a complete mess. Remnants of wooden chairs covered the floor, scratch marks adorned the walls, and shredded clothing lay scattered about. Tyraz rushed into the back room and returned a moment later.

"Nothing," he said. "But it looks the same as in here–signs of a terrible fight."

"If you didn't find a body," said Chara, "maybe your friend escaped."

Jarlen pulled Chara toward the nearest wall.

"It doesn't seem like a bear or sabretooth caused this damage," he said. "These scratch marks are too shallow to have come from powerful claws."

"I'll search outside," said Tyraz. "You wait here."

"I'm coming with you." Chara released Jarlen. "If you'll be all right on your own."

"Go with him," said Jarlen. "I'll look for more clues in here."

He leaned against the wall for support as the other two left the cabin. The back of the door appeared similar to the walls, except for a couple of deeper gouges. Jarlen snatched the closest chair leg and matched the end of it to the holes in the wooden door. Someone had smashed the furniture against the door. Either that person had very bad aim or hadn't been fighting someone else. He inched over to a pile of clothing near the back of the room. One of the leather vests had a set of teeth marks along the sleeve–human teeth. Jarlen sank to the base of the wall and sifted through the rest of the material.

Tyraz and Chara returned an hour later having learned nothing more about the fisherman's whereabouts. Jarlen handed them a few pieces of clothing with bite marks.

"There's no blood anywhere," he said, "so I doubt some creature ate your friend."

"Maybe he went into town to find help," said Chara as she tossed the vest back onto the pile. "Maybe the animal came in here after he escaped and trashed the place looking for food."

"And maybe it wasn't an animal," said Jarlen. "Something might have caused the fisherman to lose his sanity and attack the cabin on his own. I don't think we should stay here tonight."

"Then let's keep going," said Chara. "This place only reminds me of all the strange events we've witnessed recently."

"Jarlen's done enough walking for the day," said Tyraz. "He

has to rest."

"I'll rest once we make it to Kroflund." Jarlen stood on his own and headed for the door. "As I recall, the outskirts aren't too far from here."

Tyraz barged ahead of him to take the lead.

"Tell me when you need to stop," he said. "Chara, don't let him away from your side. It's going to be a dark night, and he could easily trip on a stray rock or fallen branch."

The brief rest had refreshed Jarlen, but he appreciated Chara's help. They marched quietly behind Tyraz, following the river upstream for a couple hours before a loud shriek pierced the air. Tyraz rushed toward the commotion, quickly outdistancing the others.

"Can you go any faster?" asked Chara. "Before we lose sight of him?"

Jarlen answered by increasing his pace. He felt more like himself and would have tried climbing into a tree if it were bright enough. They soon approached another shack where Tyraz had inserted himself between a small family and the old fisherman. The husband, wife, and three children huddled in their garden staring at the front door, guarded by the fisherman.

Tyraz pointed his sword at the old man, whose skin appeared quite pale in the moonlight.

"Come away from there," he said. "I don't want to hurt you."

The fisherman let out a low-pitched grown and ambled forward. His head bounced back and forth with each step, giving Jarlen a clear view of his cloudy eyes.

"He's one of them," said Chara, drawing her dagger. "Just like the dead farmer."

"No, he's not," said Tyraz. "He's my friend. Don't hurt him."

"Hurt him?" Chara crept closer. "He's already dead. He won't feel anything. You know what we have to do, Tyraz.

Don't let him harm these innocent people."

"Maybe I can help," said Jarlen.

He closed his eyes, raised his hands, and chanted, "*Alysan bans asendan eft.*"

"Nothing's happening," said Tyraz. "Are you sure you know what you're doing?"

The fisherman approached him and took a huge swing. Tyraz knocked his arm away but didn't launch a counterattack. Jarlen tried the spell a couple more times, both equally ineffective. He couldn't even feel a connection to the netherworld. He truly had sealed off the netherworld.

"My magic isn't working properly," he said. "We have to try something else. Can you capture him?"

"And do what with that infernal creature?" asked Chara. "Teach him manners? He's dead already. Let's put his body to rest."

Tyraz's furrowed brow and tense muscles belied his frustration. When the fisherman came at him again, he swung back, carving into his opponent. Metal repeatedly tore into flesh. Jarlen and the family members all turned their heads from the carnage until it was over.

"It's done," said Tyraz as he sheathed his sword.

Pieces of his friend's body littered the ground, but there were no puddles of blood. The father of the family extended his arm in gratitude.

"Many good thanks," he said. "We heard rumors about similar attacks in town, but we never thought it would happen to us."

"More attacks?" Tyraz darted away. "I'll come back for you tomorrow."

Jarlen nudged Chara in his direction.

"Go with him," he said. "I have to find out if there is another type of magic that can help."

"Don't tell me you're returning to the Forbidden Wood."

"I'm going to look through my mother's books about human magic," he said, "back in Hillswood."

"But we just found you," she said.

"You did," said Jarlen, "and you might even have helped me return to this world. I promise not to do anything like that again without speaking to you first. If something is bringing the dead back to life, we can't delay finding a solution."

He returned Chara's glare with a smile until she yielded. After a quick hug, she rushed after Tyraz. Jarlen headed into the forest with a sigh. Perhaps he shouldn't have sealed the portals to the netherworld.

Chapter X

Return of the Dead

As Chara darted after Tyraz, a sliver of moonlight reflected off the calm patch of water to her right. Up ahead, however, the river grew more turbulent, rushing through a narrow stretch over partially submerged rocks. The forest on both sides of the river thinned out, its tall trees yielding to flat farmlands and the occasional row of prickly bushes dividing the properties.

"Should we have convinced Jarlen to come with us?" she called out.

"It's not his job to protect Kroflund." Tyraz didn't slow down. "It's mine. Besides, once he's back to normal, he'll travel through the forest much faster than we could."

Chara didn't disagree, but she thought they would have been more effective as a team. The whole reason they initiated the search for Jarlen was to get answers about the dead bodies coming back to life, but they barely had time to ask him any questions before everyone went their separate ways. Hopefully he'd return soon with new information from his mother's library.

Tyraz kept increasing his pace the closer they got to the city. Chara could barely keep up with him. Her legs ached, she couldn't breathe fast enough, and her stomach kept reminding her that she hadn't eaten all day. With torn clothing and dirt covering most of her body, she wanted to head straight home for some much-needed rest, but she knew Tyraz intended to speak with his commander directly.

"Won't Aiax be upset that we didn't bring Jarlen back with us?" she asked.

"We found him," said Tyraz, "and he's gone to look for answers. That's more important. We're lucky we started the search when we did. Otherwise, he might have been sitting in that dark building for years. Hurry–it's not much farther."

Although Chara gasped for air, the rest of the night seemed peaceful around the outskirts of town. People slept quietly in their dark houses, an occasional rat roamed the streets in search of scraps, but more lights than usual brightened the center of town. Aiax must have doubled the guards patrolling the neighborhood. There might not have been any need for Tyraz and her to rush back home. With everything under control in Kroflund, they could have accompanied Jarlen to Hillswood and helped him dig through the hundreds of old tomes.

Unable to keep going without a break, Chara found the closest rain barrel and took a sip of the refreshing water. She splashed a handful on her face and leaned against the wall of a cobbler's shop. The coarse bricks felt cold against her skin, but the sturdy structure offered more than enough support. Nearby, Tyraz approached one of the night guards and was probably speaking about the events of the past few days. The peasant family must have exaggerated the rumors. Chara pushed herself away from the wall and stumbled toward Tyraz, forcing her tired legs to obey her wishes.

A shrill whistle pierced the air.

"Another one of them," shouted a nearby guard. "Don't let it go any farther."

He and three other men, including the one speaking with Tyraz, rushed toward Chara with their swords drawn. Her heart jumped as she spun around, looking for the vile creature about to pounce on her, but only the few Ferfolk graced the streets. At first, she thought the creature might have camouflaged itself until she realized the guards had targeted her. They dashed forward, focused on destroying their enemy.

"Stop," she screamed as the first sword swung downward.

The metal blade clanged against another sword, stopping only inches from her neck. Tyraz pushed the guard away and stood beside her, glaring at the men.

"Do you always attack without thought?" he asked. "You could have killed her."

The men backed away, yet kept their swords ready.

"There have been so many attacks this week," said the first guard, "and she looks no different from any of those infernal creatures."

"No different?" Chara ran her fingers through her matted hair, pulling out a small twig. "I find that hard to believe."

The first guard lowered his weapon and brought his oil lamp closer to her body.

"I suppose your skin has a bit more color," he said, "but not much."

"And what about my voice?" she asked. "Do I sound like I can only grunt or moan? Or have the dead started conversing with the living?"

"You didn't say anything until we were upon you," said the guard. "What are you doing on the streets at this hour anyway? You should be locked in your house, as per the curfew."

"We were away from town seeking an answer to this problem." Tyraz sheathed his sword and motioned for the remaining men to do so, as well. "When I heard about the frequent attacks in Kroflund, I rushed back to offer help."

"Unless you know of a way to end this evil," said the guard, "there's nothing more you can do. Whenever a dead body rises to attack, we cut it into small pieces. It's a gruesome job, but it keeps Kroflund safe."

Chara looked around. Even in the dark she could tell the streets were relatively clean. Either there hadn't been any attacks recently, or Aiax had assigned men to dispose of the remnants.

"What do you do with the...pieces of bodies?" she asked.

The guard sent the rest of the men away to continue their patrol, while he escorted Tyraz and Chara toward a graveyard. She'd never feared cemeteries before, but now that the dead bodies could come back to life, her heart beat faster as they neared the entrance. Each gravestone marked a potential spot for an undead monster to claw its way out of the ground. Every little sound caused her to jump, and the slightest breeze made her skin crawl.

"You don't have to come with us," said Tyraz as he held open the front gate. "Stay here and we'll be back soon enough."

"No place around here is safer than any other." Chara marched through the gate. "Let's get this over with."

As soon as she crossed the threshold, she tripped on a pile of soil and landed with her head facing into an empty pit. Tyraz jumped to her side and helped her up. She clung to him for an extra moment before releasing his arm. Scores of other holes littered the landscape, each with its own pile of soil nearby. The guard led them to one of the larger holes, this one filled with decomposing body parts. A rank odor wafted up from the ground, forcing Chara to turn her head.

"Why don't you fill in those holes?" she asked. "It's not only disgusting to leave them open to the elements—it's disrespectful to the families of those...people."

"We were spending too much time moving the dirt back and forth, in and out of the graves," said the guard. "Every night we'd fill in the holes, and every morning there would be new ones open. Now we keep a few of them ready for new deliveries, while the rest are covered up in the hopes they'll stay that way."

"You could have told us that back in town," said Chara. "Without forcing us to experience these noxious odors firsthand."

"That may be true." The guard drew his sword. "But I'm fairly certain you haven't seen anything like this."

He pointed into the hole. Chara covered her nose with her arm and peered down. The body parts convulsed, wiggled, and writhed, shifting positions throughout the hole. Legs, arms, and jaws moved on their own, each piece searching for something. After a few minutes, a pair of legs seemed to have joined together at the base of a skull.

"They're trying to merge into a complete skeleton," said Tyraz.

His words caused Chara to cringe. Even hacking the dead into little pieces might not be enough to stop them.

"Not necessarily a full skeleton," said the guard. "Just enough to escape the hole. We might be in control now, but once enough of these abominations come together, they'll overrun the town. There are many more dead than living."

"So just bury all the pieces apart from one another," said Chara, "or chop them into smaller bits. There has to be a better solution."

She was glad she hadn't eaten today, or the food might not have stayed down.

"We tried everything. At least this way, we know where the next creature will come from. With body parts this size, a new one forms about once per day. This latest composite should attempt its escape by sunrise. We'll have a few men waiting for it."

"You clearly haven't tried everything yet," said Tyraz. "Wait here."

He rushed back into town and returned several minutes

later with a lit oil lamp.

"Stand back," he said as he opened the cover and tossed the lamp into the hole.

Burning oil covered the body parts, sending up a blast of heat. The flames spread quickly, converting the stench of rotten meat into that of burning flesh. Soon only ashes and a couple charred bones remained in the pit. The guard stood motionless, staring at the hole.

"You...set them on fire," he said. "That's forbidden."

"Even to save the town?" asked Tyraz. "Let's do the same to the rest of these creatures."

"But..."

"They're no longer Ferfolk," said Tyraz. "Do you agree that we must protect the citizens from this scourge?"

The guard nodded but seemed unconvinced. He focused his gaze on the burnt remains, as if they'd come from a close family member. Chara kicked the pile of dirt into the hole to break its hold on the guard. Tyraz dragged him away and shoved him toward the front gate.

"Go back to your patrol," he said. "Chara and I will finish the work here."

Chara didn't appreciate being volunteered for the morbid task, but the sooner they finished, the sooner she could return home to her comfortable bed. Apparently nobody else in town would be willing to break tradition and burn the dead bodies, but until Jarlen came up with a better solution, this had to be done. She helped Tyraz locate a half dozen oil lamps, but allowed him to start each of the fires. They parted ways after the last of the fires had gone out and the sun was just beginning to brighten the cloudy sky.

As tired as she was, Chara couldn't fall asleep. She lay in bed and stared at the ceiling, obsessing over every shadow. Could the spiders and insects in her house come back from the dead? Did it matter? She probably couldn't tell the difference between a live spider and one that had died and come back to life, but she didn't want either one crawling around her body while she slept.

Instead of tossing about for the rest of the night, she lit her bedside lamp and got up. Clutter filled the house, more than she remembered from before her excursion with Tyraz. If he ever came for another visit, she couldn't let him see such a mess.

Starting in the bedroom and continuing into the kitchen, she collected anything that didn't belong or wasn't useful and tossed it into the main living area. Extra chairs went flying, empty barrels rolled from one room to the other, and more clothing than she knew she owned piled up in the center of the floor. Before long, she'd filled the entire room, and the rest of the house didn't even look less cluttered.

She climbed over the mounds of refuse and pushed against the front door, but it wouldn't open. No matter how much pressure she exerted, the door refused to budge. Behind her, the mass of garbage appeared to be growing, covering the room from the floor to the ceiling. It pressed against her body and pinned her against the door. She shook the door handle, slammed her shoulder against the wood, and screamed for help. In the past, her neighbor would come over at the slightest indication of a problem, but tonight the old lady must have been sleeping soundly in her own bed.

The debris crushed Chara against the door, making it difficult to breath. Any longer and she'd be killed by her own house full of garbage. Just when she thought she'd pass out, the door burst open.

Chara jumped up from bed. Her small lamp sat on the table nearby, and bright sunlight streamed through the window. Although the bedroom wasn't the cleanest space she'd ever seen, it was relatively empty of debris except for the thick layer of dust off to the sides. She fell back against her pillow. Somehow her dreams had to be connected to the events of the past few weeks. Since Aiax had the situation under control in Kroflund, perhaps she could convince Tyraz to accompany her back to the Arboreal Forest. And if he refused her request, she'd seek answers from Jarlen on her own.

Chapter XI

Return to Hillswood

Clouds had blotted out the moon and stars, making the night sky even darker than usual, but Jarlen kept going. If he'd caused Ferfolk bodies to return from the dead, he had to find a solution before anyone else was hurt. He didn't have time to rest, regardless of whether his body wanted him to continue or not. Traveling through the treetops had become too dangerous after the second time his feet got caught in the branches, so he returned to the ground and kept up a quick southward pace.

As an apprentice, Jarlen had pursued an interest in necromancy against his master Zehuti's command. Zehuti responded by magically sealing an important tome and forcing Jarlen to come up with a unique method to undo to the spell. Jarlen couldn't imagine what the old Arboreal would have done if he learned about this recent crisis. Even with the prospect of facing his master's harsh discipline, Jarlen wished to see Zehuti and his wife Otha again. Their wisdom had helped him overcome many seemingly insurmountable obstacles and would have been more than welcome when dealing with these bodies coming back to life.

A stray thought of one of these monsters harming Tyraz or Chara distracted him. He tripped on a root and went flying into the bushes. After brushing himself off, he continued southward. He had to solve this mystery before anything bad happened to his friends.

The sun's return to the sky chased away the nighttime chill and energized Jarlen, allowing him to increase his pace through the forest. Nothing slowed his progress, including the call of hunger, until a pair of Arboreals jumped out of a large beech tree in front of him. He veered off to avoid a collision and landed in a tangle of vines. At least they weren't covered in thorns.

"You must be Jarlen," said the older of the two Arboreals, helping him to his feet.

He wore a traditional hardened cloth vest atop a light shirt, while the younger one sported a green tunic normally reserved for tenderlings. They each carried a slender sword and had long green hair in a single braid tied with twine. Something bad must have happened in town for a tenderling to be allowed on a scouting mission.

"I am," said Jarlen. "But I've never met you before. How did you know it was me?"

"No other Arboreal travels along the ground," said the younger one.

"And your skin is quite pale," said the older. "This day might turn out well after all. We could use your assistance."

"I wouldn't usually turn down a request for help, but I'm on an important quest," said Jarlen. "One that might affect every creature in our forest."

He sidestepped the pair, but the older Arboreal darted ahead of him.

"We've heard rumors that you studied the human school of necromancy," he said. "No other Arboreal is more suited to lend us aid."

The word 'necromancy' chilled Jarlen. His quest should have rendered it defunct, nothing more than an archaic discipline in a safe world, but something had gone wrong.

"One of our elders returned to the forest a few days ago,"

said the younger Arboreal, "but his body rose that night and continues to plague us. Nobody feels safe at home anymore."

"This can't be." Jarlen fell to his knees, paralyzed with regret. "It's worse than I thought."

"What is?" asked the older Arboreal. "Have the other hamlets experienced anything similar to this?"

"I don't have news from other Arboreal villages, but the same has happened to the Ferfolk and some animals. Dead bodies rise at night to terrorize the living." Jarlen buried his face in shame. "I've ruined everything."

The two Arboreals helped him up. He gave them a quick smile of thanks but knew they wouldn't have been so nice if they believed his admission of guilt.

"Whatever you've done can be undone," said the older Arboreal. "The flower petals still greet the morning sunlight every day."

For now, but what if one day only darkness met the sun because of his mistake? Jarlen would not let that happen, yet he couldn't ignore their plea, especially if the undead creature threatened their family or friends.

"Show me," he said. "I'll do what I can, but then I must return to Hillswood forthwith."

The younger Arboreal spun around. "Someone else is here. Were you traveling with others?"

Jarlen was about to shake his head when Cassor and Eslinor dropped out of the trees behind the group. Eslinor rushed over to Jarlen, wrapped her arms around him, and squeezed tightly.

"I was so worried about you," she said. "Especially when Cassor told me you wouldn't wake up."

She examined him from head to toe before releasing him.

"How did a Ferfolk and a human manage what an Arboreal couldn't?" she asked.

"They did nothing special to rouse me," said Jarlen. "They just dragged me through the forest toward Kroflund. I don't remember much between my time in the netherworld and the bumpy ride on that makeshift sledge."

"Either way, I'm glad my services were proven unnecessary."

She stepped backward to allow Cassor in for his greeting. The Arboreal veteran hugged Jarlen twice as hard and for twice as long. His eyes conveyed a feeling of warmth and caring, but his clenched jaws and furrowed brow betrayed his true concern for the situation. He knew who was at fault. Jarlen glanced at Eslinor. Her smile didn't fade, whether she suspected his involvement or not.

"Don't be so happy that I've returned," said Jarlen. "I'm afraid that I've caused the dead to come alive and haunt the living."

"If that truly is so," said Eslinor, "then you are uniquely qualified to fix whatever you think you've done."

Her words of encouragement filled Jarlen with hope. The solution might not be easy to find or implement, but his friends had convinced him that it was possible.

"I hope to find answers in my mother's library, but first I promised to help..."

"Ieden," said the older of the two Arboreal strangers. "And this is Bresil. Come this way. Between the five of us, the former elder will have nowhere to hide. I just hope we can help him find peace."

Ieden led them to a small hamlet tucked within a copse of ironwoods. Arboreals in full leaf armor guarded each tree, as if the Ferfolk army were marching against them. No wonder they'd sent a tenderling to look for help. The rest of the town remained sheltered in their homes, afraid of the monster Jarlen had released upon them. He was glad that he'd decided to help. Nobody deserved to face such a horror.

As Jarlen wandered around the village, he gazed at the treetops, each one housing an innocent family of Arboreals. Although he'd felt like an outsider when growing up, always treated more like a human than an Arboreal, he missed his home in Hillswood. Many of the tenderlings who used to tease him had sacrificed themselves to save both the Arboreals and the Ferfolk from the evil lyche. They might have seemed cruel when they were younger, but they'd all proven themselves heroes. Jarlen had done the opposite and unleashed a terror upon society. He'd face whatever punishment was necessary, after he corrected his mistake.

"I found him," Cassor called out from nearby.

Jarlen rushed over to where an old, withered Arboreal plodded around the trees at the edge of town. Evidently the creature had difficulty climbing through the branches. Scratches covered its skin, and torn clothing barely covered its body. Leaves and twigs had embedded themselves in the creature's matted hair, and a layer of dried mud had encased its hands and fingers.

The others joined Cassor in the branches above Jarlen but didn't move against the creature. They probably didn't believe what they saw.

"Can you speak?" asked Jarlen as he approached the dead Arboreal. "We're here to help you."

The creature responded with a guttural moan as it leaped at him with its arms outstretched. Jarlen stepped backward but tripped on an exposed root, sending him to the ground. The creature caught him by the leg and dug its sharp fingernails into his skin. Jarlen screamed in pain and kicked it in the face. Instead of letting go, it caught his other leg and opened its mouth for a bite.

Cassor jumped down and landed on the creature's back, forcing it to release its hold. Jarlen pulled his legs against his body and put his hand over the wound, while Cassor drew his sword.

"Can you do anything to return his body to the soil?" asked Cassor.

"I don't think so," said Jarlen. "Necromancy no longer works properly. Tyraz's only solution has been to carve these creatures into little pieces."

Ieden landed on the ground between Cassor and the creature.

"You cannot violate his body like that," he said. "He was one of our elders and deserves respect."

Cassor squeezed the hilt of his sword but remained next to Jarlen.

"Look at its eyes. That creature is no longer Arboreal," said Eslinor, "but I agree with Ieden. We must find another solution."

She climbed down from the branches, placed a pair of leaves on Jarlen's leg, and sang quietly until the leaves hardened into a bandage. The gash stung at first but the pain soon abated.

"We can trap the creature," said Cassor, "but what should we do with it?"

"We'll bring it back to Hillswood and hope to find a more permanent solution." Jarlen stood with Eslinor's help and leaned against a trunk. "I promise to do whatever is necessary to end this scourge."

Cassor glanced at Ieden before staring into the branches at Bresil. Jarlen knew they were communicating without words but could only understand bits and pieces of their conversation. Zehuti and Otha had helped him learn about the different expressions and gestures, but he'd never mastered the silent language.

Ieden and Bresil disappeared into the forest, while Cassor kept his sword pointed at the creature. It appeared to understand the danger of the weapon and backed away. Cassor followed it at a distance, never allowing it to get too far from him. Jarlen limped after them with Eslinor's help.

They'd gone about a hundred paces when Ieden and Bresil returned with armfuls of large leaves. Cassor sheathed his sword, raised his hands, and chanted. Ieden tossed his bundle into the air, as did Bresil. The leaves swirled around the creature and attached themselves to its body. They linked together and contracted, eventually encasing the creature in a hard shell that left nothing uncovered. The creature squirmed in its bonds but couldn't break free. Ieden grabbed it by the head, Bresil took the feet, and they carried it away.

Cassor inspected Jarlen's leg and gave Eslinor an approving nod.

"Can you make it back to Hillswood?" he asked.

Jarlen pulled away from Eslinor and marched into the woods. This was his responsibility. He would not fail.

After a long hike through the forest, Jarlen welcomed the sight of Hillswood. An enormous banyan dominated the center of town, sending its branches hundreds of paces from the trunk to bury themselves in the ground. The rest of the homes spread out from the banyan forming two large spirals. Everyone stopped their activities to greet him with kind words and warm hugs. He promised to tell them all about his adventure after he got some much-needed rest, but he knew any festivities would have to wait until he'd ensured their safety.

Ieden and Bresil left the encased body just past the outermost spiral, where Cassor recruited a few Arboreals to guard the prisoner day and night. The two strangers asked to remain in Hillswood until Jarlen had found a solution. They obviously wanted to ensure their elder's body was treated with respect. Both Cassor and Eslinor agreed but had to confirm their decision with Aquila to make it official. Although the request was minor, Jarlen knew it could take hours or days for them to offer a formal response. He headed straight for his home, climbed the trunk, and collapsed into his branch bed.

Arboreals never slept the way humans did, instead meditating for several hours starting at midnight. Jarlen, however, always found himself falling asleep whenever he attempted to mimic their behavior. This time might be different. He closed his eyes and cleared his mind, but images of the dead Arboreal kept forcing themselves into his thoughts. The harder he tried to ignore the visions, the more vivid they became.

The dead Arboreal tore itself out of the cocoon and climbed into his bedroom. It snapped at him and raked him across the leg, shredding the leaf bandage that Eslinor had created. Jarlen knew none of this was real and turned his head to focus on all the work he had to accomplish. No matter how hard he concentrated on his plans for the next day, he knew he wasn't alone in the room. When he looked back at the creature, Zehuti's head topped the decaying body.

"Have you forgotten all that I taught you?" asked his master.

"I remember every incantation," said Jarlen. "But none of your lessons had anything to do with necromancy. Should I use elemental magic to burn these creatures?"

"I'm not talking about spells."

The creature pulled its head off its body and tossed it at Jarlen. As it flew toward him, its features softened and its hair lengthened until the head resembled that of his mother.

"I would listen to your master," she said. "Arboreals are resistant to change for good reason."

He ducked as the head sailed above him and disappeared through an opening in his wall. The headless creature fell to its knees and scratched at the ground outside the banyan tree. Its fingers did little more than shift the topmost layer of dirt.

Jarlen inched closer until his foot hit a solid object. He bent down and picked up a shovel.

"If you want to return to the soil," he said as he started digging, "I can make a hole for you. Stand back."

No matter how hard he slammed the shovel down, the metal blade would not pierce the ground. Around him, a dozen other headless creatures tried digging their own holes, but neither pickax nor spade were more effective than the shovel. The creatures were stuck above ground, ready to overrun the town.

Jarlen threw the shovel aside, closed his eyes, and ran. He had to get away, but it felt like his feet weren't moving. His body had become lodged in a deep hole. Around him, his tenderling friends were busy digging more holes. Some dug into the soft ground with their hands, while others used small spades or shovels. A young sapling grew out of every hole except the one that had caught him. He couldn't find a mature tree in any direction.

"Can you help me out of here?" he asked, but the tenderlings ignored him as they continued their work.

Something moved below him, pushing him upward. A tree had sprouted at the bottom of the hole, wrapping several branches around his legs and body. The tree grew taller, carrying Jarlen up into the sky, where the brilliant sun blinded him.

Jarlen awoke to a bright ray of sunshine in his eyes. He yawned and stretched his arms before sitting up. He didn't remember the last time he slept and would gladly suffer through many more nightmares to feel this refreshed every morning.

Not a single leaf was out of place in his bedroom, a sure sign that someone had taken care of his home while he was gone. He smiled as he climbed from room to room. It had to have been Eslinor. She'd been close friends with his mother and had taken care of him after his parents had died. He almost expected breakfast to be waiting for him, but he knew the elders had already resumed their discussions after last night's meditation. It was just as well; he had a lot of research to begin.

After discovering his mother's secret library during his quest to stop the lyche, Jarlen had moved all her books into a room deep within Hillswood's Gathering Tree. The cozy chamber had remained unvisited since then. No other Arboreal showed any interest in human magic, but one day that might change. Until then, the new library served as his own private study.

As soon as Jarlen reached the center of town, he was summoned into the elders' meeting chamber. Cassor, Eslinor, and Aquila were seated around a large branch table, munching on an array of brightly colored fruits.

"Please dine with us," said Eslinor. "You must be hungry."

A single flick of her wrist caused a fourth seat to form across from her. Branches from the floor rose up and weaved themselves into a chair for Jarlen. With a slight bow, he joined them at the table and selected a red apple.

"Cassor has told me you claim responsibility for these strange occurrences," said Aquila.

"None of this would have happened if I didn't seal the rifts between this world and the netherworld." Jarlen finished the apple in four bites. "Now I must find a way to undo the damage that I caused."

"And what if this solution makes things even worse." Aquila pushed the plate of fruit closer to him. "We have much more to discuss before making any decisions. Perhaps you should delay your research until we have come to a consensus."

Jarlen jumped up from the table.

"That couldn't possibly help," he said. "You have to admit that more knowledge is always better than less. What I find might even aid your deliberations."

"He has a good point," said Eslinor. "We know very little

about human magic. Cassor, what do you say?"

Cassor's gaze shifted from Aquila and Eslinor to Jarlen. The scar on the side of his face seemed darker than ever.

"Learn what you can from your mother's library," he said, "but come to us before you take any action."

"I promise," said Jarlen as he left the chamber.

He understood their hesitation. If he'd been more careful before closing the rifts, none of this might have happened. Next time, he'd be sure to know what he was doing, but he dared not wait for the elders to complete their discussions. They could spend the next few months in the meeting chamber, and too many lives were at risk.

Chapter XII

Ancient Wisdom

Jarlen's mother clearly had no interest in necromancy. It was the least represented school of human magic in the library. There were many more tomes about history and culture than information about bones and death. Jarlen had organized the room by subject, piling up all the non-magical texts in the far corner, but after several hours agonizing over ancient symbols, he still hadn't found anything helpful. He'd gone through the single necromantic tome in great detail and moved on to the related schools of sorcery and alchemy, tossing aside one book after another until he could barely move around the room. It seemed as if the number of items recovered from his mother's library had expanded since he'd moved them from the deep hole in the ground to the banyan tree. It would take another few weeks to sift through them quickly and decades to study—time he didn't have.

Jarlen remained in the room the entire day, keeping track of the passing time by the amount of sunlight filtering through the branches. As the last few rays disappeared, he realized he hadn't eaten anything since last night, and he'd found nothing related to dead bodies coming back to life. He threw the latest tome aside and grabbed another, promising himself to stop after completing a few more chapters.

Eslinor interrupted his reading when she entered the room with a plate of sliced fruits and whole nuts. She pulled the book away from him and replaced it with the food. He rubbed his eyes, angry at first, but the ancient symbols on the latest page had defied interpretation. He needed a break.

"Can you truly concentrate on your work without light?" she asked as she sat next to him. "I could barely see the words you were staring at."

She placed the book down out of Jarlen's reach.

"Your mother was just as passionate about her work," she said. "Once she started learning a new topic, she wouldn't quit until she'd mastered it. Such fervor often confused your father. Arboreals never understand the need to rush."

"So how did they get along?" asked Jarlen as he cracked open a pair of walnuts. "I don't remember them ever fighting."

"Nor do I," said Eslinor. "If they had disagreements, they hid them well, but they respected each other's differences. Your father allowed her to pursue her quest for knowledge, and your mother accepted the slower pace of the Arboreals."

"Apparently my mother was good at hiding things," said Jarlen. "I never suspected she was a wizard."

"Not many Arboreals approved of her passion, but your father always defended her, choosing acceptance over exclusion. I'm glad to see you're much the same."

"You mean choosing a forbidden topic to study?"

"That and your closeness with Tyraz. Despite your father's tolerant views on relations with other races, we're still quite removed from the Ferfolk. Perhaps your generation will bring our people together."

She took the plate from him when he was finished and placed it atop the old tome. Jarlen wanted to continue his research but felt it would have been rude to ask her to leave so soon.

"There seems to be more books in here than in my mother's library," he said. "Where did the other ones come from?"

"We combined most of the texts from the elders' libraries

with your mother's cache. It didn't make sense to have all this knowledge spread throughout the forest." Eslinor crawled over to the pile of history tomes. "You don't seem interested in these."

"They're not about human magic," said Jarlen. "I might read some of them later–after I've found what I'm looking for, but I don't have time for them now."

Eslinor dug through the pile, selected one of the books, and opened it to the middle. She scanned the pages with a smile.

"These might not teach you necromancy or elementalism," she said, "but that doesn't mean they're devoid of information."

She handed him the book and pointed at a detailed drawing of a skeleton.

"I realize this text only concerns the human body, but others could contain more clues."

"Looking through them all would double my work," said Jarlen with a sigh. "You should let me get back to reading...if you don't mind."

"Or..." Eslinor tapped on the far wall.

The branches parted and a hand reached through carrying a firefly lantern. Eslinor hung the lamp above her head and grabbed the nearest book.

"I could help you go through this pile if you tell me what you're looking for."

"That's the problem," said Jarlen. "I'm not sure what I need to learn. Something related to death or the netherworld would be best, but I'm ready to accept anything."

"We have a few more hours until midnight," she said. "Let's get started."

Jarlen pushed the plate aside and returned to the page he'd been studying. The ancient symbols appeared more understandable than they were before dinner. It could have been the added light or the recent meal, but having Eslinor's assistance didn't hurt. He gave her a quick grin and continued translating the page.

The fireflies had long since gone to sleep, leaving the small chamber in complete darkness. Eslinor had left before midnight and urged Jarlen to do the same, but he wanted to get in as much reading as possible before retiring for the night. He blindly crawled around the piles of books toward the exit but soon changed his mind. Why bother going back home only to sleep for an hour or two and return here in the morning? He found an empty spot on the floor, lay down, and closed his eyes.

Zehuti would have known what to do. He might not have understood the exact incantations necessary to stop the dead from coming back to life, but he would have guided Jarlen to the proper texts, regardless of his own views about necromancy. No other Arboreal cared about human magic as much as his old master. Although Jarlen had friends both here and in Kroflund, he felt alone in his quest for knowledge, even with Eslinor's assistance. She only read through the endless volumes to help her friend, not because the ancient knowledge interested her. Perhaps he should have tried to find Zehuti's spirit when he'd sent his mind into the netherworld. Now it was too late. He'd destroyed the links between the two worlds, and nobody else could help him.

A loud screech caused Jarlen to jump up. Several more growls and yelps followed the eerie noise, too close to have come from outside of town. Perhaps the dead Arboreal had broken free of his bonds and was attacking the citizens. Jarlen couldn't allow anyone to get hurt. He rushed out of the library and flew down through the branches toward the commotion, shivering in the chilly night air. The moon shone just bright enough to light the way, giving life to a pale shadow that kept pace with him. A layer of dampness coated the tree limbs, transferring onto his hands as he went along. He wiped his fingers on his shirt and pulled it tighter against his body to conserve the warmth.

Near the base of the Gathering Tree, a muscular blaeculf faced off against a smaller coyote. Neither animal was a common sight within or near an Arboreal habitation–blaeculfs preferred the dense jungles to the south and coyotes favored the edge of the wastelands. Even stranger, both creatures usually hunted in packs, yet Jarlen could detect no other animals in the area. He sneaked closer, remaining high above the ground.

A mat of black fur covered the blaeculf's body, although several bare spots dotted the shoulders and haunches. Blood stained most of the coyote's fur, and one of its hind legs appeared to be broken. This fight should have ended quickly with a blaeculf victory. The dark beast was twice the size of its gray opponent with a fierce temperament to match its bulk. Arboreals would often remain many trees away from a pack of blaeculfs on the hunt.

Jarlen was about to return to the library when a moaning growl came from the coyote. It leaped forward and sunk its teeth into the blaeculf's neck. The two animals wrestled each other to the ground, barking and yelping loud enough to wake the entire hamlet. As the tussle continued, Jarlen noticed that a large chunk of flesh had already been torn from the coyote's neck. There was no way the creature could have survived the attack.

A group of Arboreals soon gathered in the branches around the fight, including a few curious tenderlings. Jarlen waved a warning to them, but they ignored his frantic gestures and focused on the battling animals. He couldn't risk causing a panic if they realized the coyote had come back to life, and he doubted any of his magic would be effective. The spectators pointed at the creatures and gestured among themselves. If they didn't know something was different about these animals, they would soon. Jarlen couldn't wait any longer without acting.

"Get out of here," he shouted and hopped to the ground a few paces from the animals. "Take your fight elsewhere."

He stared up into the trees.

"I have this under control," he said. "It's just a couple of lost animals. Go back home and finish your meditation."

The two creatures paused their battle to stare at him through pairs of gray eyes. Both the coyote and the blaeculf must have died, which is why this fight had lasted so long. They might tear into each other for the next ten weeks if he didn't do something, but first he had to lure them far from town. The Arboreals seemed even more interested than before, climbing down for closer looks. Jarlen's heart beat faster, knowing the danger he'd put himself in, but he had to protect the innocent citizens. He waved his arms at the animals, shouted out another taunt, and darted away, hoping they'd follow.

A flurry of paws pounding against the ground answered his question. If either of the two creatures had been alive, it would have easily outrun him, but death must have slowed their muscles. His heart thumped in his chest, trying to keep up with his legs. He tried not to think about dying and coming back to life if either animal caught him.

Running as fast as he could, he kept just ahead of the pair until he cleared the hamlet's outermost spiral. He would have gone farther, but thicker vegetation slowed him, allowing his pursuers to close the gap. If only he'd learned to control living plants like a true Arboreal, but he always had a stronger connection to the dead.

He found a wide trunk to hide behind as the two creatures came to a stop. The smell of living flesh seemed to have made them forget about their feud. Jarlen doubted he could rekindle that mutual anger, but he had to try. He climbed into the tree and found a branch over the creatures' heads. They stared at him the whole time, probably waiting for him to fall so they could feast on fresh meat. He wrapped his feet around the branch and hung downward.

"Do you want a taste of me?" he taunted, waving his hands. "I'm right here."

The blaeculf jumped first, coming up just short and landing closer to the coyote.

"Not bad," said Jarlen as he stretched farther downward. "Does this help?"

The coyote leaped upward and brushed the tips of his fingers with its snout. When it came down, its front paw smacked into the blaeculf's face, evoking a fierce growl. The blaeculf snapped at the coyote, initiating another round of snarling. Jarlen should have brought a sword with him. He had no idea how to put these creatures to rest without carving them into small pieces, but he appeared to be safe for a while.

"What's happening here?"

Cassor's voice came from a few trees away and startled Jarlen. His legs loosened from the branch and he fell headfirst to the ground. The two creatures ignored each other and pounced at him. They soared over an intervening bush, but a pair of vines caught them before they touched down. Long green tendrils wrapped around their bodies and pulled them high into the tree as Cassor alit next to Jarlen.

"You shouldn't have taken on those beasts by yourself," he said as he helped Jarlen to his feet. "There could have been more of them nearby."

"I didn't want to cause a panic in town," said Jarlen. "What are you going to do with them?"

"Let's hold them with the reanimated Arboreal for now." Cassor sent the vine-encrusted creatures westward. "Until we find a better solution, I'll post more guards around town. I'm afraid this situation is only going to deteriorate the longer it takes to get answers."

Jarlen felt guilty enough already. He didn't need Cassor reminding him of his mistakes. They returned to the Gathering Tree together, where a large crowd had congregated in the branches. Aquila and Eslinor were assuring the citizens that Hillswood remained safe from this new threat. Cassor joined them and added his own words of support. Eventually the crowd dispersed, each Arboreal off to start his or her day, but Jarlen worried that this false sense of peace wouldn't last. The dead greatly outnumbered the living, and he might have initiated a war between the two. He returned to the library and collapsed against a pile of books. If he couldn't find answers in here, he feared there might be none.

Another growl woke him up, but this one had come from his stomach. Bright sunlight filled the room, pointing out the big mess of books strewn across the floor. With a sigh, Jarlen lugged a handful of tomes from the center of the room to the side, stacking them neatly against a few references about sorcery. Perhaps he'd see something he missed if he reorganized the library. Next time he'd return items to their proper places after finishing so he wouldn't have to waste daylight cleaning the room. He continued sorting out the texts until Eslinor arrived carrying a woven twig basket.

"I thought you might be hungry," she said. "You haven't left this room in two days other than your brief excursion with those beasts last night."

Her quick song caused a table and two chairs to form out of

the branches from the floor. She set the basket down and took one of the seats, motioning for Jarlen to sit across from her. A sweet, fruity smell filled the room, making him even hungrier than he already was. He hopped onto the chair and reached for the basket, but Eslinor's stern glare warned him to be more patient.

She handed him a leaf plate from the basket before lifting out a dark violet tart. Crushed nuts and seeds formed the crust, and a circle of edible flowers adorned the top. Eslinor must have spent hours preparing the dish, which looked too extravagant to eat.

"Why did you bring such a fancy meal?" asked Jarlen. "Is today special?"

"I'm just happy that you're home," said Eslinor as she served him an ample slice while taking a smaller one for herself.

Jarlen's mouth watered just looking at the food.

"Did it take you long to prepare this?" he asked.

His first bite filled his mouth with tartness, which slowly faded to sweet. The type of berries she'd used eluded him, but there could easily have been two or more varieties. She might have spent days scouring the woods for the proper ingredients.

"Working with elderberries requires patience," said Eslinor, taking small bites of her slice. "The traditional method of preparation includes peeling each berry by hand, discarding the skins, and bathing the pulp in an acidic bath for a week. You must take your time to deliver such unique flavor, but when I was younger, I thought I could speed up the process. First I tried leaving the skin on the berries, but a single taste after the bath gave me terrible nausea for three days. Next I reduced the soaking time, but even a single day shy of a week caused the same digestive problems. Undaunted I mixed the berries with every possible soothing agent I could think of, but nothing helped. I still remember each night, wracked with cramps."

She served Jarlen another piece after he finished his first. He could have eaten the entire tart himself.

"Did you ever find a faster way to prepare the berries?" he asked. "It's difficult to know what you might want to eat so far in advance."

Eslinor smiled at him, displaying a full mouth of purple teeth. The stains didn't detract from her beauty at all.

"Sometimes we must stick with what works, no matter how much better you think you can do. Now I enjoy following the instructions handed down to me and hope to pass them along one day."

Jarlen held up his plate for another piece.

"One more slice but that's all," said Eslinor. "We'll leave the rest for Cassor and Aquila. This is one of their favorites, and I'm out of elderberries."

After Jarlen finished eating, the table and chairs merged into the floor as Eslinor left the room. Jarlen returned to the sorcery pile, opened the top book, and began reading. The delicious meal had filled him with hope. One of these books had to have some answers.

Chapter XIII

Remains of the Dead

In the early morning darkness, Chara lit a candle and wandered into her kitchen. She knew it was empty, but she still hoped to find something to eat–a scrap of dried meat, a potato that had rolled under a chair, or a handful of raw grain to crunch on. Working in the cemetery for most of the night had given her a big appetite, making her regret not keeping a fully stocked pantry at home. She'd worry about that later, when she had extra time.

Fresh spider webs lined her cupboard, and not a single crumb contaminated the layer of dust collecting at the base of the walls. Even the pests would have had difficulty sustaining themselves in this house. Chara would have welcomed her neighbor showing up with freshly baked bread, but she remained alone for the entire morning, searching her house until it was light enough to snuff out the candle. Without a morsel to eat, she'd have to buy some food.

By the time she'd scrounged up a few coins to pay for breakfast, lunchtime had already passed, but Chara could still have a delicious meal at one of the taverns in town. On her way to the front door, she bumped into the basket that her neighbor had given her. Maybe she'd return it later and get one last home-cooked meal before she ventured back to the Arboreal Forest. Even better, she should fill the basket with a few treats as a gift for the old woman.

Chara headed to the marketplace with the empty basket

dangling on her arm. She never told her neighbor that she'd planned to be away before her search for Jarlen. The old woman had probably worried about her while she was gone and definitely would have visited this morning after seeing the candlelight moving about the house. Something must have happened to her. Chara shook her head to clear her thoughts, but the empty basket kept drawing her gaze.

She rushed to the first open shop and asked the merchant if he'd seen her neighbor recently, repeating the question to everyone she met, but the old lady hadn't come to the center of town recently. Food and gifts would have to wait. Chara hurried back home and rapped on her neighbor's door.

Nobody answered.

She tried the latch, found it unlocked, and pushed the door open. The front room appeared spotless, more organized than Chara's house even after she'd just finished cleaning, but a stale odor hung in the air. She'd encountered the same smell recently–in the graveyard last night. The stench of decay seemed to come from the kitchen.

"Please no," said Chara as she held her breath and darted to the back of the house.

When she reached the kitchen, Chara exhaled in relief at the sight of a bare floor and empty chairs. The smell hadn't come from her neighbor's decomposing body. A quick sniff of the overpowering odor led her to a large cooking pot perched above the logs in the fireplace. Perhaps the old lady had forgotten to start the fire, leaving her next day's meal to rot overnight. Maybe her tinderbox was empty, and she'd gone out to collect hay or kindling, or maybe she needed a new flint and had gone into the foothills to find the stone herself. Chara stepped toward the covered pot, too small to hold a grown Ferfolk but larger than necessary to cook one meal for a single old lady.

She grabbed a fire poker and shoved the lid off, causing a loud *clang* against the bricks. The pot responded by moving on its own, shaking once and then rocking back and forth on the spit. Whatever it contained wasn't completely dead. She peeked inside to find the dismembered remains of a small animal, perhaps a dog or a cat. Half the bones had been picked clean, while others still held lumps of rotting flesh. If Chara had eaten anything for breakfast, it would have made a quick return. At least she was no longer hungry.

Chara staggered backwards and knocked into a chair on her way to the door. The feet of the chair scraped against the floor, evoking a few *thumps* from above. The old lady must have locked herself upstairs, terrified of her meal refusing to stay dead. A deep sense of regret overcame Chara, forcing her legs to wobble. The poor woman shouldn't have had to suffer alone. She shook off the terrible feeling, bounded up the staircase two steps at a time, and stopped in front of a closed door.

"It's me, Chara," she said as she gave a few knocks. "I'm coming in to help you. I'm sorry I was away for a few days."

The old lady didn't respond, probably too frightened to speak. Chara opened the door to find her neighbor just inside the room, lunging at her with a kitchen knife. The blade sliced through Chara's sleeve, drawing a thin line of blood. She hopped away as the old lady stumbled forward.

"Everything will be fine now," said Chara, holding the wound. "I'll clean up your kitchen, and we'll cook something more palatable together. You probably have a big bin of potatoes somewhere. Put the knife down and help me find a clean cloth for this gash."

Dozens of bite marks marred the old lady's arms and legs, and dark red stains covered her clothing. She clung to the knife and pushed herself up from the floor with a scratchy groan. When she raised her head, a pair of solid gray eyes stared at Chara.

"Please tell me you're alive," said Chara as she backed up toward the staircase.

The knife offered hope. She'd never seen any animated corpse use a weapon before, but her neighbor's terrible wounds combined with grunts instead of speech could only mean one thing. She had died, but why could her corpse handle a weapon while none of the others could? The old lady was always cooking something. Perhaps wielding the knife was more instinct than thought, which would make dead soldiers even more dangerous. Chara refused to imagine a warrior that couldn't be killed, continuing to fight no matter how seriously wounded. If another war broke out between the Arboreals and the Ferfolk, nobody would survive.

Chara turned and ran–down the stairs, out the door, and kept going until she reached a group of town guards.

"Something happened to my neighbor," she said. "I think she died, but I'm not sure."

"We have another one," the lead guard called out. "We'll take care of it, young lady."

A nod to his men sent them back toward the house.

"She's a good woman," said Chara. "Make sure she's not alive before you..."

"We know how to deal with these abominations."

So did Chara. She wiped a tear from her eye. With or without Tyraz, she had work with Jarlen to end this curse.

The gate guards allowed Chara into the military compound, not because they were friendlier or more tolerant than the rest of the Ferfolk community. They'd heard about her involvement in defeating the lyche and knew she was dedicated to resolving the current situation. Although the complex spanned a good portion of the city, she didn't have to ask where to find Tyraz. There was only one possible place he could have been. Chara headed straight for Aiax's command center, but she'd only gone halfway when Tyraz intercepted her.

"I'm glad you came," he said. Dark spots under his eyes indicated he hadn't slept recently. "They won't listen to me."

"About what?"

"About cremating the dead." He took her hand and urged her toward Aiax's building. "Maybe you can convince them that it's necessary to protect Kroflund. Humans never cared what happened to the bodies of their dead."

Chara pulled away from him and crossed her arms.

"What is that supposed to mean? That we're uncivilized beasts?"

She couldn't believe Tyraz had made such a biased statement. He'd always seemed more accepting than the others.

"I'm sorry," he said. "I only meant that humans had no set rituals concerning death. If you explain this to Aiax and Septu, they might be more willing to compromise. Most of our men are already dedicated to patrolling the graveyards, and the situation will only worsen as more people die."

"Animals too," she said. "Don't forget what happened to the fish."

"Exactly." Tyraz urged her forward. "Tell them what you know. The more they hear the truth, the more they'll realize there's no choice."

Chara wasn't surprised that Tyraz couldn't convince Aiax with Septu around. The tall lieutenant had always opposed Tyraz. This might have nothing to do with Ferfolk traditions. Septu had probably placed his feelings of jealousy in front of his duty. Chara had to separate him from Aiax before pleading her case.

She followed Tyraz a few steps when a vision of her neighbor stopped her. The old woman fought off armed guards, who sliced into her with swords and doused her with flaming oil. She screamed in pain, trying to put out the fire. Chara couldn't bear to see the old woman or anyone else in such a gruesome struggle, especially if any part of them was left behind in the animated body.

"I can't do it," she said. "What if the creatures aren't truly dead? What if we're torturing them, causing them to die in agony and despair when we should be trying to cure them?"

"You know that's not true. You've seen it for yourself–in the graveyard."

"But she always treated me so well. I've never met a Ferfolk as kind as her." Tears flowed down her cheeks. "They can't...we have to save her...somehow."

Tyraz put his arm around her shoulder and brought her close. The warmth of his body comforted her, pushing aside her terrible thoughts. It wasn't her fault that her neighbor had died, yet she still felt guilty.

"I'm sorry that a friend of yours is gone," he said, "but we have to put her body to rest–if not for any other reason than to protect everyone else in town. She wouldn't have wanted to harm anyone."

Chara knew he spoke the truth but still found it difficult to accept. She dried her cheeks and gave him a weak smile.

"We can try to convince Aiax once more," she said, "but then we have to help Jarlen find a solution. Nobody else should suffer from this curse."

"We can pack supplies and leave by sundown."

Tyraz led her into the command center, where Septu stopped them in the hallway with a stern look.

"Aiax has already made his decision," said the tall warrior. "You have your orders. I suggest you follow them."

His shaggy hair set him apart from the other soldiers in the compound, even more than his towering height. He placed his hands on his hips, blocking the path to Aiax's room. With such an imposing figure in the way, Chara doubted Tyraz's ability to get past his rival. If Septu wanted to fight an unwinnable battle against the dead, let him. They had a more important mission to complete.

"We only need a few minutes with Aiax," said Tyraz. "He hasn't heard from Chara on this issue."

"We don't need advice from humans or females," said Septu, "but either way, Aiax has already left to discuss the matter with the town council."

"Discuss what matter? I thought he was against cremation."

"He was until I convinced him otherwise." Septu stepped forward and glanced at Chara. "Are you heading out, or will I have to take your place? She's no Ferfolk, but I wouldn't argue against spending a bit of time with her. You know where the Arboreal lives, I assume?"

Chara glared at him. Aiax had probably ordered Tyraz to retrieve Jarlen, but either way she'd never work with Septu even though she was wrong about him. He apparently placed duty before feelings, but his condescending attitude disgusted her.

"We're going now." Tyraz backed away from the tall warrior. "I'm sure you have orders, as well."

He spent an extra moment glaring at Septu before turning for the door. Chara didn't look back.

"Were you planning to go to the Arboreal Forest without me?" she asked as soon as they left the building.

Tyraz's silence answered her. She should have been more upset, but she knew his only reason was to keep her safe. He should have known better.

Every item in Tyraz's room had its own place, including the supplies he'd already picked up for his trip. His bed looked as if nobody had ever slept in it, a large trunk held all his clothing neatly folded, and a single chair accompanied a table tucked into the corner. Two backpacks sat upon the table, one of which overflowed with dried meats, hard cheeses, and thin loaves of bread. He'd packed enough to avoid eating Arboreal food for weeks. Tyraz fastened the top, grabbed the second backpack, and filled it with the remaining gear.

"We'll stop at your place on the way out of town," he said.

"Never mind that," said Chara. "I'm ready to go. It's already getting late."

"We left too quickly last time," said Tyraz. "This is your chance to bring whatever you might need."

"If you mean palatable food, I think you have us covered for the month." She strolled to the window and peered outside. "Otherwise, I'm good."

Lamplighters circled the compound, adding a flickering orange glow to the darkening night. Flames danced within the nearest lantern, prompting Chara to draw the shades and hop back to the center of the room. Perhaps they should wait until morning if every fire made her think of her neighbor suffering at the hands of those hoping to protect the town. The old woman didn't deserve to have her body butchered and set aflame. Perhaps the Ferfolk burial customs had some merit.

Chara's grandfather would have gotten along well with her neighbor, if he could get past the fact that she was a Ferfolk. They might even have moved in together. He'd provide fresh fish every day, and she'd cook the catch into a scrumptious feast. Chara would have lived with them in Luceton, helping out in the kitchen or on the boat, until she met someone for herself. Life would have been much simpler and much more joyful. Maybe it was better the old woman had died. She didn't have to witness these mounting horrors.

A rapping at the door caused Chara to jump. A pair of Ferfolk soldiers in full armor stood outside. Although their skin blended with the hardened leather, chain links woven into the chest, leg, and arm pieces made it easy to distinguish the two. Long, serrated swords lay at their sides–battle weapons more fearsome than the everyday sabers Chara had become used to seeing.

"There's been a change of plans," said the first soldier. "Aiax needs you at once."

"This can't be good," said Chara. "What happened in the past few hours?"

"We weren't given the details," said the second soldier, "but we heard rumors."

The first soldier stepped inside the room and leaned into Tyraz. Chara inched closer to them.

"The council didn't agree with Aiax's suggestion," he whispered, "so he decided to take over the city."

"That's impossible." Tyraz pushed the messenger back outside. "Aiax would never resort to violence against his own people. Where is he?"

The guards led him toward the center of the compound with Chara following a few steps behind. In the course of one day, Aiax had gone from opposing the idea of cremation to starting a military coup to enforce the solution. Something didn't make sense. The rumors had to have been false.

Along the way, they passed several groups of soldiers marching toward the front gate. Each of the men wore the same outfit as the messengers. Either there had been an outbreak of living dead, the peace-loving Arboreals had initiated an attack, or Aiax was indeed taking command of the city. Chara clenched her teeth and curled her fingers into fists. Violence would only make the problem worse. Surely they understood the need for restraint.

Aiax stood outside the command center barking orders at

anyone who approached him.

"You can't do this," said Chara as she marched up to the grizzled Ferfolk. "Kroflund has been a free city for ages."

Tyraz tugged at her arm, but she shrugged him off. She didn't care that Aiax commanded the entire Ferfolk army. He would listen to her.

"And why wouldn't it remain free?" asked Aiax.

"Because you're using might to force your will upon the people."

"Only to protect them." Aiax waved away the two messenger guards. "This was Tyraz's idea, anyway. You should be just as angry with him."

"He never intended to start a coup, only to stop the dead from returning to life."

An initial smile on Aiax's face turned into a hearty laugh. Chara wanted to yell at him but held her voice.

"This is nothing of the sort," he said. "The council still rules the city, except in the single matter of what to do with corpses until this situation is resolved."

"Then why do you need me?" asked Tyraz.

"We can all agree that no living Ferfolk must be harmed," said Aiax. "Many citizens will oppose cremation, just like I did at first. It will take every soldier in this army to protect the town for the next few days. Once we've proven that Kroflund is safe again, you can resume your quest to find a permanent solution."

"But what if burning the dead doesn't help?" asked Chara.

"You've already shown fire to be an effective weapon," said Aiax. "What could possibly go wrong?"

Chapter XIV

For the Greater Good

Jarlen leaned against the branch table in the middle of the library. He and Eslinor had gone through every book and scroll in the room and laid out anything that referenced death or dying. Old tomes lined the table from one end to the other with various scrolls filling any gaps. Jarlen had difficulty interpreting the archaic dialects in the older texts, but he persevered, eventually translating everything they'd found except for a single, ancient scroll. Neither Jarlen nor Eslinor understood any of the strange symbols, but Eslinor recalled seeing similar characters on some of Kuril's belongings. While she tracked down the items in question, Jarlen kept looking for any clue, no matter how small.

Several tomes described methods to bury the dead from each of the four races. Each ceremony included unique rituals to prepare and inter the body, but all seemed designed to help the spirit during its transition between worlds. Somehow Jarlen had interrupted the natural order, forcing the spirits to roam the land or return to their broken bodies. It didn't matter that he was trying to help. He had caused this terrible situation, and only he could fix his mistake. The proper solution was to restore the links between this world and the netherworld that he'd sealed.

The minimal necromantic information he found was from the books he'd originally studied during Zehuti's guidance. He'd already memorized each incantation and used most of them at some point. At first, many of the spells didn't work as he'd expected, mostly due to his inexperience, but he'd become quite proficient recently. More advanced books on the topic must have existed in the past, but the passage of time would have destroyed them. If he wanted more powerful magic, he'd have to recreate the more intricate spells on his own. Unfortunately, he didn't understand how the necromancers from long ago had performed their research. Was it strictly trial and error, or had they methodically analyzed prior knowledge to come up with new theories?

Jarlen shoved all the books onto the floor. None of them had done anything except waste his time. He kicked over a few piles. The longer it took him to find a solution, the more people would be hurt by the living dead. He slammed his fists against the branch table, shaking the tree. The fight between the blaeculf and the coyote had only been the beginning of this curse. As more animals and Arboreals died, curiosity would eventually turn into fear and panic. Nobody could find peace when surrounded by dangerous creatures. He wouldn't have been surprised if some citizens had already started barricading themselves in their houses.

"Those books don't deserve your wrath," said Eslinor as she entered the room and restored the nearest stack. "You should go out for a few hours, while the sun still shines."

"I don't deserve a break," said Jarlen. "Not until I make some progress. Did you find anything?"

There was no point dawdling outside while innocent people were in danger.

"I might have." Eslinor took him by the hand and pulled him toward the doorway. "But you'll have to indulge me first. A walk around town will clear your head and make it easier to concentrate."

Since she hadn't brought anything into the room, she must

have planned this distraction. Arboreals never thought time mattered, and Jarlen wasn't sure if he agreed with their relaxed attitude. He couldn't, however, dissuade Eslinor from delaying his research and had to accept her invitation. She smiled over her shoulder as she brought him outside.

Several Arboreals waved to Jarlen as he climbed through the Gathering Tree. Tenderlings attended classes in the outer branches, sprouters kept watch over their seedlings, and gardeners harvested fresh greens at the peak of their flavor. Either they hadn't yet realized the danger, or they trusted Jarlen and the elders to guide them safely through this latest threat. He could never live with himself if he let them down.

Eslinor led him southward until they reached the swamp at the edge of town. Polsor had lived nearby, but since then, few citizens ever visited the area, giving Eslinor a private spot for the picnic she'd prepared. No wonder she refused to let him remain in the library. Several dishes of aromatic food rested on a large limb that stretched far over the pond. Jarlen looked for any invading insects, but Eslinor must have enchanted the area to keep the food safe. She'd gone through so much trouble for a single meal. He appreciated the effort but still didn't want to waste more time away from his studies than necessary.

Jarlen draped his legs over the thick branch and stared at his reflection in the calm water below. Did Eslinor know this was where he'd first encountered Polsor after Oengus's spirit had taken over the elder's mind? He'd been searching for deadly nightshade when Polsor tried to convince him to give up necromancy. Had that been the Arboreal elder talking, or the evil spirit? Jarlen had always assumed Polsor wanted him to become more Arboreal, but perhaps the spirit feared he might learn how to send it back to the netherworld. Now that spirit would have gotten its wish. With the links to the netherworld severed, it could have caused havoc in this world with no fear of being sent back.

"Your mind is elsewhere," said Eslinor. "Come, I'll show you what I found."

She'd probably spent as much time preparing the feast as searching for Kuril's belongings yet seemed willing to give it all up to indulge Jarlen's thirst for answers. He couldn't refuse her hospitality.

"I'm sorry." Jarlen took a fresh apple from her basket. "I won't think about the research until we're done eating. Tell me about these dishes you prepared."

He took a small bite of the fruit, savoring its crisp crunch followed by subtle sweetness. As he shifted his position on the branch, a leaf fell into the water, sending ripples all the way to the other side. A moment later, the water in the pond had settled back down, its surface as flat as a polished shield.

Jarlen wished he'd never translated the last scroll. Maybe he misinterpreted the ancient symbols, or maybe the old journals that Eslinor had uncovered were wrong. Maybe they were written in a different language that coincidentally had similar characters. He returned the scroll, unfurled alone on the table. The writing seemed to tie all the other information together, explaining how deaths enhanced the links to the netherworld, especially through sacrifices. Ancient people must have started their funerary rites to block any spirits returning from the netherworld. If it were possible to undo his sealed portals, it would have to be through a live sacrifice.

The scroll taunted him, daring him to follow through with the plan. No other Arboreal would have considered the possibility, but Jarlen never truly fit in with them. He'd spend his years as a tenderling isolated from the rest of his peers, subjected to their laughter and pranks. Eventually, Zehuti and Otha took him in, fueling his interest in human magic and further distancing himself from the Arboreal community. So why not try a sacrifice? If it worked, nobody would think less of him than they already did.

He couldn't do it–he couldn't kill an innocent animal, but perhaps Tyraz would. Ferfolk didn't place as high a value on life as Arboreals did. No. How could he ask his friend to commit such a deed to fix a mistake he had made? This was his responsibility alone. He stumbled out of the library into darkness. The sun had already set, but it hadn't yet reached midnight. Although not many Arboreals were out at this time, Jarlen preferred not to interact with anyone. He climbed to the ground and headed for his house.

The altar outside of Kroflund would have been a good spot for the sacrifice, but Jarlen preferred to be as far from civilization as possible for this experiment. He didn't know what would happen after reopening a link to the netherworld. At best, the spirits of the recently deceased would finally be at peace, but if a creature from the other side forced its way through, he needed time to warn everyone before it attacked. He'd build a new altar somewhere to the southeast, far from both the Arboreals of this forest and their cousins who lived in the southern mountains.

Jarlen collected supplies from his house, including the ceremonial dagger with a jade handle that had belonged to his master Zehuti. On his way out of town, he passed Eslinor's tree and whispered a quick goodbye. He wasn't sure he could face her or any other Arboreal again after the sacrifice. This could be his last few moments in Hillswood, and he finally felt a stronger connection to his people. He ambled toward the edge of town, recalling memories both good and bad, stretching a hike that should have taken minutes into a journey of several hours.

As he distanced himself from the hamlet, more animals than

usual appeared around him. Squirrels waited on thin branches for him to get close before scurrying up the trunk, deer stood munching tender leaves and twigs several trees away, and birds lined the lower canopy. Were the animals drawn to the smell of food he carried in his pack, or did they want his help against the undead plague? Jarlen focused on the ground directly in front of him and hummed an Arboreal lullaby to himself. He couldn't listen to the melodious tweets without imagining the jade knife silencing the poor creature forever. The animals, however, seemed to become more comfortable with him the deeper into the woods he traveled. Dozens of creatures turned into scores, and sounds amplified until he could no longer keep them out of his head.

"Go away," he shouted and waved the dagger. "I don't have anything for you except a quick death."

A few birds on the lowest branches hopped higher into the tree, and the nearest pair of deer looked up at him, mouths holding steady on their last bite. He veered off his path toward the deer.

"You want to help me?" he called out as he leaped over a patch of ferns. "I'll show you what I need from you."

The deer bounded away before he reached them. Jarlen drove the dagger into the ground where the deer had stood moments before and fell down beside it. He shouldn't have scared the animals away. This was their home. At least nobody saw him act so irrationally. He looked up into the trees to confirm that he was alone, feeling blood rush into his cheeks. The wind ruffled a few leaves high above his head.

Two more days of hiking brought him to an outcropping of large rocks. He would have preferred to be farther from Hillswood, but a relatively flat boulder made a perfect base for his new altar. A nearby stream offered a supply of decent-sized stones to line the area. Jarlen wasn't sure if it was necessary, but he tried to match the layout of the altar outside Kroflund as closely as possible. By evening, he was satisfied with the preparations, but he worried that the waning light might cause him to miss something. He needed to have a clear view of the area to ensure nothing unexpected came through the opening. His sacrifice would have to wait until morning.

The night refused to end. Jarlen could neither meditate nor sleep. He lay awake on a branch, wondering why he ever chose to seal the portals between worlds. There had been no problems for millennia, and he thought he could make things better? The evil spirit that had inhabited Polsor's body and the destructive lyche had escaped the netherworld, but an inexperienced necromancer and a young Ferfolk had stopped them. The world would continue to exist without his interference. Perhaps the elders were right. Maybe he shouldn't even try to fix his mistake, but what if he'd altered a fundamental part of nature? What if his error caused irreversible damage if left as is.

He slid off the branch in the dim, morning light to search for an unsuspecting animal. If Tyraz were here, he would have justified the sacrifice by offering to eat the remains after the ceremony. Jarlen only wanted to put this past year behind him—fix his mistake, apologize to the poor animal, and never see this altar again. He crept through the woods until he found his victim, a muskrat that had gotten caught in a tangle of vines. The animal had chewed through half of its restraints and bared its teeth at him when he reached in.

"I have to do this," he said as he grabbed the animal by the scruff of its neck. "Your death will save countless others."

The muskrat squirmed in his grip, flailing its legs. It didn't care about noble causes. Maybe it had children to feed, or a pregnant mate. Jarlen held it away from its body on his way to the altar, but it never stopped struggling. He could drop it and find another animal to sacrifice. Or he could forget about this plan and hope this terrible situation resolved itself. He didn't have to return to civilization. He could wander the land on his own, avoiding any contact with Arboreals or other races. It wouldn't be much different from his current life. Of course, Tyraz and Chara would track him down like they did before. They'd never allow him to live in isolation, even if he pleaded his case to them.

Jarlen marched to the altar and held the muskrat against the cold stone. He made one quick slice with the knife while chanting the spell to call forth a skeletal servant. As the warm blood flowed over his fingers, he glimpsed the red sky of the Lava Plains. A moment later, the vision disappeared, leaving him staring at the still carcass in his hand.

He dropped the knife as his knees buckled, sending him to the ground. Jarlen wiped his hand on his shirt but kept his eyes focused on the sacrifice. The dead muskrat remained motionless on the altar the entire time. Something definitely had happened. He'd contacted the netherworld briefly before the link closed again. The sacrifice had almost worked, but killing more animals wouldn't help. The passage to the netherworld closed too quickly after its death. To open the link permanently, he needed something with a stronger spirit.

Jarlen pushed himself away from the altar. He wouldn't do it. Killing an animal was bad enough. He could never commit murder, even with a willing subject. He jumped to his feet and ran. It didn't matter where, as long as he was far from the altar.

Exposed roots tripped him several times, but he didn't deserve to travel through the treetops. He'd violated one of the basic Arboreal instincts–to protect life. He could have blamed his human half, but wouldn't anyone have done the same to protect friends and family? The elders would have had to agree given enough time for their discussions, but the more he assured himself of their eventual understanding, the worse he felt. His actions had been despicable. He shouldn't have killed the innocent muskrat, but would he have thought differently if the sacrifice had succeeded?

The next time he tripped, his body wouldn't allow him to get up. He rolled onto his back and gazed at the sparse bits of blue visible through the thick foliage. The slightest breeze obscured his peek at the sky, covering the tiny openings with a wall of leaves. After catching his breath, Jarlen hopped onto the lowest branch and climbed the trunk until he broke through the emergent layer. Bright sunlight warmed his face, forcing him to cover his eyes with his hand, still stained with blood.

Jarlen remained at the top of the tree until pinks and oranges lit the sky. He'd never kill an innocent person, but forcing open a link to the netherworld required a live sacrifice. Only one option remained. As long as he completed the incantation, it didn't matter what happened to him. Positive this plan would work, he slid down the trunk and returned to the altar as the moon rose. The muskrat carcass was gone, probably taken by a hungry predator, tired of fighting its prey long after the supposed kill. At least the poor creature's body had not gone to waste.

If he restored the link to the netherworld tonight, everyone would be safe, and Tyraz would eventually learn about his sacrifice. If the link didn't remain open, however, his friend deserved an explanation. Jarlen found the jade knife and carved his final words to Tyraz into the base of the widest trunk near the altar. He apologized for causing so much chaos and thanked Tyraz for his friendship. With blade in hand, Jarlen climbed onto the altar and began the incantation.

As he neared the end of the chant, he took the knife in both hands and raised it above his head. This had to work, and it was a fitting punishment for his naïve rush to seal off the netherworld. He pointed the tip of the blade at his neck, ready to end his life.

"No, Jarlen," shouted a female voice.

Eslinor flew down from an overhanging branch and crashed into him. He hit the boulder hard, pinned under Eslinor's body.

"The muskrat," she said as she pulled the bloody knife from between their bodies. "I don't think..."

When the knife clanged against the stone, an explosion flung Jarlen off the altar. He sailed through the air, collided headfirst against a solid trunk, and passed out.

Chapter XV

Up in Flames

The pyres lit the night sky almost as brightly as the sun on a cloudy day. Towers of billowing smoke rose upward, glowing bright orange from the flames below. Chara's entire body reeked from the acrid fumes, and a layer of sooty ash covered her head. Although the noxious odor disgusted her, she knew she could get through it, especially since they were nearing the end of the bodies. One more night of this horrendous work should do it. She had to ignore the terrible smell, just like when she first learned how to clean fish.

Perhaps her grandfather shouldn't have taught her this skill on the hottest day of the year, but they'd returned from a particularly successful fishing trip with a bountiful catch. He probably wanted help to prepare the fish for salting before they rotted in the fierce sunlight. As a young girl with a sensitive nose, Chara already had one arm draped across her face to keep out the unwanted odors, but her grandfather would have none of that.

"Make the first cut here," he said as he sliced into the fish's side behind its head.

He drew the knife along the bone until it came out near the tail. It looked so easy, but Chara wasn't interested in trying if it meant taking her arm away from her face. She could handle the smell of live fish, but once that odor mixed with death, she preferred to be elsewhere. Her grandfather flipped the fillet to continue the lesson.

"Hold the back end firmly between your thumb and palm, cut down with the knife, and pull the skin off."

With a couple yanks against the blade, the skin separated from the fillet. Her grandfather tossed the skin into a small bucket. Some people enjoyed the skin as a snack, after the scales had been scraped off, but Chara hated how tough and chewy it became. Instead, she'd bury the skins for a week or two before using them as bait on a future trip.

Chara shivered. When she was younger, she'd never thought about attracting fish with their own skins. Did they know they were eating one another? Or was there not enough food to go around in the ocean? Either way, Chara promised herself to use live bait whenever she fished again. The fire in the pit burned brighter, ending the tortured afterlife of the corpses with a blast of malodorous fumes.

Before her filleting lesson, Chara's job was to wash the deboned fish in fresh water, cover the strips in salt, and place them in a large barrel. Well-prepared meat could last months, but no part of the fish went to waste. Bones would always go into a large pot to make broth. The first day or two, Chara loved the taste of fish soup, but by the end of the week, she could barely force it down her throat.

Her grandfather offered her the knife with an encouraging grin. She took the blade, held down the next fish with all her weight, and dug in. The sharp knife crunched through the bones, nearly taking off the entire head.

"Not so hard," said her grandfather. "We're not soldiers attacking the enemy. Let the blade do the work, and if it doesn't cut on its own, it's time for sharpening."

He flipped the carcass over, placed his hand atop hers, and guided the knife along the bones. The meat came off with little effort. A quick tug on the tail against the blade along with a slight back and forth motion separated the fillet from the skin.

"Your turn," he said, releasing her hand.

From then on, he only observed her progress. It didn't matter if their salted fish would have a bone or two in it. He let her prepare the rest of the catch on her own. Even when she cut into her hand, he didn't take back the knife. He patched her up, gave her another pointer, and kept the fish coming.

As the flames from the pyres dwindled, Chara sent her two assistants back to the military camp. Their commander would surely wake them at sunrise, if not before, and there was little for them to do here except bury the ashes. Chara grabbed the shovel and started filling in one of the pits where the fire had already died out. One more night of this–only because the citizens would protest if she tried to cremate any bodies during the day. She tamped down the soil and moved to the next hole. Perhaps this was just a new way of life for the people of Kroflund. Cremation versus burial. The Ferfolk would eventually get used to it, maybe even start some new traditions. With a yawn, she finished her work and headed home.

Chara couldn't sleep. She lay in her bed, staring at the ceiling until the patch of sky visible from her window started to brighten. A bump from somewhere outside drew her attention. She rolled out of bed and leaned against her windowsill. Faint hints of red and orange outlined some thick clouds, while a dark figure dragged a large chair out of her neighbor's house. Nobody should have been there, especially before the remains of the old lady had been cremated. Chara rushed next door to confront a middle-aged Ferfolk.

"What are you doing?" she asked. "That chair doesn't belong to you."

"The old woman's dead," he said. "She doesn't need furniture anymore."

Chara latched onto a leg of the chair and tugged, but the

strong Ferfolk just pulled her along with it.

"She's not even buried yet," said Chara. "You would defile her house before her body's in the ground?"

"I've heard the rumors." The Ferfolk yanked the chair away from her. "You don't intend to bury the poor woman or anyone else that dies. No traditions, no rules, everyone takes what they want. This is the new world."

"As you wish."

Chara darted into the house and bolted the door shut. Already most of the furniture was gone, along with any gold or silver items. Her footsteps echoed against the barren walls as she charged into the kitchen and jammed the sole remaining chair against the back door. If people planned to pick the house clean, she'd make sure nothing of value, either monetary or sentimental, remained inside. She owed her neighbor at least that much.

By the time she'd found an oil lamp and a tinderbox, enough light streamed through the small windows not to need them. Nobody else, however, would claim those or any other of the old woman's possessions as their own. Chara emptied a burlap sack of potatoes to carry everything she wanted to protect from the greedy Ferfolk, and started in the upstairs bedroom.

A collection of pillows adorned the old woman's bed, each one intricately decorated with images of flowers. The roses sewn into one pillow looked so realistic, Chara thought she could smell the delicate aroma. Someone had spent months creating these works of art, destined to be discarded by the insensitive treasure hunters. Chara stuffed them all into the sack and moved to a heavy, wooden dresser across from the bed.

She dug through the drawers, tossing the clothing aside. The Ferfolk could keep all those rags, except for one blouse that had caught her eye. With a high neck and rugged weave, it had to have come from Luceton. Chara pressed the shirt against her face and took a deep breath. She didn't care if she imagined the scent, but she smelled the crisp ocean air on a calm summer morning. The old woman must have lived in Luceton at some time, and she might still have family there. If so, they deserved to know she'd passed, and Chara would see that they did once she'd completed her responsibilities in Kroflund.

With even more reason to collect the old woman's personal possessions, Chara scoured the rest of the house, making several trips back home to empty the sack on her floor each time. She finished her work in a few hours and left both doors open to allow other neighbors to scavenge anything that remained. Exhausted, Chara collapsed into her chair and stared at the towering pile. Her neighbor's entire life had been reduced to a mound of clothing and household items in the center of her floor. Was this her destiny, as well? Fill her house with meaningless belongings to be raided as soon as she died? She let out a sigh and dug through the pile for the tinderbox, planning to use it during the next cremation.

"You look tired," said Tyraz as he approached Chara. "This is the last batch of bodies for now. I can take care of them myself. Go home and rest."

Two soldiers marched behind him, each one carrying a pair of buckets filled with oil. Their stern faces displayed resentment for the assignment, but neither one would dare defy an order from Aiax. Although Aiax no longer carried out the tradition of execution for disobeying a direct command, all his men feared whatever punishment he meted out.

"I couldn't sleep last night," said Chara, "and I doubt tonight will be any different. It'll be months before I can get this rank odor out of my mind, let alone my clothing. Shall we get this done so we can move on with our lives already?"

"I know how you feel." Tyraz opened the gate for her. "But

you mean more than turning over cremation duties to someone else. You want to see if Jarlen has any answers for us."

Chara gave him a quick smile and brushed against his shoulder on her way into the cemetery. Patches of grass dotted the ground, surrounded by lumps of soil. The terrain appeared to belong in a Terun mine rather than a Ferfolk city.

"Your idea to burn the bodies has been working well," she said as she stifled a yawn. "I'm sure Jarlen will come to us when he learns anything. No need to rush him."

Tyraz stopped in front of her and held her gently by the arms. She wanted to pull him closer but feared the move would only remind him of old arguments.

"No doubt," he said, "but something else changed your mind about our trip into the Arboreal Forest. You can tell me."

"We're burning her today."

"Your neighbor, yes, I'm sorry, but it has to be done. Her spirit will finally be allowed some peace after tonight."

"I hope so," said Chara. "She might have family in Luceton. I plan to head up there tomorrow and let them know what happened."

"What about our banishment?"

The people of Luceton had banned her, Tyraz, and Jarlen from ever returning, blaming them for damage done by the lyche and his minions.

"They didn't know what they were saying." Chara put her hands on his arms. "Besides, don't you think they're having the same troubles as we are. Once I convince them to listen, they'll welcome the knowledge that I bring."

"Now that we have a solution, Aiax intends to send a legion to help them with their dead," said Tyraz. "I'll volunteer for the mission."

He pulled his arms away before leading her to the last set of mass graves. Once they finished burning these corpses, Aiax would handle any new deaths. Their morbid job was done, but she'd gladly accept the same responsibility in Luceton to be by Tyraz's side each night. A brief image of Jarlen looking for them in Kroflund crossed her mind. As long as they left word for him to await their return, she wouldn't have to worry about missing their Arboreal friend. The hike to Luceton was under two weeks when the weather in the Pensorean Mountains cooperated.

Chara stood at the edge of the pit but gazed into the nearby forest. Not a single breeze rustled the leaves, and no animals made a sound. Nature respected this somber moment, allowing Tyraz and Chara to complete their job in peace. The only noises came from within the hole, pieces of bodies squirming about, trying to form enough of a creature to escape their fate. They didn't realize all this was to help them find rest.

"I'm glad her family wasn't here to witness this," said Chara. "A funeral is bad enough, but watching your loved one struggling to escape the flames would be horrible. I couldn't handle it."

"It isn't their family members down there," said Tyraz with a nod to the soldiers carrying the oil. "They're creatures from the netherworld, maybe even demons, but I agree this must be done without spectators."

A flurry of dark wings took to the sky from the nearby trees, causing Chara to jump. The birds soared overhead, disappearing in every direction except due south. Tyraz and the soldiers paused briefly at the sudden activity but soon resumed their duties. Chara grasped the old woman's tinder box as she whispered a quiet farewell to her neighbor.

As if resigned to their destiny, the body parts stopped moving. Chara let out a breath of relief. There wouldn't be any battles against flaming corpses tonight—only one last bonfire and she could focus on grieving with her neighbor's family in

Luceton.

The soldiers dumped the oil into the hole and took their positions a few paces back, while Tyraz and Chara lit a few pieces of kindling. They tossed the burning sticks into the pit, igniting the entire mass. Flames shot upward, warming the chilly air but sending out the sickening smell of burnt flesh. Chara could have left this final task to Tyraz and the soldiers, but she wanted to know that her neighbor had moved on. Peace at last.

Chara stepped back and covered her nose with her arm. Tyraz braved the smell, but she could tell he had difficulty maintaining his composure. He overlooked the pit with a furrowed brow and his hand squeezing the hilt of his sword. She would have edged closer to him, but he'd only get more frustrated, unwilling to show any sign of weakness in front of his men. Instead, they watched and waited on opposite sides of the pit.

The fire died down after several hours, leaving behind the ashes of at least a dozen Ferfolk. With bodies carved into small pieces, Chara couldn't tell exactly how many had been cremated. As the last few embers turned dark, the pile of dust at the bottom of the pit swirled around. Chara couldn't feel the slightest breeze, but perhaps the last of the flames had kicked up a small wind within the hole.

Instead of settling back down after a few seconds, the circling ashes spun even faster, rising upward from the center of the pit. As the ashy cloud grew taller, it seemed to become darker, turning from steel gray to charcoal. A pair of smaller eddies pulled material off opposite sides of the column, forming into appendages that resembled arms. The top of the column formed into a globe shape that housed two glowing yellow spots. Eyes.

"Get back," Tyraz shouted at Chara as he unsheathed his

sword. "This has to be some kind of demon."

The two soldiers joined him near the pit with their weapons ready. Chara put her hand on Tyraz's dagger, glad that she hadn't returned the weapon to him. The demon moaned during its final spin and lunged forward. Tyraz's sword sliced straight through its body, apparently without dealing any damage. The two soldiers had similar difficulties with the creature as they jabbed its airy body. Weapons were useless against a creature without substance. Hopefully the same would be true of the creature, but Chara feared its touch might be dangerous. Tyraz dived out of the way, barely escaping a direct hit. The demon soared past him, flew into the sky, and turned around for another pass at its opponents.

This time, it went after the nearest soldier, passing directly through his body. The soldier gasped once and collapsed onto the ground, while Tyraz and the other Ferfolk continued searching for the creature's weak spot. Their weapons, however, didn't affect the demon in any way.

The downed soldier rolled onto his back. At first, Chara thought the demon was as powerless to affect the living as the metal blades against its body, but the soldier's skin appeared even more leathery and cracked than before. His gaunt face resembled a fisherman's after being stuck on the ocean without fresh water for a week. The Ferfolk pushed himself onto his feet, leaving his weapon behind, and stumbled toward the melee. His cloudy gray eyes focused on Tyraz.

"The dead soldier is coming for you," shouted Chara as she pulled the dagger from her belt.

Tyraz broke off from the combat to intercept his former comrade. He seemed hesitant to attack, probably wanting to make sure the Ferfolk had actually died, but this was no time for inaction.

"Stand down," said Tyraz, keeping his sword between him

and his new opponent. "I don't want to hurt you. Our healers might be able to help if you don't force my hand."

The dead soldier swung a fist at him, but Tyraz easily dodged the clumsy blow. Nearby, the other soldier had given up attacking the demon and was desperately trying to avoid any contact. The demon, however, grew faster and more agile with each pass. Eventually it collided with the Ferfolk, sending him to the ground. Now Tyraz was outnumbered with no way to win the battle. The demon hovered above the pit, eyed Chara, and turned for its final opponent.

"Tyraz," shouted Chara. "Don't let it touch you."

With Tyraz focused on the dead soldier, he didn't notice the more immediate threat. Chara launched the dagger at the demon. The blade sailed through the demon's yellow eye, eliciting a piercing shriek from the creature. Tyraz looked up in time to avoid both the falling dagger and the demon coming toward him.

"Its eyes," said Chara. "Go for its eyes."

Ignoring the two dead soldiers, Tyraz focused his attacks on the demon's yellow eyes, furiously stabbing and slicing with his sword. Chara was sure the blade had hit the glowing orbs twice without any effect, but when the sword came backwards through the demon's head, another shriek gave Tyraz all the information he needed. Only the back of its eyes were vulnerable. Three more swings turned the demon into a pile of lifeless ash, simultaneously causing the dead soldiers to collapse.

Chara rushed over to Tyraz and held him tightly. He returned the gesture only for a moment before turning his attention to the soldiers. After several minutes, however, the bodies still hadn't moved.

"Do you think those men will come back to life?" asked Chara. "Should we cremate them?"

"I don't know," he said. "But something was different this

time."

"Of course—this was the first demon to arise from the ashes of the dead."

"More than that," said Tyraz. "These bodies looked different from the other animated corpses. Something has changed—and I doubt it was for the better."

Chapter XVI

The Fall of Luceton

Tyraz hadn't spoken about his conversation with Aiax since they left Kroflund several days ago, and Chara didn't want to bring up the subject, especially with other soldiers around. It had taken an hour for Tyraz to plead his case before Aiax allowed him to lead the mission to Luceton. The Ferfolk commander didn't appreciate the ethereal demon killing two men and blamed Tyraz for their deaths. Chara would have argued that it was impossible for him to have known what would happen, but Tyraz accepted the responsibility. Aiax eventually gave Tyraz veteran soldiers to assist with Luceton's problems, so any punishment for the unfortunate deaths couldn't have been too severe.

"We'll stop here for the night and purchase any necessary supplies," said Tyraz as they approached the Tooth of the Gods. "We'll double up in rooms except for Chara."

The Tooth, as it was called by most people, was a large mountain in the Pensorean Range that housed Terun City above ground and the Undercity below ground. From a distance, it appeared as if a giant had taken a bite out of the peak, but up close Chara couldn't tell it apart from any other mountain. Most Teruns lived in one of the two sprawling establishments, the Undercity being far more prestigious. Tyraz rented a few rooms in one of the inns on the side of the mountain, where all the merchants and traders lived. Only miners, smiths, and farmers resided in the Undercity, although the Teruns welcomed most visitors to their subterranean world.

"Since we're here," said Chara, "we should check if the Teruns have had problems with their dead."

"That's not our mission," said Tyraz. "We're only spending time in Terun City to replenish our supplies and rest for the next leg of the trip. It's another week to the coast."

"I know how far it is." Chara gazed up the trail that wound its way toward the Cold Ocean. "I used to live there."

Tyraz stopped in front of a stone door that appeared to have been carved directly into the mountain. A squat Terun woman with chalky skin answered his knocking and invited the group into an entry way with a low ceiling. Even Chara had to duck to avoid brushing the top of her head against the hard stone.

"Four large rooms for us," said Tyraz, handing the innkeeper a few silver coins, "and a smaller one for her."

The Terun woman stepped in front of Chara with a smile, rubbing the back of her index finger against Chara's forearm.

"I have not seen your kind here since I was small," she said. "I thought you were all gone. You'll take my room for the night, the best on the hill."

"Many good thanks," said Chara, "but I don't need special treatment. Any room will do."

She secretly hoped the Terun would ignore her comment. It felt good to be treated with respect.

The innkeeper led them through a dark hallway lit only by glowing lichen on the ceiling, showing them to a set of rooms that seemed to be part of the mountain. The tables, chairs, and even the beds were all made of stone, possibly chiseled from a single piece of rock. Chara slapped the back of a chair with her palm. The wooden furniture of the Arboreals was luxurious in comparison.

"Meals are served when the bell rings," said the innkeeper.

"Don't be late."

After Tyraz and the soldiers piled into their rooms, Chara ran after the Terun.

"Excuse me," she said, "but have there been any...difficulties...with your dead?"

The Terun woman's brows furrowed as she pursed her lips.

"In Kroflund," Chara continued, "the recently buried have come back to life and attacked the citizens. Has anything like this happened in Terun City?"

"Our dead stay dead," said the woman as she turned back down the hall. "And you should leave them be."

Chara returned to her room, which appeared to be no fancier than the soldiers' quarters. Perhaps only a Terun could tell the difference between various types of stone. She sat on the cold bed but couldn't close her eyes. How could both Ferfolk and animals have returned from the dead but not Teruns? Were they truly that different? Tyraz might not have been interested in the reason, but she had to know. After the soldiers retired for the night, Chara sneaked out of her room to investigate this curious situation.

Night and day looked the same underground, but fewer Teruns roaming the tunnels of Terun City implied that many of them had gone to sleep. Chara didn't know where to find a Terun cemetery, if they even had any, but she enjoyed investigating the different lifestyle of the Teruns. She passed several alcoves that appeared to be meeting spots with benches carved from the walls, some of which also contained stone murals and sculptures. Eventually the passageway ended at an enormous cavern, large enough to swallow Luceton. Sounds of metal clanging against rock echoed from the dark depths, proof that the miners were still busy at work. A narrow path led downward from the tunnel along the cavern wall, disappearing behind a curve after several paces. Under a dim green glow from the phosphorescent lichens, Chara headed into the Undercity.

As she made her way along the treacherous path, Chara kept near the wall, afraid that one false step would send her plummeting to the cavern floor. Initially she thought the trek would be easier during the day, but knowing how high up she was might have intimidated her even more. She stopped and tossed a pebble over the side, listening to it knock against stone on its way down. The plunking sounds faded away without any definitive smack against the ground. As nervous as this hike had made her, she refused to turn back before reaching the bottom.

Chara pressed herself against the stone wall when heavy footsteps approached from behind. A pair of Teruns hiked past her at a quick pace, stopped, and turned around.

"You should come back when the sun is out," said the closest Terun. "Its rays shine through holes in the roof to shed light on the town."

His gray skin picked up the greenish tint of the ever-present glow, making him appear like a short Arboreal. Both Teruns carried a stack of empty sacks over their shoulders and had small pickaxes attached to their belts. A fine layer of pale dust covered their fingers and boots.

"I would like to have a better view of this wonderful place," said Chara, "but I don't have the time. My friends are leaving at sun up."

"There's not much to see at night," said the Terun. "Shops are closed, and you may not go near the mines."

Chara wished she had a week or more to explore the Undercity, but she needed to find answers and return to the inn before Tyraz noticed she was gone. She didn't want to argue with him, but more importantly, she didn't want his men to know she'd disobeyed his order.

"Where's the nearest cemetery?" she asked.

The Teruns glanced at each other in confusion.

"Where do you bury your dead? Teruns die, don't they?"

"Why do you want to see the dead?" asked the second Terun. "Let them sleep."

"That's exactly why I must see them," said Chara. "The Ferfolk dead have been restless this past fortnight, digging out of their graves to attack the living, and the same has happened to some animals."

"If you must." The first Terun dumped his sacks onto his friend's pile. "Come with me."

The two Teruns continued down the trail, but when they reached the bottom, Chara's guide veered off to the side. In the distance, huge stalagmites rose from the ground, many of them dotted with glowing lichen. Chara guessed the large structures housed families who worked in the Undercity. The Terun guide skirted the more populated area, eventually leading her to an open patch of ground. Thousands of mushrooms in various shapes and sizes grew in neatly arranged rows. Chara followed him past the mushroom fields to a spot where the rocky ground had been broken up into chunks the size of small boulders. Her feet slipped several times while traversing the uneven ground, but she made it to the center without falling.

"Is this what you want to see?" asked the Terun, spreading out his arms.

A slight odor of rotting flesh wafted upwards. They had to have been standing atop some recently buried bodies. Chara knelt and tried to loosen one of the large stones, but it wouldn't budge.

"Can you help me with this?" she asked.

"It would take three of us to move that stone," said the Terun, "but I would not do it with ten of my friends. The dead should be left where they are."

It probably didn't matter if the Terun bodies had come back to life. They couldn't dig themselves out unless they worked together to move the boulders. Chara suppressed a chuckle. The Teruns had inadvertently solved a problem that had plagued the Ferfolk and probably the Arboreals. Perhaps the people of Luceton had also found their own method to cope with this curse. She hoped so. They didn't deserve such a gruesome fate, even after they forbade her from ever returning.

The incessant peal of the mealtime bell signaled morning's arrival. With her chamber too dark to see her fingertips in front of her eyes, Chara rolled over in her bed. She'd lain out the pillows underneath her to make the stone furniture more comfortable, but it didn't help much. Her back ached from the restless hour or two of tossing about. With any luck, the rest of the group would forget about her and head out soon. She'd catch up to them after a good sleep. Unfortunately, a pounding at her door interrupted her return to dreams.

"Breakfast is ready," said Tyraz from outside her room. "Gather your supplies. We leave directly after the meal."

Chara groped around in the dark for her pack. She could have lit a candle on the stone dresser, but she wasn't ready for too much light. With no windows to the outside, the rest of the inn would be relatively dark. She opened the door to see Tyraz ready for the upcoming hike with a smile on his face.

"Don't tell me you enjoy sleeping on rocks," she said.

"Better than in a tree." He grabbed her pack and slung it over his free shoulder. "You look like you haven't slept in days. Can you make it to the next campsite? I plan to hike until sunset."

"I'll be fine." Chara shuffled ahead of him toward the dining area. "But I'd be better if we left in a few hours."

"If you couldn't sleep the entire night, how will a few more hours help?"

She sped up, nearly jogging to the first empty table, and collapsed into a stone chair. Tyraz dropped the packs onto the floor and sat across from her. He stared into her eyes with a puzzled look that morphed into a smirk.

"You didn't even try to sleep," he said. "You went searching for dead Teruns."

"I had to know how they were affected," she said and waved for the innkeeper's attention.

The Terun woman brought them a couple mugs of fungal ale along with a plate of hard cheese and dried mushrooms. Chara dug into the food, hoping a full stomach would help her body forget about its lack of rest.

"And," said Tyraz, surprisingly accepting of her disobedience. "What did you learn? Did any of them come back from the dead?"

"They might have," said Chara, "but we'll never know. The Teruns bury their dead under so much rock that the corpses could never free themselves. If nothing else, we found an alternative solution for any Ferfolk who oppose cremation."

"Perhaps." Tyraz joined her finishing off the food and drink. "But is it any better if they knew their loved ones were trapped below tons of rock, desperately trying to dig themselves out?"

"You've already agreed those bodies are not their loved ones anymore." Chara bent over to grab her pack, conveniently hiding a yawn from her companion. "Let's go. I need a bit of sunlight to refresh me."

They emerged from the inn to a rainy day. Chara groaned. This was going to be a long hike.

So much dried mud covered Chara's legs that her pants could have stood on their own. Rain had followed them for days and had only recently stopped, although the threatening sky could easily unleash another downpour at any moment. Chara sniffed the air, detecting a familiar briny scent, although it was probably her imagination since the ocean was still far to the north. It would be another couple days before the first signs of blue water would be visible on the horizon.

The Ferfolk soldiers stopped and drew their swords. On the trail ahead of them, a ragtag group of people were charging forward, quickly closing the distance. Tyraz sent Chara to the back before taking his place in the lead.

"Who are you?" he called out. "What do you want?"

The newcomers halted about fifty paces away. Eight Ferfolk men surrounded a few women and children. Their bodies and clothing were as dirty as Chara's, and many of them appeared thinner than anyone in Kroflund. They must not have eaten in days and probably had gotten little sleep.

"We need help," said the closest Ferfolk, trying to catch his breath. "Luceton–overrun."

Tyraz sheathed his sword and approached the group.

"Did corpses come back to life?" he asked.

While most of the Ferfolk nodded, the children grabbed onto their mothers.

"Aiax sent us to help," said Tyraz. "We have a temporary solution."

"You're too late," said the Ferfolk. "I don't think anyone else made it out of town."

"That can't be." Chara nudged her way through the soldiers to Tyraz's side. "Someone must have figured out what was happening, or at least told you to evacuate. The dead could never outrun you."

"These poor folks have never seen anything like that before," said Tyraz. "Don't forget, we had an advantage after all our encounters with the dead."

Chara fell to her knees. "If that's true, then the humans might also have been wiped out."

"Does that matter? You never expected to see any of them again."

"Still, now I might truly be the last of my kind. I had always imagined the humans finding a new home and starting a new civilization."

The temperature seemed to have dropped, sending chills throughout her body.

Tyraz called four of his men forward.

"Escort them back to Kroflund," he said, "and make sure they have a good meal in Terun City. Take Chara, too."

"I'm going with you." She pushed his hand away when he offered it and stood on her own. "Regardless of what they said, there might yet be survivors."

"Then we go now," said Tyraz, "double pace."

As they hiked over the final hilltop, the Cold Ocean revealed itself, reflecting the steel blue sky, but a rank odor of decaying bodies had replaced the crisp scent of the water. The small town of Luceton stood in the distance, a cluster of tiny houses nestled against the shoreline. Chara gazed at the hills to the east of the settlement, where she'd grown up. The familiar cliffs to the east of town still held back the fury of the sea, which pounded against sand and rock, never ending. A wave of hope flooded her mind. Perhaps a few people survived. Maybe her grandfather was home, preparing his latest catch over a roaring fire. She wiped away a few tears and took a deep breath, wondering if it would have been better if she'd listened to Tyraz and returned to Kroflund.

Tyraz led the group down the trail to the outermost huts, many of them once housing the few pack animals in Luceton. Any horses or cows had escaped or been eaten. The old shacks were empty with no signs of damage to the structure.

Other than the lack of people, the town seemed the same as ever. Cormorants and gulls filled the sky with their loud squawking, and a constant breeze blew in from the north. A few paces down the road, however, revealed the first set of corpses.

The body of an old Ferfolk lay in a trampled garden. Insects covered any skin not hidden behind torn, ratty clothing, and chunks of its arms and legs were missing. Tyraz and the soldiers surrounded the body and prodded it with their swords.

"This one's not coming back to life," said one of the men.

"The curse must have been lifted," said another.

"I hope so." Tyraz stepped away from the body. "These past few weeks have been difficult, but I'll remain skeptical until we hear from Jarlen."

He continued down the street, ignoring the few scattered corpses, until they reached a pile of dead Ferfolk near the main wharf. At least two score bodies had been stacked up in the center of town. A flock of gulls hovered nearby, occasionally pulling off a piece of carrion, although they seemed more skittish than usual. The soldiers charged forward to scare off the birds, while Tyraz examined the ghastly pile.

"Who would do something like this?" he asked, mostly to himself, as he circled the mound.

Chara instinctively pulled out her knife. The living residents had fled, and the dead bodies never exhibited any cooperation or intelligence. Something else was around here.

"Get back," said Tyraz as he positioned himself in front of Chara. "I don't think we're alone."

His men formed a line on either side of her, awaiting his command. Chara followed his gaze to the bottom of the pile, where several bodies moved.

"I was wrong," said one of the soldiers. "The curse is still with us."

"This is different," said Tyraz. "I don't think these corpses are moving on their own. I think something is underneath them."

Chara rushed forward.

"Maybe someone is trapped under there," she said. "We have to help him escape."

"Don't get too close to the bodies." Tyraz held her back with a gentle grip on her arm. "That pile is too large for someone to survive at the bottom. We should–"

The moving bodies exploded, sending pieces of flesh everywhere, and a large creature emerged. With the claws and beak of an eagle attached to the body of a wolf, it couldn't have come from this world. It leered at the newcomers, piercing them with its bright red eyes, and pounced.

The nearest soldier took a heavy swing at its neck, but his sword just bounced away as if he'd attacked solid rock. Another soldier lunged forward, jabbing at its midsection, but he fared no better.

"You will not plague this land, demon," shouted Tyraz as he moved into an attack position.

The demon raked him with its front claws, but he blocked the blow with his sword. The metal bit into the creature, drawing a thin line of black blood and evoking a loud shriek. It stumbled backward, probably not expecting to have been harmed by anything in this world.

"I got this one," said Tyraz. "Make sure there are no more demons around here, but don't engage them. Your weapons can't break their skin."

Chara circled the mound of bodies but found nothing else moving. She returned to battle, where the demon's beak had locked onto Tyraz's blade. He tugged at the sword, but the creature wouldn't release the weapon. The rest of the Ferfolk soldiers were conducting a thorough search, poking the sides of the pile and shifting a few of the loose corpses. Chara couldn't wait for them to return to the battle. She leaped onto the demon's back and wrapped her arms around its neck, trying to jam her knife through its fur. Unfortunately, her blade was as ineffective as the soldiers'. At least she was safe for now. As long as the demon held onto Tyraz's sword, it couldn't snap at her.

"What are you doing?" shouted Tyraz. "Get off that beast before it kills you."

Chara felt the demon's muscles tense as it pulled harder at the sword, but Tyraz didn't let go. Neither would Chara. With her face buried in its matted fur, she caught a whiff of brimstone mixed with death. This creature had come from the netherworld, and even if they destroyed its body, Chara didn't know if they could send it back. Where was Jarlen when they needed him most?

One by one, Tyraz's men noticed the struggle and rushed forward into the battle, grabbing the demon's legs until it finally released the sword. With its mouth free, it tore into the closest Ferfolk, but couldn't free itself from the rest of the men. Tyraz plunged his blade into its beak and up through the back of its head. As soon as the demon collapsed, Tyraz rushed forward to check on the wounded soldier, but it was too late. The demon had torn through his neck, creating a pool of blood on the ground. Chara thought she saw a shadow rise from the demon's body and float eastward, but it might have been her imagination.

"We'll bury him and everyone else in this town before returning home," said Tyraz. "Go find picks and shovels. We have a lot of work to do."

After the others scattered into town, Tyraz took the fallen soldier's sword and jammed it blade down into the ground.

"This wasn't your fault," said Chara. "He gave his life to protect everyone from that demon, not just you."

"I know, but that could easily have been you lying there," said Tyraz. "What were you thinking? You're no soldier."

"As the last human, I have to set a good example for my kind. Otherwise, what would the legends say about us?"

Chara gave him a weak smile, but he only scowled at her. Regardless of what he wanted, she'd risk her life again to protect his, and he'd do the same for her. He'd be a hypocrite if he didn't accept her decision to help. Chara stared at the demon—the second one they'd seen in as many weeks. Jarlen might have lifted the curse of the dead coming to life, but at what cost?

Chapter XVII

Netherworld Released

Jarlen couldn't move his hands to scratch an itch on his neck. He opened his eyes. Leaves, branches, and vines covered his head and body, pressing down against him, but a few rays of sunlight broke through the debris. Either he wasn't dead, or this was a part of the netherworld that he hadn't yet visited. The itch grew more intense–perhaps an insect crawling across his skin. As long as it didn't start feeding, he could ignore it. He tried to bend his legs, but vines held him firmly in place.

"Hello?" he called out. "Can anybody hear me?"

The only response came from a nearby animal that scurried away–a chipmunk or squirrel. This wasn't the netherworld. Jarlen relaxed slightly, thankful he was still alive. The explosion that had thrown him backward must have buried him in this mess.

Jarlen struggled to free himself for several minutes, but each time one piece of vegetation loosened its grip, another one tightened against his limbs. To escape, he would need help to clear everything out at once, but if he'd just restored the connection to the netherworld, calling spirits through might not be wise.

"Eslinor," he shouted. "Where are you?"

She had to have survived. He didn't want to consider the alternative, although he knew only death could have formed the new link between worlds. Why had she followed him into the forest? She should have left him alone.

Jarlen tugged once more at his bonds but couldn't move. One simple spell wouldn't harm anyone, after which he promised to stop contacting the netherworld. Concentrating on the closest few branches, he recalled one of his earliest and most helpful incantations.

"*Segnian bans, segnian beame,*" he repeated, increasing in volume each time.

One by one, the vines and branches surrounding his body became brown and brittle, crumbling to dust at the slightest touch. Soon, Jarlen had dug himself out of a huge mound of underbrush, emerging into a scene of utter destruction.

Not a single tree remained standing within twenty paces of the altar, and all vegetation had turned black. Closer to Jarlen, trees had fallen backward away from the boulders, most of them propped up by the trunks and branches behind them. Several paces farther from the altar, the forest eventually returned to a healthier shade of green, although the colors weren't as rich and deep as Jarlen remembered.

He took a step into the destruction, ran his finger across the ground, and brought the black ash up to his nose. Surprisingly, he couldn't detect any scent of burnt leaves. The acrid smell was particularly offensive to Arboreals, but this vegetation had not seen flames. Something else had covered everything in this dark substance. He inched forward, glad that he hadn't been injured other than a few scrapes, and reached out for the nearest black leaf, crumbling it into a handful of dust. The vegetation had been affected by something similar to his spell but had become black instead of brown. He continued toward the altar, leaving a trail of dark footsteps behind.

Other than a thin coating of ash, the boulders of the altar seemed unchanged. His jade knife lay on the ground in a circle of dried blood. He wouldn't have picked it up, except that it had belonged to his master Zehuti. The old Arboreal would never have approved of his recent behavior. Jarlen felt as bad as if he'd received a full day of chastising from both Zehuti and Otha.

Since his spell to free himself from the vines had succeeded, he must have opened a link to the netherworld. He could think of no other explanation for the damage done to the forest, but should he close it again or assume he'd fixed the problem he originally created? Either decision could be correct, and either one might cost more lives.

Jarlen sat on the stone altar and stared at the scene. At least no other Arboreal would see what he'd done to these plants. He dreaded bringing Eslinor's body back to Hillswood, but she deserved a proper ceremony. Her body had to be somewhere nearby. He kicked up the black ash, weaved over and under the fallen trees at the edge of the destruction, and continued his search far into the unaffected part of the forest. Even though he knew she'd sacrificed herself, he kept calling for her as loudly as he could until his voice gave out. Eventually he collapsed on the ground against an old willow trunk. Eslinor had given her life to help fix his mistake, and he swore not to let her memory fade. As soon as he returned to Hillswood, he'd convince the elders to allow a year of grieving instead of the more traditional two months.

After thinking about all the times she'd taken care of him, he stood up and wiped a spot of black ash off his pants. It must have coated his clothing when he was climbing around the fallen trees. With one last glance in the direction of the altar, he set out northward for home.

By late afternoon, Jarlen's hunger had forced him to search for food. He circled the nearest group of trees, pausing at the carcass of a squirrel in some brush. Long ago he'd kept a squirrel as a pet, and the lifeless body brought tears to his eyes. He would have buried the dead animal but a few more carcasses nearby caught his attention. They seemed to form a line heading deeper into the forest.

Jarlen followed the trail of bodies to a mound of carcasses in a small clearing. A slurping sound came from behind the pile, causing chills to run through Jarlen's limbs. He backed away, checking each to footstep to ensure he didn't snap any twigs. Whatever predator had collected so many animals might have family nearby, and Jarlen didn't want to interrupt their meal. After a few steps, his stomach gurgled. Jarlen stopped and gazed at the center of the clearing, hoping the noise hadn't been loud enough to give him away. The head of a large eagle peeked out from behind the pile, its beak stained dark red from its victims' blood. Jarlen turned and ran.

From behind him, a heavy set of paws slammed against the ground when he expected to hear flapping wings. He glanced over his shoulder at a creature that had to have been a demon. Its body resembled that of a blaeculf, but bony knobs stuck out of its fur near every joint. Long talons tore at the ground with every pounce, and bright red eyes stared back at him. Even if he carried a decent weapon, he couldn't fend off such an imposing creature. Tyraz would have had a chance, but Jarlen didn't even know if his friend was still alive.

He leaped onto a branch and climbed to the canopy, but the demon followed him into the trees. It soared from one limb to the next as easily as it tore across the ground. He couldn't fight the beast, and he couldn't outrun it, but he refused to give up. The bizarre creature didn't belong in this world, and nobody else could send it back.

The demon came closer with every leap, and Jarlen knew he'd have only one chance. He hopped to the ground, faced his pursuer, and belted out an incantation to control undead plants. Vines in front of the demon turned brown and shot out from the tree, tangling its legs before it reached him. The creature snapped at each tendril, easily biting through them, but there were enough vines in the area to give Jarlen a few extra minutes.

Sending the demon back to the netherworld would require separating it from its body, but Jarlen still had no weapons other than his ceremonial jade dagger. Vines weren't strong enough to overpower the demon, but a tree might be. Jarlen focused on a nearby mahogany and repeated his incantation.

The demon ripped through the last of the vines and landed on the ground with an angry snarl. It pounced forward, fully aware that Jarlen was calling for more help. Jarlen ignored the beast and finished his spell, hopefully calling forth a spirit to inhabit the tree. He ducked around a thick trunk as the demon drew close enough for him to smell its foul breath.

"You're going back to the netherworld," he said. "Give up now to avoid much pain."

The demon answered with a growl and reached around the trunk to swipe at him. Jarlen was temporarily safe if he kept the creature on the opposite side of the tree, but this strategy couldn't last more than a few minutes. After another swipe from the other side, the demon stepped back, screeched loud enough to force Jarlen to cover his ears, and split its body in half. No blood spilled from the tear, which quickly sealed itself by pulling its fur together. Its head and two front legs hopped around one side of the trunk, while its tail and back legs went the other way.

Jarlen fell backward in surprise, but before either half could reach him, the tall mahogany leaned over and grabbed both halves of the demon in its extended branches. A set of brown leaves encased the struggling creature, squeezing until it went silent. With its body crushed, the demon couldn't resist Jarlen's magic. He sent the fiend back to the netherworld and released the spirit that had inhabited the mahogany tree.

Leaning against the nearest trunk, Jarlen let his body sink to the ground. He couldn't have accidentally found the one demon that had made it through the portal. Many more must have come through. Before tracking them down, however, he had to ensure that no others could breach the void between worlds. So much for his vow to give up necromancy.

It took another day of constant hiking to return to the altar. No new footprints dotted the ashy coating on the ground, but that didn't mean flying creatures hadn't emerged recently. The more Jarlen tried to fix his mistakes, the worse things got. First, he'd caused the dead to come back to life by sealing the links between worlds, and now he'd released demons by opening a new portal. Maybe it would be best if he just ended his life. That would ensure he could never cause any more harm.

No. He couldn't abandon his friends and allow demons to roam freely. He had to return everything back to the way it was before he learned necromancy, allowing spirits to pass from this world to the netherworld, while blocking demons from coming through. Without more research on the topic, his only choice was to try the same incantation that he'd used to seal the gateways in the netherworld.

He stood on the stone altar, closed his eyes, and chanted, focusing only on this side of the portal.

"It's too late for that," came a deep voice from behind the felled trees. "But I'd like to thank you for your help."

Jarlen finished his incantation before gazing at the newcomer. A pale man with a pair of bull horns adorning the top of his head stepped into the clearing. He was easily twice as tall as Jarlen and wore a robe of animal hides. Three paces brought him next to the altar, where he leaned against one of the boulders, displaying fingers that ended in sharp points.

"You seem familiar," said Jarlen, "but I'd remember a horned giant."

"We've met before," said the newcomer. "I helped you in the netherworld, and you graciously returned the favor."

"Dis?" Jarlen climbed down from the stone on the opposite side of the altar. "You don't belong in this world."

"Why? Because it's not part of the netherworld?" He burst into a fit of laughter. "That won't be the case for long."

"I won't let you harm this world," said Jarlen. "I'll send you back and seal the portal again. I don't care if the dead won't stay buried. It's better than allowing demons through."

Dis straightened up and spread his arms.

"Do what you must."

Jarlen wished Tyraz was here with him. Together, they would have thought of a way to combat the archfiend, but Dis's confidence overwhelmed him. He could only stare back with his mouth open.

"In that case," said Dis, "join me and you'll receive an entire realm of your own."

Jarlen smiled at the one piece of good news he'd encountered in the past few weeks. Dis couldn't have said anything more encouraging except perhaps offering to return home on his own. The demon prince still needed something to complete his plan to conquer this world–something Jarlen could provide. He stepped back onto the altar, more confident than before.

"How do I know you won't just kill me once I start trusting you?" he asked as he hopped down next to Dis.

The archfiend headed back to the forest, waving at Jarlen to follow him.

"You don't," said Dis, "but if I wanted you dead, you've already given me enough chances."

"Where are we going?" asked Jarlen, allowing Dis to increase the distance between them.

"We need more animals." Dis stopped between a pair of ironwoods. "As many as we can find."

"So that's why you released the other demons," said Jarlen as he slowed down. "To collect dead bodies for you."

Dis scowled at him.

"I need them alive," he said. "Come along. You're falling too far behind."

Jarlen stopped and shouted his incantation, calling spirits into the trees on either side of Dis. They responded by wrapping their branches around the demon lord and squeezing.

"Release me at once," he called out, "and I'll forget this little misunderstanding. You don't want me as your enemy."

He flexed his muscles, bending the tops of both trees. It wouldn't be long until he freed himself. Jarlen bolted in the other direction. He would need help from both the Arboreals and the Ferfolk to defeat the demon lord, a creature far more powerful than the lyche.

Exhausted after a full day of running, Jarlen collapsed on the bank of a small stream. He stuck his head into the water and gulped down a few mouthfuls of the refreshing liquid. He didn't know if he was happy that Dis hadn't followed him or worried that the demon lord was continuing with his plan back at the altar. Either way, he had to reach Hillswood as quickly as possible. He forced himself up, hopped over the stream, caught his foot on an overgrown root, and came down hard. Everything went black.

When he awoke, he was lying on a branch bed at the top of a tree. Although the room was dark, Jarlen could tell it was neither his home nor the Gathering Tree from the strong smell of birch. Nobody in Hillswood took up residence in birches because of the thin bark. He sat up and rubbed the bump on his head, sore but not enough to keep him down. Somewhere nearby, water trickled over rocks. Jarlen climbed through the doorway and onto the outer branches for a better look at where he was. None of the trees looked familiar.

"We're in a small hamlet south of Hillswood," said Cassor as he climbed onto the limb behind Jarlen. "Have you seen Eslinor? We think she might have been looking for you."

The words hit Jarlen in the stomach. How could he ever explain what had happened to her?

"I didn't listen to you and Aquila," he said. "Now everything's worse."

He moved closer to Cassor, lost his grip, and slipped down a few branches before he caught himself. Cassor quickly positioned himself beneath Jarlen in case of another accident.

"Tell me what happened," he said. "We'll figure it all out."

"I couldn't let the dead overrun this world. I had to fix my mistake. Eslinor came to stop me, but the knife..." He drew the jade knife from his belt, stared at the red stain on the blade, and let it slip from his fingers. "She saved my life, but her death connected the two worlds again."

Cassor sat back against the trunk and folded his arms. He'd known Eslinor for a long time and probably didn't believe she was gone. Jarlen wanted him to say something, sorrow for her death, assurance that it wasn't his fault, anything, but the elder just breathed deeply and gazed at nothing in particular. Soon, his eyes returned to Jarlen's face.

"That must be how the demon came to this world," said Cassor. "Now we have to find a way to send it back."

"You saw Dis?" asked Jarlen, wondering how the demon had traveled from one spot to the other so quickly.

"The creature didn't identify itself." Cassor climbed onto Jarlen's branch and put a hand on his shoulder. "It ravaged Hillswood, taking many of us prisoner. Very little remains of our beloved hamlet. Our weapons could do nothing against its tough skin, and it froze any plant that came too close to its hairy body."

Jarlen's heart dropped as he swooned on the tree limb, but Cassor tightened his grip to keep him in place. Dis wasn't the only demon lord that had come through the portal. Mammon must have joined him, and possibly others.

"Did this demon have long white fur?"

Jarlen already knew the answer, yet he still cringed when Cassor nodded.

"That would be Mammon," he said, "one of the demon lords. Dis is south of here, preparing to turn our world into part of the netherworld. Mammon might be doing the same— or they could be working together to destroy our world."

"Can they do that?"

"It doesn't matter," said Jarlen. "They're collecting living creatures for a massive sacrifice, probably to open more connections to the netherworld. We have to stop them."

Cassor hopped downward from branch to branch and returned with the jade dagger.

"Do you know how to defeat a demon lord?" he asked as he handed the weapon back.

"Not yet," said Jarlen, "but first we have to save the Arboreals that Mammon took. We might not have much time before he's ready for the sacrifice."

"I sent a few men after them," said Cassor. "They haven't reported back yet, so there's hope the prisoners are still alive. Come. It shouldn't be difficult to find them."

"I'm surprised you didn't try to free them yourself," said Jarlen.

The elder looked back at him, his worn face showing signs of concern.

"I would have," he said, "but I knew you had to be involved somehow."

Jarlen didn't think it was possible to feel any worse than before, but he'd betrayed everyone. He gripped the jade knife until his knuckles paled. One quick slice, and he wouldn't have to worry about any of this. Instead, he slipped the blade into his belt and followed Cassor to the next tree. He should have learned more about necromancy before trying to change the world, but there was so little information about it. As soon as he banished the demons back to the netherworld, he promised himself to document everything he knew so future generations wouldn't face the same problems. Unfortunately, he had no idea how to destroy a demon lord.

Chapter XVIII

On the Trail of Fracodians

Chara had seen enough death for one day. While Tyraz and the soldiers buried the Ferfolk bodies, she hiked up the seaside cliffs toward her old home. It hadn't been more than a couple years since she lived there, but it felt much longer. Her little shack still stood, set back from the precipitous drop to the shoreline, but nothing remained inside. Much like her neighbor's house in Kroflund, looters had taken everything, leaving only the walls, floor, and ceiling. Even the front door had been removed from its hinges, although a piece of leathery fur hung from an exposed nail. At least some animals might have found shelter inside the hut, protected from the furious winds coming off the water.

She followed the worn path leading from her home to the edge of the cliff and sat overlooking the Cold Ocean. The sea had claimed her grandfather and lured the rest of the humans away from Luceton, but she still missed the crisp air and the waves crashing against the rocks. Gulls squawked incessantly as they dropped clams and mussels from high above the ground, probably angry that their easier meal had been taken away. The birds shouldn't have been feeding on the dead bodies anyway; it wasn't their natural source of food.

A set of rushed footsteps came from behind. Chara didn't have to turn around to know Tyraz was approaching.

"We've been called back to Kroflund," he said. "It's urgent."

"How did they get a message to you so quickly?" asked

Chara as she pulled herself away from the scenery.

Tyraz pointed at a small speck in the sky, heading for the mountains.

"Trained hawk." He returned to the trail leading into town, urging her to follow. "Only for the most dire circumstances."

Chara hurried to his side, jogging down the slope. Could it be any worse than the demon they fought near the wharf? It had to have been, or Aiax wouldn't have sent a hawk. Chara stumbled as her legs grew weak. Had the people of Kroflund suffered the same fate as those in Luceton? She couldn't handle anything so terrible.

"Do you know what happened?" she asked, hoping that he didn't know more details.

She needed to maintain the possibility that Kroflund still stood. Tyraz handed her a small, rolled-up scroll. She held her breath as she unfurled the paper to reveal a message in Aiax's handwriting:

Under attack–need your sword

"I've already sent the others ahead," said Tyraz. "We'll meet up with them when they set up camp for the night."

"Maybe we can find the Luceton horses," said Chara. "They'll bring us back much faster than we can hike."

"I can't risk the chance that the animals are all dead." Tyraz sped his pace down the slope. "A single hour could save hundreds of lives or more back home."

"That's if you get there sooner," said Chara, "but I'm not a soldier. What could I do with a single knife? Skin a few fish for lunch? I'm staying behind to search for the horses. Even one of them alive would help."

She stopped at the bottom of the cliff, forcing Tyraz to do the same.

"It's too dangerous for you to stay here alone," he said.

"What if there are more demons around?"

"This is not a discussion."

Tyraz stepped toward her, probably thinking he could carry her out of town. She placed her hand on the hilt of her knife, not as a threat but as an indication that she could protect herself. When Tyraz kept coming toward her, she backed away. Secretly, she hoped he wouldn't give up, that he'd force her to join him on the return trip to Kroflund, but he must have known she was right.

"Don't spend too long on this quest," he said as he turned toward the mountains. "Only death remains in Luceton."

"I promise."

Chara headed for the barns on the outskirts of town. Since she'd arrived in Luceton, she hadn't found the bodies of any horses, and the animals couldn't have just disappeared. She approached the first building, where a mixture of hay, dirt, and manure covered the floors, with heavier concentrations in each of the stalls. The villagers had apparently ignored the horses for some time before the animals escaped. Perhaps they'd gotten so hungry that they were forced to break out of their stalls.

To test her theory, Chara examined the stall doors in more detail. None of them had been destroyed, but a heavy object had crushed most of the latches. Either the horses had become smarter, yet not smart enough to open the latches, or another creature had released them. Teruns or Ferfolk would have known how to operate a latch, so it had to have been Fracodians. That would explain the hardened patch of skin she'd found on the door to her shack. If she hurried, she could reach Tyraz to give him the news, but he'd assume the Fracodians had already killed the horses. She'd have to track them down herself to see if any had survived.

Most Fracodians roamed the eastern portion of the Pensorean Range, but searching from here to the Great Ocean would take years. Chara gave herself two days to track them down. After that, it wouldn't matter if she found the horses alive. It would be too late to help Tyraz reach Kroflund any faster. She headed out of town with a spring to her step, away from the setting sun.

The terrain grew quite rough the farther east she went, hopefully forcing the Fracodians to remain on the rare paths through the mountains. Chara chose the widest trail, noting the trampled bushes here and there. Excited that she'd soon find mounts for everyone, she darted up the path, keeping her eyes down to avoid twisting her ankle on any loose stones. She didn't have time for any mistakes.

After turning a tight corner, she collided with the rotting carcass of a horse and flew forward onto the ground. Chara sat up, scratched but otherwise unhurt. The unfortunate horse had died several days ago. Insects covered the exposed flesh and were probably hidden within the matted fur, as well. She backed away from the horrendous stench, wondering why the Fracodians had left the animal behind. It had to have been alive when they freed it; they wouldn't have carried such a heavy load all this way.

Chara wrapped the bottom of her shirt over her nose, found a stick nearby, and inched closer to the carcass. She poked the body in a few spots, sending up a flurry of bugs. A sharp blade had torn through the horse's neck, opening a gash from one side to the other. Chara dropped the stick next to the carcass and hopped off the trail, where she found several burnt pieces of wood surrounded by a circle of rocks–the remains of a campfire. The Fracodians must have intended to eat the horse. Chara chuckled. That didn't work out too well for them after the body came back to life, but did they keep the rest of the animals or send them away? If the Fracodians remained on this trail, she'd soon find out.

After another day of hiking, Chara finally heard grunting in the distance. She scooted off the trail and waited for nightfall before edging forward. A flickering light came from up ahead, most likely the Fracodians' campfire. From the variety of sounds, there had to be at least four of them. Tyraz would have forbidden her from going any farther, but he was well on his way to Terun City by now. She unsheathed her knife as she closed in on the group.

The Fracodians were as ugly as she remembered, with hairy skin and faces more reminiscent of bears than of humans. Unlike the settlement on the Cursed Island, these Fracodians wouldn't hesitate to attack her. The island Fracodians had surprised her with their ability to speak and their peaceful demeanor. Until she'd met them, she'd only known Fracodians as monsters to avoid. She crept closer to the camp. Six Fracodians surrounded a large fire, with a single horse tied to a nearby bush. It would have been so much easier if these were the island fishermen. A simple trade would yield the mount. Chara sighed and skirted the area, heading toward the horse.

She hadn't gone far when the Fracodians stopped grunting. Two of them stood and sniffed the air, turning in all directions. Chara held steady until they returned to their seats. They knew they weren't alone, and one misstep would send them straight to her. She planned to find a good hiding spot, wait until they fell asleep, and free the horse. Once she was atop the mount, she could outrun them, even though she knew little about riding horses. Unfortunately, the Fracodians didn't agree with her plan. One of them remained awake to guard the campsite.

Chara picked up some dirt and rubbed it between her fingers. If the Ferfolk town guards had mistaken her for the living dead, perhaps she could also trick the Fracodians. The dead horse had already spooked them once, and they weren't nearly as intelligent as Ferfolk. She tore holes in her shirt and pants with the knife, covered her skin in dirt, and crumbled bits of leaves and twigs into her hair. Her ruse wouldn't last long, but she only needed a few seconds of confusion to free the horse. Taking a deep breath, she stumbled into camp, moaning as she went along.

As soon as the Fracodian glimpsed her, he grunted at his comrades and fell backward. Chara didn't wait to see how convincing her disguise was. She darted to the horse, cut through its rope, and hopped onto its back. The Fracodian must have realized his mistake and rushed forward, but Chara grabbed onto the horse's mane and dug her heels into its side.

"Go fast," she shouted. "Or we're both dead."

Either the animal understood her, or its captors had mistreated it. Free from its bonds, the horse charged at the guard and knocked him over on its way back to the trail. Chara patted the silky fur of its neck with her free hand. They had a long way to go before they were safe, but she promised to treat it well.

Chara couldn't get the horse to gallop, but even at a slower pace, it was still faster than she could have hiked. Besides, the mountain path often ran across steep slopes, making it treacherous to navigate too quickly. She rode most of the night, giving the horse a few minutes to eat and rest whenever they found some greenery. By the end of the next day, she hadn't passed the dead horse. A large scavenger might have taken it away, but she thought it more likely that the dead were coming back to life again, which would explain Aiax's urgent request for Tyraz to return. Now it was even more crucial that she bring this horse to Tyraz. She slipped off its back after the sun had set.

"Only a short rest tonight," she said as she led the horse to a small stream trickling downhill. "Don't go wandering off. You have an important task."

She took a few sips herself, located a flat spot under a lone pine tree, and closed her eyes. An unusually warm wind blew in from the east, making the otherwise chilly air more tolerable to Chara in her tattered clothing. Apart from the rush of water nearby, Chara heard no other sounds. Even the horse remained silent, forcing Chara to check if the animal was still around. It had given up on the stream, with its head in the air and its ears pointed forward. A grunt echoed from up the trail. The Fracodians must have caught up to her. She rushed to her mount and climbed onto its back.

From her higher vantage point, she glimpsed a pair of glowing red eyes in the distance, but they weren't from the Fracodians. The reanimated carcass of the horse she'd found on the trail was trotting toward her. Unlike the cloudy gray eyes of the previous bodies that had come back to life, this one stared ahead with burning hatred. This dead creature was different from all the ones before, and Chara didn't care to find out why.

"Don't let it catch us," she said as she urged her mount forward.

The horse understood the danger and took off at a quick pace. Chara couldn't hold on tight enough and flew off, crashing onto the hard ground. She rolled onto her back and sat up, her hands sore and bloodied from scrapes.

The undead horse stormed past her, almost crushing her underfoot. The gash on its neck had spread open, displaying the set of bones underneath, and its teeth all ended in sharp points. It wobbled with every step, its legs ready to collapse at any moment yet held together by sheer will. Chara's horse could outrun this creature, but it would eventually tire and be caught. She couldn't let that happen.

"Don't you want me instead?" she shouted as she returned to her feet. "I'm a much easier target than that other lame creature."

The undead horse stumbled as it came to a halt and turned to face her. This was no animal that came back from the dead. It was either possessed by a demon, or it was the demon itself. Chara froze under its piercing gaze, transfixed by the red eyes. It sauntered toward her, ready to take over her body, but she wouldn't let more people die. She had to help Tyraz reach Kroflund faster. If she hadn't told him about her neighbor's family in Luceton, he never would have volunteered for the mission. It was her fault for taking him so far from home, where they desperately needed him.

She backed away from the creature, heading toward the nearest cliff. She knew a fall, no matter how bad, wouldn't stop the demon but would slow it down enough for her to find and calm her mount. The possessed horse moved forward, never taking its eyes off her, never blinking. At this speed, her trick wouldn't work. She turned and ran.

The demon horse let out a grunt and took off, quickly closing the distance despite its uneven gait. Chara rushed toward the precipice, hopped off, and caught the edge with her hand, stopping herself from plummeting downward. Another inch and the fall would have crushed her. Her pursuer leaped at her but went too far, tumbling into the valley below. The next time, it wouldn't be fooled so easily. She had to reach Tyraz before the demon found her again.

Chara pulled herself up from the edge and collapsed on her back, breathing heavily. Myriad stars lit the night sky, but this wasn't a time for sleep or dreams. She brushed herself off and jogged in the direction that her horse had fled. Perhaps she could get some rest while allowing it to carry her, otherwise she'd be awake for the foreseeable future.

As she backtracked to the small stream and followed her horse's path, Chara worried that the frightened animal might have tripped and hurt itself. It also might have veered off the main trail. Although intersections were rare, she didn't have time for a single wrong turn. Her heart beat faster as she increased her pace, until she was running through the hills. The slope grew gentler the farther she went, and soon she'd reached the first few shacks of Luceton. Her horse stood near the old barns, munching on a patch of tall grass. She darted to the animal and wrapped her arms around its neck.

"I'm so glad you made it back safely," she said. "And not just because we need you."

She nudged it away from the barn, using all her weight.

"The demon is sure to find us if we stay here. We have to go now."

As if it understood her words, the horse finished its last bite and yielded to her pressure. After one final glance at Luceton, she climbed onto its back and trotted away. It had been a good place to live, and she knew people would fill its streets again one day.

Time had passed. Chara wasn't sure how long she'd been riding. Hours blended with one another, and it didn't matter if the sun was up or the moon. She forced herself to stay awake. The skin on her lips cracked during the daytime heat and stung whenever she took an infrequent break to sip from a stream running down the mountainside. The horse seemed to sense the urgency and kept going despite the lack of food. She promised her mount a life of green pastures and plenty of treats after this ordeal was over.

The sight of The Tooth rising over the other peaks in the distance lifted her spirits. She could definitely make it that far without collapsing, and once she reached the home of the Teruns, someone would help her find Tyraz. Each time she turned another corner, however, another mountain inserted itself between her and The Tooth. Somehow, she must have gotten disoriented and was traveling in the wrong direction. Chara urged the horse to turn around. It whinnied at her but eventually gave up objecting. She didn't know how much time she'd lost, but even an hour was too much.

Ahead of her, the mountains blurred, blending in with the sky. The Tooth had disappeared. Maybe she'd passed it already. Chara looked back as the surroundings spun around her head. She slid off the horse and landed on some hard rocks.

A refreshing sip of cold water flowed down her throat, while a rough hand held up the back of her head. Chara opened her eyes, squinting in the bright sunlight. Tyraz knelt beside her with a pouch of water in his other hand.

"How did you find me?" she asked, struggling to sit up on her own.

"We weren't much farther up the trail," he said. "When the horse came to us, I knew you had to be close."

"Go, now." She pushed him away. "Aiax needs you."

Tyraz dropped the water pouch and grabbed her hands.

"Both you and the horse need food and rest," he said. "We'll spend the night in Terun City and leave at sunrise tomorrow."

"But Aiax..."

"Will see me much sooner thanks to you." He waved to his men, standing a few paces away. "Help me carry her into town."

Chara would have preferred to walk, but her muscles wouldn't listen. She allowed Tyraz's strong hands to lift her off the ground, thankful that she'd completed her mission.

Chapter XIX

The Siege of Kroflund

It didn't matter that Chara had opened her eyes. The room appeared the same with them open or closed. She knew from the cold stone beneath her body that she was in a Terun bed. Perhaps she was still in the innkeeper's bed and had only dreamed the events of these past few days: the pile of bodies in Luceton, her search for a horse, and luring the demon to fall off the cliff. Her tension eased as she imagined the Luceton villagers waking up to a new day of sailing and fishing, but what if her dream had been a premonition?

She jumped out of bed and opened the door, ignoring a few aches from her muscles. Pale light flowed into the room from the glowing lichens in the hallway, revealing her torn clothing and scratched skin. Unable to deny the truth any longer, she sank to the floor. There had been so much death.

"Good, you're awake," said Tyraz as he marched toward her. "I didn't know if I should let you sleep any more. It's time to go."

"I was only able to find one horse," said Chara, staring into the dark room. "Go help Aiax. I'll get to Kroflund eventually."

Tyraz held out his hand, but Chara remained on the floor. She didn't want to encourage him. Aiax needed his help as soon as possible. She'd only slow him down.

"I'm not leaving you here," he said.

"Why not?" Chara shifted herself farther into the room. "Because you want me to see another city ravaged by demons?

Terun City seems to have been spared so far. I'll be safe here."

With a sigh of frustration, Tyraz picked her up and carried her outside. A blustery wind bit through her tattered clothing, causing her to shiver. She nestled closer to Tyraz's body for warmth, waiting for him to hold her tighter. Instead, he put her down and waved to one of his men, who brought him a heavy cloak.

"This should keep you warm," he said as he covered her shoulders and led her through the circle of soldiers.

The Ferfolk had gathered several paces away from the horse, which stomped on the ground and whinnied. The poor animal was scared. It needed a familiar face. Chara left Tyraz behind as she calmed it with soft steps and soothing words. She gave it a firm pat on the back and stroked its neck.

"I'm here," she said. "I'm not going to leave you."

She knew Tyraz could have handled the horse on his own if he tried, but she was glad he wanted her help. Even riding together on the single mount, they'd still reach Kroflund much faster than hiking.

"Are we ready to go?" he asked.

Chara gave him a quick smile and hopped onto the horse. Before joining her, Tyraz ordered his men to bring as many Teruns back to Kroflund as they could convince. The Teruns must have heard about Luceton, and if Kroflund was also under attack, it was only a matter of time before Terun City was in danger. Chara pulled the cloak tighter around her body and urged the horse down the path. Compared to the Ferfolk soldiers, she would have had an easier time convincing the Teruns to send an army, but it didn't really matter if they were successful. With demons around, Kroflund would need more help than a few axes or picks.

The meager supplies from Terun City had long since run

out, but Chara and Tyraz were nearing Kroflund. Unfortunately, she wasn't expecting a lavish meal anytime soon. They dismounted a good distance north of the Sinewan River and continued the rest of the way on foot. Chara promised the horse she'd come back for it and sent it into the foothills. The woods seemed quieter than usual, not much different from when the animals had been spooked near the cemetery. Something terrible must have happened in Luceton to have such a lasting effect. She followed Tyraz through the thinning trees until the water came into view.

No fishermen lined the banks, no ferries carried people across the river, and no longshoremen loaded supplies onto merchant ships. In fact, no boats were docked outside of town, except for a single raft on this side of the river. Chara headed toward the bank, but Tyraz pulled her behind a large tree.

"Not until we know what's happening," he whispered as he pointed downstream at a long-eared animal creeping through the bushes. "That's not a rabbit."

As if it had heard him, the creature turned its head, displaying a set of glowing red eyes. It hopped forward on legs of uneven sizes, hissing as it went. It knew someone else was nearby, someone who didn't belong.

When the demon was within ten paces, Tyraz drew his sword and leaped out from behind the tree. The rabbit demon swerved out of the way faster than Tyraz could react, but his sword clipped its hind leg, causing it to stumble. Tyraz lunged at the creature with a big swing and cleaved its body in half. A gooey black substance oozed out, turning red after a few seconds.

"Quick," he said, "before any more of these scouts show up."

"How do you know it was a scout?" asked Chara as she rushed toward the river.

"Small and fast with good hearing. What else could it be?"

He kicked the raft off the bank and guided it to the other side with a long, wooden pole. Without much current in this section of the river, the raft floated directly toward the Kroflund dock. Chara still hadn't seen any people in town and shuddered to think they'd all been killed like the Luceton villagers. She stared at Tyraz. What if he and his few soldiers were the only Ferfolk left in the world?

As soon as they touched the far riverbank, Tyraz led her to a hiding spot next to an old guard house and peeked out at the empty streets.

"Not a single person," he said, "and no signs of a battle. Aiax would never let the city fall without a struggle, but no blood has been spilled."

"Maybe the battle was in the hills east of town," said Chara, "or in the woods to the south. We should keep to–"

"How did you get out?" came a voice from behind them.

Chara spun around to see a tall man with jet skin strolling toward them. A row of sharp knobs ran from the center of his forehead down the back of his neck, and he sported similarly adorned arms. Tyraz edged out in front of Chara and held his sword up.

"Who are you?" he asked. "And where is everyone?"

"You look familiar," said the demon, "and the girl–but not from here."

He circled them yet kept his distance.

"Yes, definitely familiar."

If Chara hadn't known he was a demon, she would have thought him handsome, although the sharp teeth peeking out from his grin gave her chills. He never blinked as he sized up his opponents.

"It's you," he finally growled. "These eyes see differently, but I recognize both of you."

He seemed to grow an extra foot taller while the knobs

along his back sharpened into fine points and his claws doubled in length.

"I've never seen you before," said Tyraz, "and if you come any closer, that'll be the last you see of anyone."

The demon ignored his warning and charged forward. Tyraz hopped up to meet the attack with a swing of his sword. The blade bit into the demon's outstretched hand, causing him to howl in pain and step backward.

"This isn't over," he said as he continued backing away.

"We have to find everyone before that demon returns with help." Tyraz pulled Chara up. "There's not much time."

"But he's scared of your sword," said Chara. "You can fight back."

"Maybe against him and another one or two." Tyraz hurried down the street toward the military compound. "But I have a feeling there are many more demons around here. Let's hope that Aiax still lives."

Chara rushed down the street after Tyraz. They passed empty market places and abandoned buildings on their way through the center of town. Wilted vegetables and rotting fruits covered one farm stand, but no rats feasted on the bounty. They knew to keep hidden, if they hadn't been taken, as well.

"Maybe we should have followed that demon," said Chara. "He ran away because he was afraid of you. We could have used that to our advantage."

"He wasn't afraid," said Tyraz without stopping. "He didn't want to risk injury when reinforcements were nearby."

Another few blocks brought them to the military compound, where a demon's body lay separated into four parts, each one held to a broken cart by a thick chain. Near the wall, two other demons marched in opposite directions carrying two-pronged pole arms. Each creature had a triangular head atop a gaunt body. Their bones showed through tight skin as they patrolled the area.

"The soldiers must be trapped in there," said Tyraz. "Stay out of sight while I free them."

He charged at the guard demons without waiting for a response from Chara. The nearest one let out a loud shriek from its circular mouth and pointed its weapon at Tyraz. Its companion joined the fight from the other side as a third demon approached from the sky. Huge bat wings sent out gusts of wind with each flap, while angry snorts came from its bovine head.

"Another one's coming from above," shouted Chara. "Don't let them surround you."

One of the triangular headed demons turned its attention to her, but Chara didn't run. Although her legs trembled under its fierce stare, she had to keep it away from Tyraz until he was ready, and there was no reason for her to be afraid. With no Ferfolk bodies in town, these demons didn't want to kill anyone. This reluctance to kill gave Chara an advantage.

Near the fortress gate, Tyraz knocked the pole arm aside with his sword and stepped close enough that the demon couldn't threaten him with the long weapon. The demon swiped at him, but he dodged its sharp claws and cut into its side with his blade. A few more opportunities like that and he'd be victorious. The demon, however, continued to attack without pause, bashing Tyraz's leg with the shaft of the pole arm. It wasn't surprised by the wound, so at least one other Ferfolk soldier must have had a weapon similar to Tyraz's.

Chara's opponent pointed its blade at her, keeping it only inches from her stomach.

"What are you going to do?" she asked. "Kill me?"

She stepped to the side, but the demon blocked her with the pole arm and nudged her into the street. Far stronger than it looked, she couldn't resist. She stumbled into the street, trying to avoid getting accidentally sliced by the demon's blade. Nearby, the flying demon hovered above Tyraz, ready to grab him as soon as he lowered his sword. Chara shouldn't have let him rush the gate without a better plan, unless he intended to be captured. He should have told her if that was his plan, but Chara had no better ideas at the moment. The demon marched her one block eastward, when the fortress gate opened and Aiax appeared.

Chara's captor immediately rushed at the Ferfolk commander, who had already taken a chunk of flesh off the flying demon's leg with his own sword.

"Come with me," he shouted at both Tyraz and Chara. "Quickly."

Chara darted toward the gate, while Tyraz and Aiax carved into the triangular headed demons. The flying demon took to the sky, drawing the commander's ire.

"It won't be long before it brings reinforcements," said Aiax.

"Even sooner than you think," said Tyraz. "A tall black demon escaped me earlier today."

"Obidicut," said Aiax. "We have to learn where he's holding the townsfolk, but first we need a plan to defeat this infestation. That was the last time we'll see a minimal complement guarding this base."

The inside of the compound was as barren as the rest of the city. No soldiers exercised on the grass or marched through the streets. Aiax headed straight for the largest building, banged on the door three times with an increased pause between each knock, and ushered Chara and Tyraz to temporary safety.

Dozens of Ferfolk lined the hallway. Civilians stood beside warriors, all looking to Aiax for guidance. He pushed through the crowd, speaking only to assure them he had a plan to take back the city.

Two guards stepped aside when he reached his command center, a small room with a few chairs gathered around a circular table. Septu rose when Tyraz entered the room.

"So the rumors were true," he said. "You returned."

"Don't start with me," said Tyraz. "It's been–"

Septu silenced him with a firm pat on his shoulders.

"The first piece of good news in weeks," said the tall warrior. "It took you long enough to get here."

Aiax held a seat out for Chara and sat in his chair last.

"We only have a few weapons that can pierce the demons' skin," he said. "I've spread them throughout the compound to counter a direct assault, but with enough demons, we'd never win."

"That means there aren't too many of them yet," said Tyraz.

"There are enough to pin us down." Aiax placed his sword on the table and wiped the black ichor off with a rag. "And new ones keep appearing. We're almost out of food and water. Another day's worth at best."

"The demons don't seem willing to kill anyone," said Tyraz. "Do you know where they're taking the prisoners?"

"Eastward," said Septu. "Along the river."

"To the altar," said Chara. "I'm sure of it, but how can one extra sword help?"

Aiax's pained expression showed that he didn't like relying on others.

"I also sent word to the Arboreals and the Teruns," he said, "but they haven't responded yet."

"My men will bring the Teruns with them," said Tyraz. "We have to be ready when they arrive. There might only be one chance for victory."

"How can the Teruns be more effective against the demons than us?" asked Septu. "They're not warriors."

Aiax returned his sword to his sheathe and paced the room.

"I'm counting on them bringing their best weapons to share with us," he said. "How far behind you are they?"

"We could all have been here sooner if the Teruns kept some good horses," said Tyraz, "but the hike will take an extra few days."

"That's too long to wait in this prison." Aiax leaned against his chair. "We need water soon or hundreds will die, but if we bring the good weapons away from the compound for too long, the demons will swarm in and take more prisoners."

"Then we'll have to bring all the Ferfolk with us," said Tyraz. "Maybe they can hide in the forest instead of these buildings."

"That's exactly what we've been planning," said Aiax.

The Ferfolk commander opened the door and summoned a few soldiers.

"Send word to everyone," he said. "We meet at the western gate within the hour, but wait until my signal before moving into the open."

As the soldiers put their fists together and left to carry out their orders, a chill ran up Chara's arms. If the demons returned too soon, the rest of the Ferfolk would be taken prisoner, and it wouldn't be long before they ended up like the Luceton villagers.

"Tyraz and I will go east," she said when Aiax turned to them, "to draw the demons away from you and the townsfolk."

"As will I," said Septu. "I've had enough hiding and running."

He glanced at Aiax. "At your command."

Aiax gave them a single nod and disappeared out the door. Chara knew he didn't expect to see them again, but she'd prove him wrong. As she headed for the hallway, Tyraz stopped her with a gentle grip on her arm.

"You're going with Aiax," he said. "Septu and I will lure the demons into the hills."

Chara squirmed away from him.

"You don't even have a weapon that can harm a demon," he said. "And if we found an extra one, you wouldn't know how to use it. Do you just want to sacrifice yourself?"

Septu blocked the doorway and said, "I agree with Tyraz. You'd be most helpful with the civilians. We can't have another person to worry about when we're fighting demons."

"So don't worry about me." Chara ducked under his arm into the hallway. "And stop wasting time arguing. You'll never convince me otherwise."

"Are you sure she's not part Ferfolk?" asked Septu as he followed her out of the room.

Tyraz mumbled something and took up the rear.

Outside the building, a flying demon hovered high above the compound. It made tight circles in the sky, always centered around Chara and the others. It was clearly waiting to see what they did. The rest of the demon army couldn't be far. Tyraz stopped about fifty paces from the outer wall, where a pair of mismatched creatures waited.

"They came through already," he said and drew his sword. "I won't let them get away this time."

Septu copied his motion and charged toward a white demon that appeared to be composed of icicles. Farther away, a frog-shaped demon took one huge hop and landed within ten paces of the tall warrior. Its black tongue shot out of its mouth, but Septu countered with a compact swing. His blade nicked the tongue, forcing it to recoil into its master's gaping maw.

"You haven't tasted this metal yet," he shouted. "Now for some more."

Tyraz rushed past him to take on the ice demon, but why send only two into enemy territory? Either the demon in charge didn't know what he was doing, or this was a trap.

Chara looked up to an empty sky–definitely a trap.

"Let them go," she shouted. "They're a distraction."

"We can't let any demons see Aiax and the others," said Tyraz severing a frozen arm from his opponent. "Just keep an eye out for more of them."

The ice demon backed away slowly, as did the frog demon. Tyraz and Septu pressed forward after their opponents until they reached the wall's shadow. Chara remained far from the battle, gazing at the stonework at the top of the wall. The square lines and right angles seemed to shift, turning into rounded corners and extending to sharp points.

"There's more of them on the wall," shouted Chara too late.

A dozen stone demons leaped down and surrounded the warriors, with more forming every second. While Tyraz and Septu defended against their new opponents, the frog demon hopped over everyone and landed near Chara. Its tongue shot out and grabbed her leg before she could move.

"Let me go," she growled and stabbed it with her knife.

The blade merely bounced off the rubbery appendage as the demon dragged her toward its greedy mouth. She dug her feet into the ground, slowing her motion for a moment, but the frog demon pulled harder to dislodge her. It didn't care about taking prisoners. It wanted her as its next meal. When she was close enough to feel its hot breath against her skin, the flying demon screeched downward and tore her away. Its talons dug into her shoulders, drawing thin lines of blood as it carried her upward, over the wall to the east. Far below, Tyraz and Septu had destroyed several stone demons, but the circle of enemies had gotten tighter around them. Soon they'd have no room to swing their weapons, no chance to escape the fiendish trap. Septu launched himself at a stone demon about to pummel Tyraz. He cleaved into its side, protecting his companion, but another two demons crushed him between their bodies. Tyraz knocked them away too late to save Septu. The Ferfolk's plan for a secret escape had failed.

Chapter XX

Temptation

The flying demon separated Chara from Tyraz. She didn't worry that he might be killed, because the demons preferred to keep everyone alive, but she imagined many possibilities worse than death. Obidicut might torture Tyraz as revenge for his part in defeating the lyche, or perhaps he'd force Tyraz to watch as someone else was tortured, someone he cared about. Chara shuddered. That would be her.

She struggled in the flying demon's talons, but if she freed herself so far above ground, she'd only plummet to her death. Perhaps her death would be best, so Tyraz didn't have to watch her suffer. She'd take the memory of the humans with her, leaving this world to the Arboreals and the Ferfolk–if they ever defeated the demons.

High above the forests and farmlands, the demon veered off course and circled back toward Kroflund. It obviously didn't want anyone to know where it was going, not even its brethren that had captured Tyraz and killed Septu. From the outline of the Sinewan River, Chara guessed the demon was carrying her due west, past where Aiax had planned to lead the Ferfolk citizens. Either this demon wanted her for its own purpose, or Aiax would be leading his people into another trap. Chara couldn't sacrifice herself yet, not until she warned the others.

Blood stained her shirt where the demon gripped her shoulders, but it had been long since she felt pain. They'd flown past

Kroflund, past the western farms, and up into the Pensorean Foothills before they descended to the treetops. The demon dropped her the last several feet and returned to the sky, allowing her to crash through the branches and smack into the ground.

"Many good thanks," she called out. "If you were going to throw me down, you could have done that closer to the center of town."

"But then I wouldn't have been able to speak with you in private."

A dark figure strolled toward her from a cluster of crooked trees. Rows of sharp bumps lined his head instead of hair, and curved spikes accentuated each of his joints. His eyes glowed orange, chilling Chara when she stared at him.

"Obidicut," she said. "I thought you were gone forever after Tyraz scared you off. I'm not surprised that you cowardly sent a servant to abduct me."

The archfiend reached out to help her up, but she scooted away from him and stood on her own.

"Don't mistake caution for fear," he said as he retracted his arm. "I have orders to complete, and it would have delayed Mammon's plan if I had to nurse any silly wounds."

"Call it what you want." Chara looked around but didn't see any other demons. "We both know Tyraz would have defeated you back at the river."

She wondered how fast Obidicut could run. He had a much longer stride, but perhaps he couldn't move his legs as fast as she could. A guttural grunt from Obidicut turned into a roaring laugh.

"Defeat me? If I weren't sworn to keep you all alive, your little friend would have been dismembered before he drew that infernal blade."

"In that case," said Chara, "I'll take my leave."

She darted away. It didn't matter which direction she chose, as long as she could escape the archfiend. Once she felt safe, she'd double back toward Kroflund and warn Aiax that the demons weren't just east of the city. Whatever Mammon and Obidicut had planned, she'd rescue Tyraz and stop them together. She glanced over her shoulder. The archfiend hadn't even moved yet, giving her hope for an easy escape until she collided with a deer that must have just come out from behind a tree. The creature gazed at her through bright red eyes before trotting away. Obidicut didn't have to move to keep her from escaping. He controlled one or more animals in the forest, forcing them to do his evil bidding. Chara would also free those innocent creatures from his spell.

Obidicut ambled forward with his sharp teeth visible through a smug grin.

"You can't escape," he said.

"And you can't watch me forever," said Chara. "Don't you have responsibilities to your master?"

"He's not my master," growled the archfiend. "I'm helping him carry out his plan, nothing more."

"I don't believe you're helping him because he's your friend." Chara backed away in step as Obidicut advanced. "What did he promise you?"

"A realm of my own." Obidicut peered past her, probably getting another animal ready to block her path. "But he'll yield more than that if he wants to keep the peace."

"What do you want with me anyway?" asked Chara. "If you want revenge, then take it already. I'm bored with this conversation."

"At first I wanted to tear all of you apart," said Obidicut, "but you're not like the others. You're the last of the humans—a survivor—someone more likely to listen to reason."

"Since when does a demon care about reason?"

Obidicut scowled at her but quickly regained his composure.

"We are broga," he said. "Mammon doesn't realize he can't treat everyone the same. Fear might keep his realms under control in the netherworld, but it won't work here. I'll convince him to adjust his plan, but I'll need someone here to interact with the inhabitants."

"Reason or not," said Chara as she matched his stance with hands on her hips, "none of us will rest until every last...demon...has been banished to the netherworld."

The archfiend's eyes appeared to glow brighter and his features seemed to harden until a shadow crossed his path. One of the flying demons circled once and returned whence it came.

"We'll continue this discussion later," said Obidicut. "Mammon calls."

He followed the flying demon's path, soon disappearing in the distance. Chara didn't move for several minutes, wondering if the possessed forest creatures would block her escape again. Eventually, a hawk soared high above, and a pair of squirrels chased each other through the branches. The animals had apparently returned to their normal lives, and so would she.

Chara considered returning to Luceton, taking one of the now abandoned boats, and searching for the humans. They might have survived the Cold Ocean and the dead coming back to life. She didn't have to be the last of her kind. Either she'd find her people in their new home, or she'd die trying. Scouring the entire world for a group of humans seemed far easier than defeating the demons, but she wouldn't abandon the Ferfolk while Tyraz still lived. She gazed north at the distant mountains. Perhaps the demons didn't know about the Terun army.

She took a few tentative steps toward the steeper foothills, watching for any strange animal behaviors, but no more possessed creatures intercepted her. Tyraz's men and the Terun army could be anywhere from the Sinewan River to Terun City, but she'd find them and come up with a plan to free Tyraz and the rest of the Ferfolk.

There were no signs of an army in the woods directly north of the river. Either Tyraz's men hadn't come this far south yet or they never convinced the Teruns to send help. Chara was furious at the thought. The Teruns never wanted to leave their underground home, but they had no choice this time. She stormed up the trail, thinking of a hundred ways to chastise them for being so self-centered. Once she reached the Tooth of the Gods, the Teruns would offer her their best weapons and warriors, or she'd carry the miserable little men out one at a time and deliver them to the demons herself. The only problem was how long it would take her to get to Terun City and back. Mammon wouldn't keep thousands of Ferfolk imprisoned forever.

Chara veered off the path when it passed some grassy fields and soon found the horse that she'd saved from the Fracodians. The animal trotted up to her and bumped her with its head.

"I know I promised you an easy life," she said as she stroked the silky fur on its neck, "but I need your help again. You wouldn't mind taking me back to the Teruns, would you?"

The horse lifted its head and stared north. Maybe it understood her, or maybe it just thought she wanted to go home to Luceton. She climbed onto its back and urged it onto the trail, hoping her good fortune would hold out.

Only one day of riding brought her to the Ferfolk's soldiers, hiking along the trail without a single Terun in tow. Chara wasn't surprised. They didn't know the scope of the danger and thus couldn't convince the Teruns of the dire need for help.

"Don't return to Kroflund yet," she said as she halted in front of them, taking up the entire path. "Demons have overrun the city and captured everyone. Aiax tried to save the citizens, but he led them all into a trap."

"We don't take orders from a human," said the lead soldier. "If the city's been taken, then we'll fight to get it back. We will not abandon Aiax."

"I didn't ask you to abandon him. You can't defeat the demons on your own. Just wait until I return with the Teruns, and then we'll drive the demons away."

"The Teruns ignored us for days. They're worse than the Arboreals. What makes you think you can convince those ungrateful worms to come with you."

"For the same reason that I have a mount and you don't," said Chara. "Go get yourselves killed if you don't believe me, but I think doing so would truly be letting Aiax down."

She prodded her horse to a canter without looking back at the men.

Chara only allowed herself and her mount a few hours of rest per day, enabling her to reach Terun City twice as fast as her return trip with Tyraz. She left the horse near an outgrowth of tall grass before the trail became too steep and continued the rest of the way on foot. She wasn't sure whom to ask for assistance, but she knew it would be someone in the Undercity. If there a Terun army, the soldiers would definitely associate with the miners and smiths more than the innkeepers and merchants. Locating the nearest tunnel, she headed deep into the mountain.

With light streaming down from the roof, the Undercity was far more inviting during the day than at night. Scores of Teruns rushed up and down the passageway, ignoring Chara's increasingly loud pleas. This is what the Ferfolk meant by Teruns ignoring them, but her mission was too important for politeness. She blocked the next Terun she saw, matching his steps to either side until he gave up trying to dodge her.

"I have much work to do," he said. "What do you want?"

"I'm looking for your best weapons," said Chara. "And–"

"Speak to one of the smiths," said the Terun as he hopped around her and dashed up the tunnel.

"I don't want to buy anything," Chara shouted after him, but he'd already vanished from sight.

She chased after him and grabbed his arm.

"None of your important work will matter if Terun City is destroyed. Is that what you want?"

"This hill will not die." He pulled away from her. "Why must you force me to be late?"

"Demons have taken over Kroflund," she said, "and they're coming for the Undercity next. Do you know what it's like to fight a demon? They'll tear apart anyone that opposes them– including women and children."

The Terun brought a chalky hand up to his chin.

"I barely escaped with my life," said Chara. "If none of you want to listen to me, I'll let them take this mountain from you. At best, you'll work as slaves for your new masters, delivering gold and gems to Mammon and his lieutenants."

"I've heard a few tales of beasts with red eyes," said the Terun. "Is what you say true? The fiends have come to this world?"

Chara stared into his gray eyes and nodded. It didn't matter that she exaggerated, only that he listened.

"Then you must speak with Drydj," he said. "Down the

path, to the right, to the end. Now I must go."

"Many thanks," said Chara as she jogged down the tunnel.

The Terun's directions led her to a wide stalagmite with a door carved into the center. When she raised her fist to knock, a young Terun opened the door.

"Are you Drydj?" she asked.

"If you are here with those men from the south," he said, "Drydj has no more to say."

"Then he can just listen to me."

She pushed her way past the Terun, crouching slightly to fit in a hallway that led into the stalagmite.

"Drydj," she shouted. "Come out from hiding, or you'll face a far worse enemy than me."

When she reached a closed door, she tugged on the handle and banged on the stone. The young Terun came up behind her and tried to nudge her away from the door. When he grabbed her forearm, she jerked away from him, banged her head against the ceiling, and fell over, pinning the young man beneath her. The door opened.

"You did not have to hurt the poor boy," said Drydj, an older Terun with a white beard on his chin and little other hair on his head.

"Hurt him?" Chara ran her hand over her bump. "Your house practically knocked me out."

She rolled to the side, allowing the servant to squeeze out from under her. After a wave from Drydj, he retreated down the hallway. Chara followed the old Terun into a small room with several chairs carved directly from the base of the stalagmite. An indentation in the far wall held three glowing stones that bathed the chamber in soft yellow light.

Drydj sank into the larger chair and motioned for her to take the other. Chara sat on the uncomfortable edge, still massaging her head.

"I know you believe that you're safe beneath this mountain," she said, "but I've read stories about armies infiltrating Terun City long ago. This fortress is not impenetrable, especially to a cunning enemy. Demons have already wiped out Luceton and taken prisoner everyone in Kroflund. How much longer do you think you have before you must face the demon army on your own? I'm not even convinced the Arboreals are still alive."

"What do the fiends want?" asked Drydj as he sat forward and placed his hands on his knees. "Food. Gold. Lives?"

"I only know that they have a plan for everyone in this world." Chara leaned in toward him. "They don't have the resources to keep the entire population as prisoners for long. Mass death will come soon if you don't send help–and everyone in this mountain will be next."

"How do you know all this? The men told me they just guessed at the need for aid."

"Those soldiers never faced the demons directly," said Chara. "I have, and I've seen them beaten. Very few weapons can pierce the demons' skin."

"Most blades are a mix of ores," said Drydj, "and there are few pure ones left. They are quite rare."

"Aiax and Tyraz must each have one. I've seen them hurt an archfiend."

Drydj didn't stop staring at her, probably trying to determine what was the truth. Chara squirmed on the uncomfortable seat.

"Since you are the last of your kind," he said, "I'll trust you, but if you have lied to me, I will ban trade for two score years."

Chara rose from the cold stone and hovered over him.

"If we do nothing, there will be no trade until the end of time. This is no lie."

Although the Teruns hated leaving the mountain, once they made up their minds, they were quick to act. It only took a few hours for Drydj to gather two score weapons that he considered "pure." Most were double-bladed axes, but a few appeared more like mining picks and a half dozen were fancy swords. One of the weapons was a curved dagger with an obsidian hilt that he handed to Chara.

"You will lead these men with this blade," he said. "Bring them back to the hill when they're done."

"I promise." She took the dagger from Drydj, exchanging it for Tyraz's knife. "And I will return for this one. Aiax and the Ferfolk will not forget your assistance in this battle."

She faced the crowd of Teruns, many of whom didn't seem to understand why they'd gathered at the end of the entrance tunnel with their rarest weapons.

"Our entire world has been under siege for the past several weeks," said Chara, holding up the dagger. "Demons have escaped the netherworld to destroy our homes, and very little can pierce their skin other than the special blades we carry. They slaughtered everyone in Luceton and are preparing to do the same in Kroflund unless we stop them."

A few Teruns, probably ones with friends in Luceton, squeezed their weapons and growled. The others most likely thought they would have been safe in the Undercity. They were wrong.

"Aiax and a few Ferfolk warriors have similar blades," said Chara, "but the demons can control the animals of this world. We can only stop them all by combining our forces. Otherwise, Mammon will overpower us one battle at a time, including anyone that thinks he can hide in this mountain."

"We do not hide," one of the skeptical Teruns called out.

"Exactly," said Chara. "We will take the battle to the demons and send them back to the netherworld. Your Ferfolk brothers would never leave you in need of help. Do not abandon them now."

Most of the Teruns raised their weapons and shouted. Chara just hoped they weren't too late to save Tyraz and the rest of the prisoners.

Chapter XXI

Rise of the Demons

"How did Mammon and his demons capture everyone?" asked Jarlen as he followed Cassor from treetop to treetop. "Not only were they in the middle of the forest, they were in your own village. They should have had no chance."

Cassor stopped on a high branch, overlooking an uncountable number of trees. Far to the north, the tips of the Pensorean Mountains poked out above the canopy. A white cap of snow topped the tallest peaks, while patches of green and brown dotted the rest. Years ago, Jarlen had dreamed of visiting the mountains, but now he only wanted his forest back.

"They turned Arboreal against Arboreal," said Cassor. "We didn't know who was friend and who the enemy. Nobody trusted anyone, and none of us were willing to harm an innocent victim. Thankfully many of us escaped into the deep forest before they could round us up."

"Then what's the point in freeing anyone?" Jarlen slumped against the trunk, his own limbs refusing to obey. "They'll just turn on one another again."

"I was hoping you could help." Cassor sat next to him. "As a necromancer, maybe you can stop the demons from influencing our friends. If not, then perhaps you'll determine how it happened so we can tell friend from foe."

He prompted Jarlen forward with a hopeful smile. Jarlen still couldn't move. He'd caused the Arboreals to fight one another, and it would be his fault if the demons slaughtered them all. He squeezed his fingers into a fist. Not while he still lived.

"I'll do what I can," he said and followed Cassor northward, suspiciously in the direction of the altar that the lyche had used to open a connection to the netherworld.

The abrupt change between lush green foliage and shriveled brown vegetation reminded Jarlen of the differences traveling from one realm to another in the netherworld. An icy mountain led to a lava-filled plain, with rain soaked hills nearby. Here, the once majestic trees had given way to crooked, wooden skeletons. Barren branches clawed at the air, grasping for the slightest touch of life. Cassor stopped at the edge of the woods, clearly distraught at the dismal sight. Even Jarlen had difficulty looking at the devastation.

"We'll get everyone back," he said, "and restore the forest. This is only temporary."

"Our people are somewhere in there," said Cassor, "if they're still alive. We won't have any cover to hide from the demons once we cross over."

"Maybe we can have some help." Jarlen closed his eyes and chanted, "*Genip greyn bans gebindan asyrian cnapas.*"

His connection to the netherworld was stronger than he could remember, allowing him to summon several spirits to his aid. Branches from the nearest dead trees broke off the trunks and merged together to form a pair of wooden servants, each with three legs, two arms, and no head.

"Are those yours?" asked Cassor.

Jarlen gave him a single nod, proud of his accomplishment.

"What about those?"

Cassor pointed past the servants to a group of animals charging forward. A few woodchucks, three rabbits, and two wolves bounded across the rough terrain, every one of their eyes glowing bright red.

"The demons must have sent them to capture us," said Jarlen. "We only have a few minutes while my servants deal with them. Once that happens, their masters will surely come to investigate."

"Let's not waste a second." Cassor leaped down from the branch and rushed into the dead clearing, giving a wide berth to the melee.

Jarlen would have preferred to summon more help, but the demons had to have known he'd called the spirits. They might even be waiting for him to try it again, ready to trap his mind in the netherworld. Instead, he chased after Cassor. They had to free the Arboreal prisoners before Mammon increased his defenses.

In the distance, scores of dead trunks formed a solid wall of wood. The prisoners had to be inside the forbidding structure, but no demons patrolled the area. Mammon would never have let such an important location remain unguarded. Jarlen slowed down.

"This is our chance," said Cassor. "Quickly."

He stopped a few paces from the dead trees.

"Can you send a spirit into these trunks?" he asked. "Otherwise it would take hours to cut through."

"That might alert the demons to our presence, if they're not here already."

Jarlen inched closer to the wall of wood while constantly glancing over his shoulder. If he knew more about how this prison had been created, he might have had a better idea how to open it. He scanned the clearing, sure they weren't alone, but other than Cassor and himself, nothing else moved. Death permeated the area. He wasn't even convinced that there were Arboreals within the circle of trunks. Perhaps the dead trees hid a new realm of the netherworld, the first one to be merged with this land.

He put his hand against the nearest trunk, but the bark felt slippery and warm.

"These aren't trees," he said as he hopped away. "These are demons."

Cassor pulled out his sword and drove it into the nearest trunk. The demon moaned but remained motionless.

"They'll hold up to a lot of pain," said a voice from behind.

Jarlen spun around and glared at the white giant ambling toward him.

"Mammon," he said. "Let them go and take me instead."

"I have no use for a single Arboreal," said Mammon, "or even a pair such as yourselves. We need every one of you."

"We?" Cassor yanked his sword back and held it in front of his body. "Who else is here?"

"Dis must be working for Mammon, but he's far to the south," said Jarlen. "I thought you two had your differences. You can't trust him."

Mammon kept ten paces away, his eyes in constant motion, probably looking for other enemies. Perhaps Jarlen should have gathered a dozen Arboreals to help free the rest, but Cassor wouldn't have allowed anyone else to risk their lives.

"I convinced him of my plan's merit. No need to worry about his loyalty." Mammon waved his arm at the wall, which opened into a small alcove. "Why don't you step back a few paces. I wouldn't want to harm you."

"You haven't killed anyone yet," said Cassor. "You won't kill us either."

"Maybe not," said Mammon, "but I don't need you with your arms or legs, and it's been so long since I've torn anyone apart."

He reached out with an upturned hand and dared the Arboreal to attack. Cassor leaned forward, but Jarlen held him back by the shirt. Mammon wasn't bluffing. He'd tear them both apart to get what he wanted, but they couldn't just yield to him. That would be handing over the entire forest to the demons. He had to try summoning help.

"Just keep him away from me for a few seconds," he said before starting another chant.

Mammon obviously didn't approve and immediately took an enormous stride toward Jarlen. Cassor stepped into the way and blocked the archfiend. His sword swooshed against the white fur without doing any apparent damage. The huge demon pushed Cassor back with little effort until he was beside Jarlen.

"Summon your little spirits," he said, "but they'll prove as powerless as that golden sword."

At the edge of the clearing, two long vines turned from green to brown, infused with a pair of spirits from the netherworld. As soon as Jarlen commanded them to ensnare his opponent, the vines snaked along the ground and wrapped around Mammon's legs, pulling him back a few feet. The archfiend grabbed the vines and tore them in half, but the resulting pieces just kept attacking. Mammon yanked them off his body and held them at an arm's length. Meanwhile, Cassor lunged at the archfiend, aiming for his exposed stomach.

"You will not take this forest from us," he shouted.

Mammon knocked the sword aside and grabbed Cassor in his free arm, lifting him into the air and squeezing. The Arboreal elder screamed in pain, unable to escape the vice grip. His face turned red as he gasped to take in a breath of air.

"Fine," said Jarlen. "We'll go into your prison. Just let him go."

He stepped through the demon trees into the alcove. Mammon tossed Cassor beside him and closed the opening with another wave. Cassor coughed a few times, trying to recover from the demon's grasp. Jarlen checked on him before taking a closer look at their cell.

Within the tiny room, the walls no longer looked like dead trees. What were trunks on the outside of the prison appeared to be a single body covered in rough scales. Near the top, long arms or tentacles blocked Jarlen's view of the sky except for a few narrow slits between the appendages.

"Can anyone hear me?" Cassor shouted at the inner wall.

"Who's there?" a voice responded. "Are you here to free us?"

Cassor breathed heavily, either a sigh of relief or still a bit out of breath.

"Yes," he said. "Don't worry. Tell everyone that Jarlen's with me. We'll do what we can to destroy this prison."

When he turned to Jarlen, his scar seemed to have taken over his entire face.

"Mammon wasn't concerned with your ability as a necromancer," he said. "Can we prove him wrong?"

Jarlen hoped so, but he'd need a stronger link to the netherworld. Perhaps this was the exact spot of the lyche's altar. Although he'd closed the link from the netherworld side, it appeared that Mammon had reopened it somehow. A single death would give him access to powerful allies.

"If my life would help," said Cassor as if he'd read Jarlen's thoughts, "take it. Anything to save our people."

Jarlen's legs gave out, causing him to collapse onto the ground. He could never take Cassor's life as well as Eslinor's. This time, he'd be the one to sacrifice himself, but then he'd have to hope the summoned spirits would obey someone else. He groaned at the thought. Anything he brought through from the netherworld would instantly turn on his friends if he weren't around. They had to find a way to free everyone without resorting to murder.

Above him, a few openings between the tentacles appeared just large enough to squeeze through.

"Give me a boost," he said.

Cassor lifted Jarlen onto his shoulders near the edge of the alcove. The tentacles at the top of the wall were still far above Jarlen, even with his outstretched arms, but if the demon's body was soft enough, he might have a good enough grip to climb. He put his hand on the wall, but the rough scales didn't yield to his touch.

"Some of the Arboreals that Mammon captured are good climbers," said Cassor. "If escaping out of the top were possible, we would have known already."

Jarlen hopped off him and returned to his spot on the ground in frustration–no way up and no way through. He clawed at the soil underneath his body, but it was so hard packed that his scratching barely made a mark. If there were bones somewhere down there, however, he might have more luck.

Placing both hands palm down, he chanted, *"Bans ent aweaxan."*

Although he couldn't summon a powerful spirit without more preparation, he only needed something that could move a few bony fingers–something to loosen the soil enough to make a small hole. As he repeated his incantation, he felt a connection to the remains of an animal. He forced a spirit into the bones with an order to claw its way up to the surface. A few minutes later, the animated skeleton broke through the top layer of soil and crawled out of the ground.

"Do it again," he said as he pointed toward the interior of the prison. "Under that wall and out there behind me. After that, you're free to return home."

The skeleton attacked the ground, quickly forming a hole to where Jarlen hoped the prisoners awaited. Screams from the other side indicated that his servant had succeeded, but also might have alerted the demon walls to possible danger.

Jarlen squeezed through the hole and pushed himself into a large room surrounding the old boulders of the lyche's altar. Scores of Arboreals huddled near the far wall, possibly half the population of Hillswood. Nearby, a tentacle from the demon wall had come down and grabbed the skeleton, which was trying to bite itself loose.

"Does anyone have any weapons?" he asked, not surprised when nobody responded.

"Jarlen, I'm so glad Cassor found you." The crowd parted to reveal Aquila. "Is Eslinor with you? I haven't seen her since you left Hillswood."

She straightened her brown dress and strolled forward, sidestepping the altar. Although she displayed confidence to calm the crowd, Jarlen could see her concern. Her flowing hair stuck next to her body, and her bright green eyes had dimmed several shades. If he told her what had happened to Eslinor, it might remove her last shred of hope.

"She didn't join us," he said. "Cassor and I came alone. We just have to free my skeleton so it can dig one last hole."

Several of his skeletal servant's bones had cracked under the tight grip of the demon. Any longer and the spirit would be forced back to the netherworld. He grabbed the end of the tentacle and tugged, but it wouldn't release its prey.

"Help him," shouted Aquila with a glance at the crowd.

A dozen Arboreals darted forward, prompting the demon walls to send down more appendages.

"This is our best chance to escape," said Jarlen. "The skeleton's claws are sharp enough to dig through this packed dirt."

Another two score Arboreals rushed over to help. Some took on the new tentacles, while others unwound the skeleton. As more tentacles came down from above, more Arboreals left the safety of the group to join the battle. Soon the skeleton shook loose from its bonds and returned through the hole into the alcove.

"Quickly," said Jarlen with a wave at the hole. "Climb through. I'm not sure how long we have before the demons realize what we're doing."

He sent Aquila through first, ignoring her objections, followed by the women and tenderlings. As long as the line of Arboreals kept moving, he knew they were escaping the prison. The alcove was too small to hold all of them.

Several tentacles had captured Arboreals and were holding them high in the air. Jarlen didn't want to leave them behind, but they all yelled at him to escape. Without his help, the demons would just recapture the Arboreals.

"I'll come back for you," he called out before squeezing through the hole.

He emerged into the alcove, where only Cassor remained.

"There are a few prisoners left," said Jarlen, "but the prison caught them."

Cassor pushed him into the hole to the outside.

"We'll return for them," he said, "but first we have to ensure that everyone else is safe."

After so many prisoners widening the hole as they escaped, it was easy for Jarlen to climb through. He expected to emerge on the other side to find Mammon and a host of demons surrounding the Arboreals, but he instead appeared in front of an army of Ferfolk. Strangely, most of them carried no weapons, and there were as many women as men in the crowd. At first Jarlen assumed that Tyraz had brought his people to help fight the demons, but an increase in shouting dispelled that idea.

"You're working with them!"

"We're trapped. Where do we go now?"

"I knew we never should have trusted them!"

"You'll never take our home."

Cassor climbed out of the hole behind Jarlen and tried to calm his people, but his voice was lost in the chorus of angry yells. Jarlen looked around for Aiax or Tyraz. They had to be nearby, but the front line of Ferfolk wouldn't let him pass.

"Don't you remember me?" he asked. "I helped save Kroflund from the lyche and the evil spirit that sent green fire against you."

"Maybe you brought them to weaken our defenses," one of the Ferfolk called back. "You and your demon army will never succeed."

A pair of hefty Ferfolk grabbed Jarlen by the arms and legs. He struggled to free himself, but these people were out for revenge, no matter who the target. Jarlen was more worried now than when he was trapped in the netherworld. An unruly crowd was just as dangerous as a few demons and far more irrational.

"Put him down," came the strong voice of Tyraz as he pushed through the crowd. "Or face my sword."

The two men dropped Jarlen with a set of grumbles as they faded into the mass of Ferfolk. They might have yielded to Tyraz for now, but Jarlen knew they weren't done with the Arboreals. If they couldn't trust their own leaders, they certainly wouldn't allow their ancient enemy this close to their home. Jarlen had to send the Arboreals deep into the forest.

Tyraz helped him up and gave him a firm hug. In that moment, Jarlen believed the demons would never win. It didn't matter that he'd caused all these problems. With his friend's help, they'd send Mammon, Dis, and any other fiends back to the netherworld, allowing life to return to normal in the forest.

"We should separate everyone before more violence erupts," said Tyraz. "Then we can figure out how to defeat Obidicut."

Obidicut? Jarlen couldn't believe another archfiend had come through the portal. How many more would they have to face because of his mistakes? He didn't deserve to be friends with Tyraz. He was as evil as the demons.

Tyraz turned to the Ferfolk, imploring them to ignore the Arboreals and keep heading east. Something must have caused them to flee Kroflund–probably the same thing keeping the Arboreals this close to Ferfolk territory.

If Mammon had corralled both the Ferfolk and the Arboreals into this small area, perhaps his plan had always been to force an encounter between the two enemies. Jarlen waded through the crowd in search of Cassor, when a flash of red caught his attention. A tall Arboreal with glowing eyes headed toward a group of Ferfolk. Jarlen darted after him, hoping he could get there before violence erupted.

"Don't let him go any farther," he shouted. "A demon's controlling him."

"A demon," screamed a young woman. "Where? Do something."

The rest of the Arboreals looked around, moving randomly to get a better view. Jarlen couldn't get through fast enough, and any more comments about demons would only put everyone into a frenzy. He should have known this was the demons' plan. They didn't harm any prisoners because they wanted the Ferfolk and Arboreals to kill one another. Such deaths probably formed a stronger connection to the netherworld.

"We have to calm down," he said as he placed a comforting hand on one arm after another. "If we don't fight among ourselves, the demons are powerless against us."

"But the Ferfolk–"

"It doesn't matter who," said Jarlen. "Don't hurt anyone."

Just when many of the Arboreals had begun to settle down, more shouts came from nearby. Jarlen excused himself to investigate. He couldn't let the demons win. Unfortunately, a dozen Ferfolk warriors had drawn their swords, ready to attack.

"Tyraz," Jarlen called out. "You have to stop the fighting. It's what Mammon wants."

The Ferfolk warriors let out war cries and plowed into the Arboreals. Jarlen darted toward the melee, noting that several people on both sides sported bright red eyes. As one of the warrior's blades cut into his opponent, the Arboreal's eyes turned back to green before closing forever. Two furious Arboreals screamed for revenge and lunged at the Ferfolk. It wouldn't take long for this to become a bloody battle.

Behind the front line, Tyraz, with his back to Jarlen, had engaged one of his own men. Jarlen had to get close enough to stop his friend. He skirted the bulk of the fighting until Tyraz's face came into view—his eyes as brown as ever, the same as his opponent's.

"Tyraz, don't harm your own men," he yelled. "Why are you doing this?"

Tyraz shook his head before lowering his sword.

"Jarlen," he said. "I was just talking to you over there. What happened? Why am I fighting?"

"Demons are controlling a few people, including you evidently," said Jarlen. "You have to calm everyone before more people die. Once we stop the fighting, we'll handle the demons."

Tyraz's former opponent gave a single nod and ran off to help, but the few minor skirmishes had already turned into a major battle, with most of the Ferfolk army involved.

A guttural laugh came from nearby. Jarlen and Tyraz followed the sound to the demonic prison, where Mammon stood with his legs apart and his furry arms crossed over his chest.

"The offer to join me still stands," he said. "As you can see, it's too late to save your world, and I'm feeling generous now."

A skeletal figure in a dark robe rose from the center of the prison, buoyed by a writhing black mass. Arms, legs, and heads appeared and disappeared in the gooey substance as it flowed outward in two thick streams, one heading north and the other south. A four-fingered hand formed in the black substance, reached in to pull out the wailing head of an old man, and dissolved back into nothing.

"That's the Black River," said Jarlen, "from the netherworld. Why did you bring it here?"

"Bring it where?" asked Mammon. "This is all part of the netherworld now. Welcome to my newest realm."

Chapter XXII

The Black Flood

Mammon grabbed the old man's head that had separated from the Black River and tossed it to the skeletal demon.

"Keep it together," he called out, "until we're ready."

The skeletal demon shoved the head into the flowing black goo and pointed at the two armies. He obviously wanted more deaths from the Ferfolk and Arboreals. Jarlen glanced at the small space between the former enemies. It wouldn't take much from the demons to reignite the war.

"Tyraz," he shouted. "Get everyone into the forest. Make sure they understand there is to be no violence between them under any circumstance."

"What's your plan?"

"We have to stop this battle and escape the demons without giving them any more sacrifices," said Jarlen. "After that, I'm not sure."

He and Tyraz inserted themselves between the two armies, convincing one combatant at a time who was the real enemy. Many of the older men resisted, wanting any excuse to resume hostilities, but Jarlen persisted. He implored them to fight the demons' interference and give peace one more chance. Eventually, a few Arboreals and Ferfolk started calming the others down until the sounds of clashing metal had completely dissipated. The demons, unwilling to admit defeat, possessed a few warriors on either side, but Jarlen located them and convinced others to restrain them instead of resorting to violence. Slowly, the Arboreals filtered back into the forest, each of them guiding one or more Ferfolk until only a handful remained on the battlefield.

"You lost," said Jarlen to the few Arboreals and Ferfolk still controlled by the demons. "Let those people go."

With a set of growls, they tore into one another. Jarlen and Tyraz saved two of them, but the rest didn't stop until their bodies lay lifeless on the ground. The skeletal demon had gotten his deaths, but Jarlen wouldn't allow him even one more.

Jarlen sent Tyraz into the woods with the two survivors as he took one last glimpse at the altar. The skeletal demon, standing over the source of the black mass, had called on a dozen demon guards to surround him. Each of the newcomers held a two-pronged pole arm, ready to skewer anyone who ventured too close. Mammon had summoned several flying demons and was in step with the southern spur of the Black River. Jarlen knew another archfiend was in a similar position near the northern branch. Did the two streams have to encircle the globe and meet up again, or were they headed to other destinations? Either way, this world didn't feel like the netherworld yet, so there was still time to save it. He only had to figure out how.

Cassor led everyone southwest toward the border between the forest and the wastelands. He claimed it was because the demons had overrun most of the Arboreal villages, but Jarlen believed it might have been to ease the Ferfolks' nerves. Coming from the desert, they'd always held a deep distrust of the forest. Jarlen had a similar feeling about the wastelands, which only held small pockets of life between vast stretches of sand and rocks. Maybe that had been a prior attempt by the demons to rule this world. Jarlen shuddered as he imagined all the trees crumbling to dust. He couldn't let that happen again.

"The scouts we left behind have finally reported back," said Tyraz as he took a seat on a downed log. "The demons didn't follow us into the forest."

Cassor and Aquila looked down at the clearing from a high branch, while Aiax stood at the perimeter. Jarlen circled the group before heading to the center.

"Of course not," he said. "They already got what they wanted—enough deaths to open a strong connection to the netherworld. I have no doubt if we didn't intervene, the Black River would have been flowing much faster."

"Was that even a river?" asked Aiax. "Parts of bodies came out of it, some of which looked Arboreal or Ferfolk. Were they demons or some other vile creatures from the netherworld?"

"Does it matter where those arms and legs came from?" asked Tyraz. "As long as our blades can send them back to the netherworld, I'll call them all filth. We just have to get our swords back."

He peered into the darkness, evidently wondering if they were truly safe from another attack.

Jarlen glanced up at the elders, who seemed to be communicating silently. He understood very little of their signs, but they had to be discussing how to rid this world of the demons. One day, he promised himself to learn the old Arboreal language, maybe after the world was free of Mammon and his army. Aquila must have noticed him staring and gave Cassor a signal.

"We noticed the southern stream," said Cassor, "is heading toward where I found you. Can you think of any reason that might be so?"

"The altar." Jarlen sank onto the log beside Tyraz. "It's heading for the opening to the netherworld that I created."

"And the one going north?" asked Aquila.

"The opening on the Cursed Island," said Tyraz as he placed a hand on Jarlen's shoulder. "This is not your fault."

"You don't know what I've done." Jarlen scooted to the end of the log. "None of this would have happened if I'd kept my promise to avoid necromancy. Everything I did just kept making things worse. Once we send these demons back to the netherworld, I'm done with it forever."

Aiax strolled closer and hovered over him.

"So if we stop the Black River, we save our world?" he asked.

Jarlen nodded blankly. He couldn't be sure, but it was no coincidence where the two streams were heading. Unfortunately, the demons had confiscated the weapons that were effective against them, and Mammon kept summoning more help from the netherworld. Stopping the river seemed impossible, and no matter what Tyraz or the others said, he was guilty.

"We'll return to Kroflund," said Aiax, "recover the swords forged from vistrium, and split up to handle both streams at once."

"Are there enough weapons for everyone?" asked Cassor. "Vistrium is quite rare."

"Only a couple dozen of our best blades can pierce the fiends' skin," said Aiax. "The rest can only hold off their attacks for a few minutes."

Cassor lowered himself to the ground and joined the others by the log.

"Then we must split up now," he said. "I'll take the Arboreals to slow Mammon, while you stop the northern stream. If the Black River reaches the Cold Ocean, we'll have lost."

Jarlen jumped up.

"You can't do that," he said. "It would be suicide to face Mammon without any way to defeat him."

Aquila hopped down to face him directly.

"We're not trying to defeat him," she said as she took his

hands in hers. "Only slow him down until you return from the north."

She pulled him close for a strong hug.

"Don't let us down, young one."

"Mammon captured Hillswood with little problem," said Jarlen. "He'll just do it again."

"He took us by surprise the first time." Cassor exchanged places with Aquila to say his farewell. "He won't fool us the same way twice. Go now–before this world is lost forever."

Jarlen wanted to go into the forest with his people, especially if there was a possibility that he'd never see them again, but nobody else could ensure the river was stopped. He held onto Cassor an extra moment before letting him disappear into the treetops. As Aquila gave him a final smile, Jarlen swore to return as soon as he could to save her and the rest of the Arboreals.

"They've made a valiant sacrifice to protect this world," said Aiax. "We must not fail our mission."

Tyraz approached the commander, ready for his orders. Jarlen took a deep breath and turned away from the trees, garnering a nod of approval from the Ferfolk.

"While we collect the weapons," said Aiax, "Jarlen will locate the northern–"

"We've split this group enough," said Jarlen. "We find the weapons together."

Tyraz's eyes opened wide and his lips parted. A Ferfolk warrior would never have interrupted his commander, but Jarlen was neither a Ferfolk nor a warrior. He realized Aiax wanted him to hide in the trees and spy on Obidicut, but there would be time for that after they armed themselves. Besides, Mammon wouldn't have left the special weapons unprotected. Although Jarlen had promised to give up necromancy after defeating the demons, a few spells might be necessary to break through their ranks.

Aiax chose his best warriors for the mission and ordered the rest of his people to join their Ferfolk cousins in the desert oases if he didn't return soon. The reminder about desert Ferfolk relieved Jarlen somewhat. Even if the demons wiped out Cassor's group, there were more Arboreals in the Southern Mountains. Perhaps there would always be someone to resist the demons if this mission failed.

Jarlen passed no demons on his way toward Kroflund. The march brought him through barren farmlands on the outskirts of town, eerily reminiscent of the Forbidden Wood. Weeds had already popped up in the fields, abandoned buildings stood quietly on the hilltops, and empty streets awaited the daily shuffle of footsteps. This couldn't have been how the Arboreals had displaced the humans. Jarlen always imagined that the humans left their cities willingly in search of a better place to live, but what if his people were no better than the demons? Maybe nobody belonged in this world except the innocent plants and animals.

They soon arrived at the border separating the military compound from the rest of the town.

"This is where we lost our swords," said Tyraz as he moved along the stone wall looking for clues.

While he was gone, Jarlen wandered through the neighborhood, wondering who would fill these streets next. Would the demons claim them as their own, or would the Teruns come out of hiding? He made his way back to the group when Tyraz returned with a scowl.

"Nothing," said the young Ferfolk. "Not even the bodies of the demons that we killed."

"There's no reason to search the buildings," said Aiax. "The weapons must be with the demons, and we know where they are—guarding the front of each black stream."

"Before we track the northern branch of the river," said Jarlen, "we should go to the altar. Without Mammon around, I might be able to learn more about his plans or at least how to block the streams from advancing any farther."

"Agreed," said Aiax with a wave to his men, "but we cannot spend much time there, especially if it's possible the river has increased its speed."

Jarlen didn't want to acknowledge that he had little hope for this plan. If Mammon were worried about being stopped, he would have killed his enemies instead of allowing them to scamper into the forest, and he certainly wouldn't have left the altar unguarded. Maybe he didn't think the Arboreals and Ferfolk would ever dare return after suffering such a crushing defeat. Jarlen would have felt more comfortable if they encountered even a single demon scout, but he followed Aiax eastward toward the source of the Black River.

As they distanced themselves from Kroflund, Jarlen asked to approach the altar alone, but Aiax ordered Tyraz to accompany him. The rest of the Ferfolk remained well out of sight from any demons that might be roaming the area. Without weapons to protect themselves, it would have been disastrous for Aiax and his men to enter battle. Jarlen had to locate the special swords before they took on whatever demons protected the northern branch of the river.

Jarlen and Tyraz snuck through the trees, watching for any demons or possessed animals, but the forest surrounding the altar seemed quieter than usual. Even the leaves remained silent, refusing to flutter in the soft breeze as if they, too, would become the next target. The robed, skeletal demon remained atop the fountain of black goo, without any apparent protection.

"If I had my sword," said Tyraz, "I could have rid this world of that blight."

Although he'd spoken softly, the demon's yellow eyes turned toward him. The archfiend pointed a bony finger at Tyraz, causing the young Ferfolk to fall backward. Several disembodied limbs formed in the black mass below the archfiend, tore themselves away from the bulk of the river, and crawled forward. Along the way, they joined together to form a creature with four arms, one leg, and two clawed hands.

"Keep that thing busy," Jarlen whispered into his ear. "I'll see what I can find around here."

He made a large circle through the forest, always remaining several paces away from the altar. The robed demon kept its eyes focused on Tyraz, allowing Jarlen to cross the southern stream and inspect the clearing from all sides. There were neither demons nor swords of any kind near the altar. Mammon must have hidden the weapons somewhere else, but it would take years to scour the entire land for his secret lair. This mission was doomed to fail. Instead of pretending he had a solution, Jarlen thought he should send the Ferfolk back to hide in the desert. Maybe the demons would leave that part of the world alone, or maybe they would just round everyone up and slaughter them.

The Black River flowed outward from the remains of the altar. If the black mass originated from the netherworld, perhaps Jarlen could use the connection between worlds to summon some assistance. Finding a solid branch to perch upon, Jarlen closed his eyes and send his mind wandering.

With little effort, he soon found himself overlooking the snowy landscape of the netherworld's Ice Mountains. Although he couldn't feel the sting of cold against his skin, he still shivered. Nobody could last too long in this frozen world. He floated toward a nearby opening out of which rang a series of sharp *clangs*. A short tunnel led him to a dark cavern filled with ice demons, many of them armed with Ferfolk blades.

The demons sparred with one another, often slicing into one another's limbs and drawing lines of black blood. Mammon hadn't hidden the special weapons. He took them to the netherworld to equip his army. This was worse than Jarlen had imagined. Now they had no way to defeat the demons back home.

He allowed his mind to leave the netherworld, bringing him to the tree branch just outside the clearing. The strange river creature had captured Tyraz and deposited him in front of the robed archfiend. Another set of limbs had formed from the river and were holding him down, probably preparing him for a sacrifice. He struggled to pull himself free, but the extra hands had grabbed onto tree roots poking out of the ground.

"Do your worst," shouted Tyraz, "but we'll never yield. This world will never be yours."

Jarlen concentrated on the vegetation nearest Tyraz and chanted, "*Genip holt gebindan astyrian cnapas.*"

The roots below Tyraz didn't respond, but a pair of vines just outside the clearing turned brown, snaked along the ground, and tugged on the disembodied limbs holding Tyraz down. Instantly, the robed demon turned to Jarlen, piercing him with its yellow stare. Jarlen teetered on the branch, catching himself just before he fell.

With a wave of its bony arm, the archfiend shriveled the two vines, turning them into a line of dust. No other demon had taken control of Jarlen's summoned spirits so easily, but this setback had given him an idea.

He stared at the disembodied limbs until he connected with the spirits trapped within them. Pleading his case, he implored them to release Tyraz and promised to free them from their suffering as soon as he could. Whether his begging helped or not, he couldn't tell, but Tyraz broke free from their grip and scrambled back into the forest. Jarlen rushed to check on him.

"What happened to you?" asked Tyraz. "You were gone for so long."

"I only just left you," said Jarlen as he led Tyraz away from the clearing. He didn't want to find out how many river creatures the archfiend could summon.

"It was no less than an hour ago," said Tyraz. "Probably more."

They stopped by an old oak tree, far from sight of the skeletal demon. Tyraz pulled some cloth over a few scratches to stop the bleeding.

"I sent my mind into the netherworld," said Jarlen. "It's a lot easier with the strong connection at the altar. I didn't realize I'd spent so long there."

"Did you learn anything new?"

"I found the swords," said Jarlen. "Mammon took them to the netherworld for his army."

Tyraz crushed a few acorns under his boot.

"So we've lost," he said. "Even if regular swords could wound those river abominations, the demon guards would destroy us before we stopped even one of the two branches."

"What if we traveled to the netherworld and stole the weapons back? We've done it before."

"How could that possibly help?" Tyraz threw his hands up. "We'd need those weapons to fight the demon army in the netherworld. Unless you have another idea, our swords are gone forever."

He was right. They couldn't take an army of Ferfolk into the netherworld without any way to protect themselves, but he refused to concede defeat.

"Maybe I can control the Black River," he said. "The robed demon is too powerful for me to try near the altar, but I might have more success near the end of the stream."

He looked up at Tyraz as a sense of dread overcame his body. As soon as he halted the Black River, a swarm of demons would descend upon him.

"I would need help against the guards," he said. "But protecting me would be suicide."

"If that's what it takes to save this world," said Tyraz, "then so be it. Let's bring our plan to Aiax before the northern branch of the river hits the Cold Ocean."

Chapter XXIII

Teruns versus Demons

The Teruns were far more accepting of Chara than the Ferfolk were. They didn't even seem to care that she was female, treating her exactly like everyone else. Although the group started out quite surly, as they put more distance between themselves and the Tooth, the Teruns' attitudes softened. The first night, several brawls broke out for the best spot under an outcropping of rock, but by the third night, a few Teruns chose to sleep beside a cluster of trees instead of on the trail. Through it all, they included Chara in every decision, from allowing her to share the night watch to waking her at sunrise for a set of intense daily exercises.

The hike into the foothills was exhausting but passed quickly. Unfortunately, the Ferfolk soldiers hadn't remained where Chara told them to stay. She wasn't surprised they didn't listen to her. The Ferfolk prejudice against women and humans overpowered their better judgment. She was about to continue the trek to Kroflund when one of the Teruns approached her holding a serrated Ferfolk sword.

"I found this blade down that hill," he said. "Is it from the men you left here?"

"I think so." Chara took the sword from him to examine it closer. The blade shined as if it had just been polished. "They were supposed to meet us nearby. Can you show me exactly where you found it?"

The Terun led her off the trail and down a steep slope to a

small stream. A circle of fist sized stones surrounded a mound of charred wood, and the bones and antlers of a large deer lay scattered nearby. This had to have been the soldiers' campsite, but Chara detected no signs of a struggle. If something had attacked the Ferfolk, either demon or predator, there would have been splattered blood or at least some broken foliage. The closest bushes, however, appeared untouched by either animal or blade.

"Night comes soon," said the Terun. "We can save some time and camp here."

A quick shiver passed from Chara's neck to her arms. She didn't like the thought of staying in this abandoned campsite until morning, but it wouldn't have been much different if they hiked another hour or so. Any predator in the area could easily track them through the foothills, and if it was something more sinister than a nocturnal carnivore, they might already be doomed.

"Fine," she said, "but let's post double guards tonight. I don't want to be surprised by the same thing that took the Ferfolk. We're not as skilled with weapons as they were, so we have to be more prepared."

"There was no fight here," said the Terun. "They must have left on their own, back to town or in search of more food."

"That's what I would have thought." Chara drove the sword into the ground. "But a Ferfolk soldier would never leave his blade behind. Their love for their weapons is probably no different from Teruns and those hammers you always lug around."

The Terun laid a hand on the hammer attached to his belt as if she were thinking of stealing it from him.

"Go find the rest of the group," she said. "I want to look around here a bit more."

While the Terun was away, Chara dug through the ashes of

the campfire and tossed around the deer bones but found no other clues. By the time the Terun returned with the others, the sun had already dipped below the western mountains. A bright reddish-orange reflected off a layer of low clouds, making it appear as if the hilltops had caught fire. The Teruns remained transfixed by the scenery until it grew too dark to see.

"If sunset is so amazing to you," said Chara, "why don't you leave that hole in the mountain more often. You'd be able to see this almost every day."

The Teruns chuckled at her "joke" before splitting up to scavenge some food. They seemed able to sniff out meaty mushrooms, always knowing which ones were poisonous and which were edible. Combined with small game, their meals were far more palatable than the Arboreal's choices. Chara remained behind to start the campfire, and soon, a crackling fire lit the clearing.

Even with the warm flames dancing in front of her, a chilly wind coming from the mountains caused her to shiver. A few flickers of light reflected off the Ferfolk sword. Chara turned her head away from the reminder of this mystery. It wasn't a coincidence that the soldiers had disappeared like the townsfolk, and she was guilty of leading innocent people toward danger.

What if the demons didn't know about the Teruns yet? Was she condemning their entire race by bringing them into battle? Maybe they could have remained hidden beneath their mountain, safe from any turbulence in the rest of the world. There was still a chance to protect them if she sent them home now. She'd just have to find a different way of helping–perhaps by accepting Obidicut's offer. At least then she could protect Tyraz. The sound of feet shuffling across dirt drew her attention.

"Did you find something good to eat?" she called out. "I'm hungry."

When only silence answered her, she drew the Terun dagger and hopped closer to the fire. Three tall men approached the campsite, each one sporting a pair of glowing red eyes. The soldiers hadn't run away or disappeared. A demon had taken over their bodies, and Chara knew exactly which fiend was controlling them.

"You didn't like that we interrupted your feeding frenzy in Luceton," she said. "Come out and face me directly if you want revenge. I led those Ferfolk to Luceton."

The soldiers kept marching forward. Even if she could trick one or two of them like she did with the possessed horse, the third one would easily kill her. The only chance of survival would be to overpower all three soldiers or destroy the demon. It had to be close by.

A few mumbles echoed from the distance, alerting her to the nearby Teruns. If they weren't careful, the demon might take them, as well.

"A demon controls these Ferfolk," she shouted. "Don't let it–"

With a roar that made her jump backward, the Teruns charged into battle. They surrounded the Ferfolk and pounded them with hammers and picks. The soldiers fought back, tearing into their opponents with nothing but nails and teeth. It seemed as if the fight should have been over within seconds, but the Ferfolk didn't go down. Their leathery skin deflected the Teruns' attacks, and their increased strength allowed them to overpower their smaller adversaries. Chara wouldn't have long to release them from the demon's influence. She sneaked away from the melee, hoping the Teruns could hold out until she located the fiend.

Chara rushed around the rocky hills until she realized she'd become quite cold. The temperature must have dropped by half in the past few minutes. Her fingers grew numb, and each breath formed a small white cloud in front of her face. The demon had to be close, but why hadn't it felt this cold in Luceton or in the eastern mountains? Something was different this time.

Ahead of her, a cold wind blew from where the air shimmered with a pale blue light. Chara crept closer, making sure each step was as quiet as possible. A few paces away, the demon they'd defeated in Luceton faced what appeared to be snow-capped mountains inside a circular opening in the sky. Two creatures, covered in ice crystals, stood on either side of the opening and chanted in a strange language. They had to be summoning more help.

Chara darted forward and leaped onto the Luceton demon.

"You didn't think I'd forget about you," she said and drove the Terun dagger into its eye. "This is for killing those innocent animals and people."

The demon wailed as it threw her off. Chara flew several paces away and landed with a heavy thud, knocking the wind out of her. Her blow must have been accurate, however, because the snowy mountains faded away as the blue light diminished. Soon, the sky appeared as dark as usual with the Luceton demon lying still on the ground. The two ice demons screeched as they scrambled toward her, furious at her interference. The crystals covering their bodies gained an extra few inches and sharpened to needle-like points as the fiends closed in for the kill.

As the first set of claws slashed down at Chara's neck, a hammer slammed into the demon's arm, shattering the limb. Six Teruns surrounded each ice demon, while a Ferfolk warrior dragged her away from the battle. He bled from several wounds and could barely move his left leg, but he smiled at

Chara as they reached a safe distance.

The Terun hammers pounded the ice demons, sending shards flying from their bodies in every direction until nothing was left of them.

"The other soldiers?" asked Chara, already having guessed the answer from the dejected look on the Ferfolk's face.

He shook his head and said, "Along with three Teruns. The Luceton demon forced us to fight one another. At one point, I thought we killed it, but it came back again a few hours later. How is that possible?"

"Jarlen would have been better suited to answer, but from what I've learned, we can't kill these demons. We can only destroy their bodies."

"Does that mean..."

"This one will come back for us after it grows another body. I don't know how long we have."

The Ferfolk helped her to her feet.

"Then we should leave for Kroflund at once," he said.

"We don't leave our dead on the ground," said the closest Terun. "The rites will start at sun up."

"Do you think I like leaving my brethren here to feed the scavengers?" The soldier towered over the Terun. "But we have an important mission to complete, and I've waited here helplessly for too long."

Chara stepped between the two.

"Let them bury their dead," she said, "while I help with the soldiers. It's still more than a day to Kroflund, and we can't do it without some rest. Can you even hike that far with your injured leg?"

"I can go there and back, but I'll wait this one night only because you freed me from that fiend." The Ferfolk spun around and limped back to bury his comrades.

Chara followed him to the campsite but found it difficult to look at the bodies. These deaths had been caused by a demon that wasn't even present for the battle. While two good soldiers and three Teruns lost their lives, the fiend was opening a portal to the netherworld to bring more evil into the world. If each demon could do the same as the one from Luceton, there was little hope for anyone to survive.

She helped dig the graves, thankful that these bodies didn't come back to life. The Ferfolk soldier said a few words of tribute before filling the holes and returning to the campfire. Chara sat between the two mounds of dirt, wondering what had happened to Jarlen. Perhaps he'd found a way to send the demons back to the netherworld and only needed a set of fresh bones for his incantations. Chara was positive these soldiers would have gladly given their bodies to defeat the demons. If she ever found the young Arboreal, she'd offer her life for the same reason.

The Teruns spent all morning preparing their ritual to bury the dead. Half the time was spent locating hundreds of rocks, each of which had to be the same size, and piling them into tall pyramids. Chara helped when she could, but the Ferfolk soldier remained at the fringe of the clearing, sharpening his sword. By noon, the Teruns had laid the dead, along with their hammers and picks, in separate stone-lined graves.

"We can't leave those weapons behind," said Chara. "They're too important to this battle."

"Their tools stay with them," said the elder Terun. "This has been our way since our race was young."

"I've already told you many times, your way will end if the demons win."

Chara reached into the grave but was held back by a pair of Teruns. She struggled in their grip, but they wouldn't release her.

"At least let me borrow these weapons," she said. "I promise to return them after we defeat the demons. We're doing this to protect your families, not to defile your traditions." The Teruns shot frustrated glances at one another, but eventually backed away from the graves. Chara bent down and collected the hammers and picks. She laid the weapons on the ground and added her Terun knife.

"You've been very generous to lend these weapons to me," she said. "They will all be returned to their proper owners after our victory."

Although the Teruns seemed to accept her promise, none of them came any closer to the weapons. It was probably bad luck for them to use another's tools without his approval. Instead, they placed one stone after another into the graves until the three pyramids were gone.

Chara waited for them to finish before waving the Ferfolk over.

"Help me carry these weapons to Kroflund," she said. "I suggest swapping your blade for one of them."

The Ferfolk's squeezed the hilt of his sword until his knuckles turned white.

"You've already seen that your weapon does nothing against a demon. These, however, will destroy those fiends. Which would you prefer in battle?"

He released his sword and selected one of the picks, swinging it a few times before letting out a brief grin.

"I'm ready to avenge my brothers," he said and scooped up the rest of the equipment.

They were still a few hours north of Kroflund when shouts rang out nearby. Chara immediately thought the townsfolk must have escaped and were being hunted by demons, a sentiment echoed by her companions. Worried about more treachery, however, she warned the Teruns not to rush into battle.

She led the group toward the noise, which sounded more like grunts and growls as they approached. When she passed over a small ridge, an unexpected sight greeted her. A black morass, about three paces wide, ran due south as far as she could see, while a swarm of demons surrounded the northernmost edge. What appeared to be limbs of creatures, both human and otherwise, reached out from the dark liquid and fell back in. Whenever a body attempted to escape from the river to either side, the demons would attack it until it returned, but anything going to the north was allowed to expand. This had the effect of extending the black mass in one direction only, but Chara had no idea why the demons were guiding it. There were no habitations to the north, except the now empty town of Luceton.

"What is that thing?" asked the Ferfolk soldier. "Could it be…"

"I hope it's not the citizens of Kroflund," said Chara, "but if the demons want it to go north, then we have to stop it."

A few Teruns joined them overlooking the Black River. If they didn't believe her before, they certainly saw the truth. At least three types of demons surrounded the northern portion of the river. Many of them were frog shaped, but there were also a few triangular headed demons with emaciated bodies. Two demons resembling the one from Luceton seemed to take the most joy in attacking the wayward limbs. Their sharp beaks tore into any arm, leg, or tail that didn't advance the river in the proper direction.

"We'll destroy every one of those fiends," growled the Ferfolk. "Who is ready for battle?"

The Teruns pumped their weapons and shouted their agreement. Chara would have preferred a planned attack, but several of the closer demons had heard the noise and broke from the rest of the pack to investigate. The Ferfolk soldier raised his Terun pick and charged forward, leading his riled army down the hill.

Chara held back. Even though her Terun dagger could pierce a demon's skin, she felt she'd be more effective watching for any surprises. She did, however, move closer to the head of the river. If she could free some trapped creatures from the black water, perhaps they'd turn on their demon captors, giving the Ferfolk and Teruns a needed advantage.

A large shadow crossed her path. One of the flying demons circled high above before disappearing into a puffy cloud. This battle had to end before more demons appeared. She rushed toward the river, making a wide circle around the fight, but a tall, dark figure stood in her way.

"Obidicut," she said, "What are you doing here?"

"Following my orders." He crossed his arms and displayed his sharp teeth through a grin. "Have you reconsidered my offer? You can't stop Mammon's plan, not even with your friends and their new toys."

Chara glanced at the battle. The gaunt, triangular-headed demons had fought the Ferfolk soldier to a standstill, while the Teruns had taken down a few frog demons. Although the fight seemed to be going well, Chara knew it would only get worse as time passed. Even if no demon reinforcements arrived, the warriors would tire out long before they defeated all these creatures. If she did nothing to help, they had already lost. She sneered at the archfiend. Perhaps the demon army would fall into disarray if they saw their leader fall.

"What exactly are you proposing?" she asked as she slinked closer to Obidicut.

"You can rule this new realm," he said, "with thousands of servants to fulfill your wishes."

"I doubt you have the authority to offer me a kingdom. Are you sure Mammon would accept these terms?"

Obidicut's smiled faded as his body tensed. Chara drew even closer, only one step away.

"I'll deal with him when the time comes," he said. "You just need to calm your people. I will not let them delay my work any longer."

Chara lunged forward with the Terun dagger, but Obidicut responded far faster than she expected. He caught her by the arm and lifted her off the ground.

"What about your master's order not to kill anyone?" she asked, struggling to escape.

"You've all served your purpose already," he said. "Mammon doesn't care what happens to you and your friends."

"Then why haven't those demons killed a single person yet?" asked Chara. "Are they incompetent in battle, or are you lying to me?"

Obidicut snatched the dagger from her hand, tossed her to the ground, and stormed toward the battle. As he closed in, the spikes on his head and neck elongated, and he appeared to gain an extra few inches in height.

"This is what I think of Mammon's orders," he growled as he plowed into the mass of demons surrounding the Teruns.

He carved into anything in his path, including several frog demons, before plunging the dagger into the Ferfolk warrior's chest. The rest of the group stopped fighting and backed away from him, demons included.

"Yield now," he said, "or I'll send every one of you to the netherworld."

High above him, the flying demon had returned. He glared upward at the newcomer.

"Go back and tell your master that I have this under control," he shouted as he pointed southward. "And stop spying on me or you're next. The Black River will reach the island on schedule."

The flying demon made a large loop and followed his instructions.

Chara knew what the demons were doing, but she had no idea how to stop them or why the island was so important. Without Jarlen and another army or two, the demons were too powerful for a handful of Teruns miners to defeat. Forcing them to continue fighting would only bring them painful deaths.

She lowered herself to her knees, watching as one Terun after another dropped his weapon. They would have been better off if she'd left them inside the Tooth. Anything that happened to them now was her responsibility.

Chapter XXIV

Betrayal

Aiax refused to risk crossing the Sinewan too close to the Black River. Nobody, including Jarlen, knew what would happen if someone accidentally touched the writhing mass of spirits. Instead, they hiked back to Kroflund to take whatever rafts had been left tethered to the piers.

Kroflund appeared even emptier than before, if that were possible. Jarlen had hoped the next time he returned to the city, it would have been to bring the displaced citizens home. Instead he was heading north on a desperate attempt to stop the Black River from reaching the shoreline. The city was dead. No Ferfolk manned the marketplace, no birds flitted from rooftop to rooftop, and no insects gathered around the gutters. This is what happens when demons wander the land.

Dozens of footsteps echoed off the empty buildings as Jarlen and the Ferfolk marched toward the port. Rats didn't even dare forage in the few stores with food left on the shelves, although everything had probably rotted by now. Jarlen tried to focus on the direction he was going because each peek to the side increased his feeling of loneliness, despite being amid a group of Ferfolk. When they reached the river front, the soldiers piled onto the few rafts available and pushed off the embankment, ready for what they considered their final stand against the demons.

"Promise me you'll find Chara no matter what happens next," said Tyraz. "I never should have let her face such danger."

"I doubt you had much choice in the matter," said Jarlen, "but I'll find her...together with you after we've won this battle."

He didn't want to consider losing his best friend in the next few hours, but there was little chance that everyone would survive.

Tyraz knelt on the raft and stuck his hand in the water.

"You're not as afraid of the river as when we first met," he said with a fading smile, "but it can still drown you if you're not careful."

"Are you trying to scare me?" asked Jarlen as he centered himself on the raft.

Tyraz wiped his hand on his shirt.

"Just warning you to keep up your guard," he said. "It may be easier for you to contact the netherworld these days, but that doesn't mean it's any safer."

"That's exactly why I'm never doing it again after we send these demons back to where they belong."

Jarlen fell forward when the raft hit the riverbank. Tyraz helped him up and patted him on the back as they hopped off. They hadn't hiked more than a few paces when a chorus of whispers ran from one person to another. A shadow crossed the river behind them, prompting Jarlen to gaze at a large, winged demon overhead.

"Do you think it knows our plan?" asked Tyraz.

Jarlen watched the creature disappear over the trees to the north.

"It's no coincidence that it travels the same direction as we do," he said, "but it might not be related to our plan. Both spurs of the Black River are important to Mammon, so he must be keeping track of its progress."

"I still don't like it," said Tyraz. "If the demon lord has

guessed our plan, we'll have to find a new way to stop him."

He trotted forward to Aiax with Jarlen following close behind. The Ferfolk commander had stopped the procession to confer with the others.

"A single demon isn't reinforcements," he said. "It's more likely a scout."

"Yet we must still proceed with caution," said Tyraz. "This is our last chance for victory."

Aiax gave a resigned stare at Jarlen. "I suppose you have second thoughts, as well?"

The commander he knew from before would never had allowed such questioning from his men, but even the great Aiax couldn't remain confident facing such terrible odds.

"Nothing has changed," said Jarlen. "We reach the northern branch as quickly as we can and send the Black River back to the netherworld. I don't care if they know exactly what we're doing. We have to try."

Aiax seemed to stand taller as he faced his men.

"It doesn't matter what demons they throw at us," he said. "We fight for our home today. They'll have to kill every one of us or accept their own defeat. Once we help Jarlen stop this branch of the river, he'll do the same to the south with the Arboreals. Let us take back our world!"

The Ferfolk shouted their support and doubled their pace to the northeast, following the path of the flying demon.

Within the hour, Jarlen heard the first sounds of battle. Shouts, screams, and *thuds* echoed through the trees, filling the group with hope that they'd found their missing brethren. When the flying demon came back toward them, a great cheer rang out from Aiax's men, assuming the battle had already been won. They dashed over the hills to find a bunch of Teruns fighting a couple dozen demons.

Several frog-shaped fiends surrounded the Teruns, while a

pair of triangular-headed demons stood back a few paces. A tall, dark figure loomed nearby with a young woman by his side. Her blond hair fluttered in the light breeze, and a piece of metal sparkled at her feet. It was Chara next to Obidicut, with her dagger on the ground. Jarlen felt ill at the thought that she'd joined the archfiend, but he couldn't deny that they appeared to be having a civil conversation.

Tyraz seemed ready to charge, but Jarlen held him back.

"We still have a plan," he said. "With the Teruns' help, it will be that much easier, especially since they've brought weapons that can hurt the demons."

"But, Chara—"

"Isn't fighting Obidicut." Jarlen released him. "They're just talking, so she's not in immediate danger. Maybe it'll help give us some extra time."

"Or maybe she'll make things worse."

Tyraz glared at the dark demon but relaxed his stance, yielding to Jarlen.

"Go help the Teruns," said Jarlen. "I'll get as close to the river as I can before trying to control it. Once Obidicut joins the battle, we'll have little time for success."

With a nod, Tyraz rushed toward the fighting with Aiax and the Ferfolk soldiers close behind. Jarlen remained out of sight until the newcomers drew the archfiend's attention. Obidicut didn't move from his spot, probably not considering the Ferfolk a serious threat.

Jarlen sneaked around to approach the river from the other side. Without demons guiding it northward, the Black River spread in all directions. Limbs stretched out from the black mass, pulling tails, eyes, and unidentifiable body parts with them. Crouched low, Jarlen crept closer until he was within ten paces. The constant gurgling must have meant the trapped spirits were hungry, ready to feed on anything they touched.

Up the hill, Chara had positioned herself to turn Obidicut's back to the river. She hadn't changed sides, but the archfiend didn't remain fooled for long. Before Jarlen could begin his first incantation, Obidicut spotted him and strolled forward.

"There's nothing you can do, Arboreal." The archfiend waved his arm, summoning an eight-limbed abomination from the Black River. "You've only brought these Ferfolk to their deaths."

"At least they'll have died protecting their home," shouted Tyraz as he intercepted Obidicut. "Do what you must, Jarlen."

The young Ferfolk held a Terun hammer in one hand and a pick in the other. He swung awkwardly at his opponent, who merely sidestepped the attack.

"Those weapons don't suit you," said Obidicut. "If they can be called weapons at all. Where's your precious sword?"

He lunged forward and wrapped his arms around Tyraz, lifting him into the air and squeezing until Tyraz gasped for breath. Chara rushed down from the hill and plunged a dagger into the archfiend's side.

"If you're going to disobey Mammon," she growled, "start with me. I'll never join you."

Obidicut shifted Tyraz to one arm and grabbed Chara's throat with his other hand. He didn't appear concerned at all with the dagger sticking out of his side. Jarlen could try to take the dagger and find a more sensitive spot, or he could ignore his friends and try to contact the netherworld. Neither option seemed ideal, but Chara had given him a clue to a third possibility.

"Tyraz's sword," he called out, catching Obidicut's attention.

"What about it?" asked the archfiend.

"I know where it is." Jarlen inched closer. "I've seen it recently."

"So have I," said Obidicut, "when your friend attacked me

near the river. Why should I care about that infernal weapon now?"

Jarlen stopped one pace from the archfiend and reached for Chara's dagger. Obidicut watched his movements closely but didn't respond while Jarlen removed the dagger from his side and tossed it two paces away.

"Let them go first," he said.

Obidicut lowered Chara and Tyraz to the ground but didn't release them. Even with both of them struggling at once, they couldn't escape his grasp. At least they could breathe again.

"Mammon took all the Ferfolk weapons to the netherworld," said Jarlen, "to equip an army of ice dem...broga."

"I suspected he was being too trusting with his plans to conquer this world." Obidicut gazed at Jarlen, probably trying to determine if he spoke the truth. "He never planned to share his power–he wanted to increase it."

"So what are you going to do about it?" asked Jarlen.

"I'm going to use these new weapons you brought to destroy him." Obidicut smiled at Chara. "You see, you have been quite helpful to me, but I no longer require your assistance."

He tightened his grip around Chara and Tyraz until they couldn't breathe.

"Do you have an army to equip?" asked Jarlen. "The ice broga are under Mammon's control, and Dis commands these other ones."

"I'll convince them to follow me, or I'll turn Dis against Mammon, as well. This time, however, he'll be my servant."

The fact that he was still talking was a good sign. Obidicut must not have known how to defeat Mammon, even with the Terun weapons at his disposal.

"Let us help you wrest the netherworld from Mammon," said Jarlen, "in return for leaving this world alone. Without an army of your own, you'll be at a great disadvantage, especially if Dis chooses not to side with you. This is your only chance for a definite ally."

Obidicut grumbled as he lifted Chara and Tyraz higher and tossed them aside. The two gasped for air, while Obidicut and Jarlen stopped the battle between the demons and Teruns. Tyraz eventually joined them near the Black River.

"How do we know we can trust you to leave this world alone?" he asked.

"Oh, I'll be back for this world one day," said Obidicut with a chuckle, "but if we defeat Mammon, I'll be busy with the netherworld for many years to come—certainly longer than your lifetimes."

"What about the Black River?" asked Jarlen. "How do we stop it?"

Obidicut led his demons southward, toward the Sinewan.

"We send Uryx back to the netherworld," he said, "but once the river stops flowing, Mammon will bring his army to investigate. We have to be ready for him."

"How powerful is Uryx?" asked Tyraz.

"The rest of the princes avoid any direct confrontations with him." Obidicut gave him a sly grin. "And he is under Mammon's protection. They key to winning this battle is finding Dis and making him question his loyalty to Mammon."

"What about Uryx's loyalty?" asked Jarlen.

"He wants only to expand the reach of his river, regardless of Mammon's plan."

"In that case," said Jarlen, "Dis is guarding the southern altar. It'll take a long time to reach him, and we'll have to make a wide circle around Mammon and the southern spur of the river."

"Not necessarily," said Obidicut with a wave to one of the triangular-headed demons.

The fiend raked the nearest Terun with his claws, sending a

spray of blood from his neck. Tyraz and the rest of the Teruns prepared to attack, but Obidicut raised his hands.

"I can send for more broga without any extra deaths," he said, "but this is the only way for me to travel back to the netherworld. Fight if you must sacrifice the rest of your lives but come with me to save your world."

Tyraz had clenched his jaws and tightened his grip on the hammer and pick. Jarlen put a hand on his shoulder.

"I don't trust him either," he whispered. "Stay here with the Teruns and do what you must if I don't return within the hour."

Chara retrieved her dagger. With one last glare at the archfiend, she knelt at the fallen Terun to stop the bleeding. She must have known she couldn't save him, but she tried anyway. Jarlen looked away, disgusted with himself for helping Obidicut.

"I'll go with you," he said.

Obidicut chanted a few words to open a shimmery portal and stepped through. Jarlen followed him to the center of the Lava Plains, just outside the city of Dis. The intense heat caused a thick sweat to cover Jarlen's body, and he wobbled from one side to the other as a quick dizziness passed. In front of him, a chorus of moans came from the uncountable spirits forever guarding the entrance to the city. A pair of triangular-headed demons watched the gate from their perches atop the wall.

"You should not be here, Obidicut," said one of the guards. "Mammon will be angry."

"I am still Lord Obidicut to you, and you'll face my wrath if you do not let me in," growled the archfiend. "I'll add you both to this gate and enter the city no matter what Mammon says."

The gates swung open, dragging the spirits on the bottom

across the hardened lava. Obidicut marched through and headed for a tall building down the main street.

"Why are we here?" asked Jarlen. "Is there an opening to the southern altar nearby?"

"I'm guessing Dis hasn't changed his favorite hiding spot," said Obidicut. "After we talk to him, I'll need your help to return to your world."

"And if I choose to leave you here instead?"

"Then you might as well get comfortable in the netherworld." Obidicut gazed at the sky with his arms spread. "Your world will become part of this landscape."

He stopped beside a pockmarked wall, shoved his arm through the stone, and pulled out a worm-like creature with a spike on its head. The worm demon squirmed, but Obidicut held it near the spike to avoid injury.

"Tell him what you saw," said Obidicut.

"Tell who?"

"Do you not recognize Dis?"

Jarlen had known the archfiends held different forms, but he didn't realize they did so simultaneously.

"Mammon doesn't intend to honor any of his agreements," he said. "He took powerful weapons from the Ferfolk soldiers and gave them to his army of ice demons. After he conquers my world, I suspect he'll return here to force this world into submission."

"Dis doesn't believe you," said Obidicut, struggling to keep the worm demon under control.

"I sent my mind back to the Ice Mountains," said Jarlen. "His army is training in a large cavern. If you think I'm lying, go look for yourself. There's nothing more I can say to convince you."

When Dis stopped moving, Obidicut opened his hand.

"Did he even hear anything I said?" asked Jarlen. "I don't see any ears."

"He heard you." Obidicut shoved Dis back into the wall. "But we'll have to wait to find out what he believes. He's known Mammon far longer than you or me, which probably makes him more skeptical about anyone else's statements about the prince."

Jarlen considered making a run for the city limits. He could leave Obidicut behind in the netherworld, but there would be at least three more archfiends left in his world. Dis might agree to turn on Mammon, if he didn't learn about Jarlen's betrayal of Obidicut. Jarlen sighed. It was too much of a risk to turn on Obidicut now, but he certainly didn't trust any of the demon princes.

They returned to the same spot where they'd arrived in the Lava Plains, but the portal was closed and Jarlen didn't have the strength to open a connection back home. He backed away from Obidicut. The archfiend didn't need him to speak with Dis–he needed his life.

"What about the river?" asked Jarlen. "There must be a gateway back home if it flows both here and in my world. We just have to find it."

"And put myself at Uryx's mercy?" Obidicut chuckled. "That will never happen."

"But he's not here," said Jarlen. "He's near the altar outside of Kroflund."

"He's wherever the Black River flows," said Obidicut. "You could have brought others with us if you wanted to live, but know that your sacrifice will help to dethrone Mammon."

In a desperate attempt to stop the archfiend, Jarlen chanted, "*Bans beorg hlifian aweaxan.*"

The charred ground below his feet rumbled as it rose to form a wall around Obidicut. Jarlen knew this protection would only be temporary. He doubted his ability to overpower the archfiend, and he wasn't familiar enough with the netherworld to hide for an extended amount of time. Inside the wall, Obidicut pounded at the sides. He'd break free within a few minutes.

Jarlen prepared to form a second barrier when a shimmering glow appeared in the air several paces away. He jumped through the portal and landed on the ground near a huge crab-shaped demon as Obidicut smashed through his prison.

"Dis," said Jarlen. "Why did you save me?"

"I didn't save you," said Dis. "I brought Obidicut through to help me against Mammon."

The dark archfiend stepped through the portal and smiled at Jarlen.

"It appears we're on the same side once again," he said.

Around them, pale moonlight filtered through the thick foliage. They were in the deep forest, probably near the southern altar. It would take days or more to reach the Black River, too late to stop the carnage between the Teruns and the demons. Jarlen scowled at the archfiends, wondering if they'd planned this from the start.

Chapter XXV

The Demon Prince

"Hop onto my back," said Dis. "I'll get us there much faster than you can run."

Jarlen backed away from him.

"First I have to close this portal," he said as he bumped into Obidicut.

"You're not closing anything now," said the dark archfiend, placing his clawed hand on Jarlen's shoulder.

Dis closed the gap, blocking Jarlen from moving anywhere.

"What do you think will happen if you close this gateway?" he asked. "Mammon will know I helped you, and he'll figure out where Obidicut went. He'll have his entire army waiting for us at the source. He's powerful enough even when we have the advantage of surprise. Don't help him further."

Jarlen couldn't argue, but he would have felt better if this link to the netherworld was severed. He pulled away from Obidicut and climbed onto Dis's back. Small spines covered the archfiend's hard shell, making the seat quite uncomfortable. Dis took off toward the north, forcing Jarlen to grab on with both hands. Within seconds, his palms were dripping with blood. While Dis kept moving, Jarlen tore off pieces of his shirt to wrap around his hands, easing the pain somewhat.

"How can you be here and in the netherworld at the same time?" he asked.

"As I recall," said Dis, "you sent your mind into the netherworld on more than one occasion."

"So?"

"So you left your body here." Dis darted around trees and under vines. "What's the difference?"

Jarlen almost fell off several times, scraping his arms and legs against the rough shell as he steadied himself.

"The difference is that my body wasn't under my control while my mind wandered the netherworld. You can't be in two places at once."

"Why not?" asked Dis. "Next time, don't send your entire mind away. Keep some of it behind in your body."

"I wouldn't even know how to do that," said Jarlen. "Besides, I've given up necromancy."

Dis leaped over a fallen log and landed hard on the other side. Jarlen bounced off his back and crashed into a dense cluster of ferns. Obidicut snatched him up with a single arm without slowing down.

"I knew you wouldn't last on him," said the archfiend. "Get comfortable–this will be a long trek."

Jarlen flopped around in Obidicut's arm as he ran, but at least his skin wasn't being torn off with every step. As they made their way through the dense forest, he wondered if it would be possible to send only part of his mind into the netherworld. No. He wouldn't return to necromancy. It was too dangerous...although...

The two archfiends ran without tiring or stopping to eat. By the end of the next day, Jarlen couldn't continue without food, even though he did nothing except lie still in Obidicut's arms.

"I have to eat now," he said. "We just passed a wild blackberry bush. This is as good a place as any to stop."

Obidicut tossed him to the ground.

"Don't take too long," he said. "Dis doesn't seem willing to slow down. The longer we delay, the more time Mammon has to learn about us."

Dis had already disappeared through the underbrush. Jarlen rushed back to the bushes and stuffed his hands and mouth full of berries, chewing them during his return to Obidicut.

"Why did you stop?" he asked between mouthfuls.

"I can't have you die out here," said Obidicut. "You might be of use at the source."

"You mean to sacrifice me?"

"Whatever is necessary to defeat Mammon." Obidicut grabbed him by the waist. "Wouldn't you agree?"

"I suppose," said Jarlen, resigned to his fate.

Although they caught up to Dis quickly, they still had a long way to go before reaching the altar outside of Kroflund. With nothing else to do, Jarlen concentrated on sending part of his mind into the netherworld. If he kept enough of himself behind to move his body around and complain every so often, Obidicut would never get suspicious.

At first, he considered the task impossible. How could he split his mind into two or more pieces? Several hours of failure prompted him to give up. He took a deep breath and exhaled slowly. His next breath happened on its own. In fact, most of his life he kept breathing without thinking about it. Perhaps this was the key to separating his mind.

He concentrated on groaning every time he changed position in Obidicut's grasp until his complaints happened on their own. With his eyes closed, he whispered the incantation to send his mind into the netherworld. He hadn't prepared any of the standard protections for his body, but if this journey wasn't successful, it wouldn't matter what became of him. Whichever demon won, Mammon, Uryx, Obidicut, or Dis, would tear this world apart.

A moment later he opened his eyes to the harsh red glare of the Lava Plains, hoping he'd left enough of himself behind to trick Obidicut. Nearby, the Black River flowed from one end of the horizon to the other. He glanced at the Ice Mountains in the distance. Somewhere up there were the special weapons that Mammon had planned to use against his brethren, but what if Obidicut and the other princes didn't return to the netherworld? Having the weapons here would be useless, unless Mammon was willing to give up his newest conquest. He must have had a plan to bring his army through a portal. The missing Ferfolk! Mammon didn't just bring the weapons into the netherworld; he brought all the Kroflund citizens. No wonder why nobody could find them. Jarlen had to save them before they were sacrificed.

He floated toward the mountains, passing from one hexagonal island to another. Bursts of lava soared through him as he ignored everything except his destination. They sky turned from bright red to bluish gray, and flakes of snow started falling. Soon, he was moving through a blizzard, up the steep cliffs, into and out of tunnels, and around dark caves. After what seemed like hours, he found the cavern with the army of ice demons, still sparring with the Ferfolk swords as if no time had passed.

Jarlen ventured deeper into the cave, avoiding contact with the demons. He didn't know if any of them were as strong as the archfiends, but he couldn't risk that one of them could stop him. The demons screeched at him, and several swung their weapons through him. He kept moving, knowing that it wouldn't be long before a more powerful fiend showed up to confront him.

In response to the added noise from the demons, a different sound emanated from one of the tunnels at the back of the cave. It sounded like distant pleas for help. Jarlen sped up, flying down a long passageway until he reached a smaller cavern housing scores of Ferfolk trapped at the bottom of a deep pit.

"Who's up there?" an older Ferfolk called out. "Can you help us?"

Jarlen wanted to do something, but without a physical form, he had few choices. Behind him, a line of demons formed in the passageway. Even if he could get the prisoners out of the hole, the demons would just shove them back.

The nearest fiend, one of the larger ice demons, took another swing at him. The sword swished through the air. If only he had control of the weapon. He tried grabbing the blade and pushing the demon's arm, but neither were effective. Only his thoughts were present, not his body. He stared at the icy creature, wondering if he could affect its mind.

Jarlen drifted closer to the demon, prompting it to swing faster and harder. He floated into its body and focused on its mind, willing it to turn around and face the other fiends. To his surprise, the demon obeyed his command.

He forced the demon to take a big swing and lop off the head of its nearest opponent. The sudden carnage caused such confusion that he was able to destroy three more ice demons before any of them fought back. Thankfully they were still quite awkward with the weapons despite so much practice. He, however, was little better. The demon fought back against him, although it had to defend itself from its peers, as well. Instead of going on the offensive, Jarlen willed the demon to block the oncoming attacks, and whenever a sword came loose, he kicked it into the pit.

Clangs of metal against stone joined his *clinks* of sword versus sword. The Ferfolk must have used the blades to form a staircase out of the pit, because several of them soon joined him at the end of the tunnel. Jarlen used the ice demon's body to protect the Ferfolk as they slowly recovered the rest of the swords and drove the ice demons from the cave.

"I don't know why you helped us," said the old Ferfolk, "but many good thanks."

Jarlen tried to speak, but only a series of grunts came out of his mouth. He was still in the demon's body. With great effort, he separated himself from the fiend and floated out of its body.

The Ferfolk stepped backward, some of them nearly falling back into the pit.

"It's me, Jarlen. Don't be scared."

"Tyraz's friend?" asked the old Ferfolk. "How did you do that?"

"Necromancy is more powerful than I imagined," said Jarlen.

"So you can send us home," said the Ferfolk.

Jarlen cringed. He could open a portal, but it would cost a life or two, far more than he was willing to pay.

"The barrier between worlds is difficult to breach," he said, "and returning the way I came won't help us. The river's my only chance. After I've reached the other side, I'll open a door for you."

"We're not staying here," said the Ferfolk. "I thought you said necromancy was powerful."

Jarlen couldn't explain his problem, because one of them would certainly offer his life. He marched up the passageway, out of the cave, and into the storm. Behind him, the Ferfolk linked arms and pushed through the snow until they reached the border between the Ice Mountains and the Lava Plains.

"You should wait here," he said. "The temperature is more comfortable, and the ice demons won't bother you."

"And what if you can't open a door," said the old Ferfolk, "or another archfiend comes for us?"

He turned to face his people, receiving a unanimous show of support.

"Wherever you go, we go."

Jarlen stopped at the edge of the Black River. He didn't

know where the river broke through the barrier between worlds, but he expected that it wasn't at one of its ends. The netherworld realms didn't fit together like the various regions of his world. The opening could be anywhere along the river—or everywhere.

"I think this can take me home," he said, "but I'm not sure. I also don't know how it will affect your bodies. You might not survive the plunge."

The Ferfolk crowded around him. He had to give them the other option, even if it meant taking a life.

"I can probably open a link to our world with a sacrifice." He couldn't look any of them in the eyes. "It's a terrible price to pay, but it might be safer than the river."

"Two unknowns, but only one of your choices comes with certain death." The old Ferfolk stepped up to the riverbank. "Show us the way."

Jarlen gave him a single nod and jumped in. As soon as he descended into the dark water, transparent hands grabbed at him but passed right through. He hoped the Ferfolk were as immune to their touch.

"We need your help," he said. "Uryx has trapped you in this river and intends to capture more spirits from my world. Please show us the way home so I can stop him."

Tortured faces drifted in front of him, wailing in agony. He couldn't tell if they heard him, let alone understood his words. Maybe they were the spirits of the Ferfolk that had just leaped to their deaths. He should have just killed one of them and opened the portal. It would have saved the rest of them a terrible fate. Another face floated by, this one looking more human than Ferfolk.

"I've seen the demons force you to perform deeds against your will," he continued. "Please do not allow anyone else to suffer."

A few more faces floated by, this time staring into his eyes.

"Once my world is safe," he said, "I promise to do my best to free you from this dreadful existence."

One spirit seemed to circle him before retreating into the distance. He willed himself to follow, keeping his eyes averted from the hundreds of moaning beings in the way.

"Stay close," he called out to any Ferfolk that could hear him.

As he progressed, the wails grew louder, but the river grew darker until he couldn't see anything. An overwhelming sense of loss flooded through him. He strained to see anything, but only blackness surrounded him. Had the Ferfolk been captured by another archfiend? Was he even going in the proper direction anymore?

Soon, a strong wave swept him up, carrying him faster and faster along with everything around him. This had to have been the fountain below Uryx in his world, otherwise he'd be lost because he couldn't control his own movement.

A flash of bright light was followed by the sensation of falling from the tallest tree. Instead of hitting the ground, however, he plunged back into the river. He knew he'd made it back home, because the spirits in this part of the river looked much different from those in the netherworld. Opaque hands, legs, and faces attached and detached from one another, and growls of anger had replaced the ever-present wailing. Although it was dark underwater, a white glow came from nearby.

Jarlen stretched toward the light and reached out of the water. Sunlight warmed his arm, enticing him to crawl forward. He sent another arm from the river and dug his fingers into the ground to help pull himself out.

"You do not belong here," a voice came from above. "You have contaminated my realm."

It had to be Uryx, but Jarlen couldn't see anything except pieces of bodies floating around in the darkness. A skeletal hand plunged through the water and latched onto his shoulder, causing a searing pain. He pulled harder with both hands against the ground, while grabbing onto Uryx's arm in an attempt to separate himself from the archfiend.

Uryx sent another arm into the water and dug his bony fingers into Jarlen's head.

"You will submit to me," he growled.

Jarlen's head felt as if he'd submerged it in the lava surrounding the hexagonal islands, and he couldn't loosen Uryx's grip. A flash of silver sparked nearby. Jarlen snatched the sword with one hand, held onto Uryx's arm with another, and drove the blade upward until the archfiend roared in pain. Free from the demon's grasp, Jarlen hauled himself out of the river. A few paces away, several Ferfolk screamed in horror and fled.

Jarlen spun around, but other than Uryx at the top of the fountain, there were no other creatures nearby. He looked down at his body and gasped. It wasn't him. His head seemed to be attached to his abdomen, and he had five or more arms extending from his torso, two of which formed his legs and feet. Only one of the limbs looked human; the rest ended in clawed hands.

A few more Ferfolk emerged from the river, apparently unchanged by the trip from the netherworld. Jarlen was glad they escaped. Uryx was probably so focused on controlling him, that he allowed the rest of them to go free.

"It's me, Jarlen," he said, but most of the Ferfolk scattered at the sight of him.

Two soldiers, still holding their weapons, remained within ten paces. They held their blades defensively but pointed at Uryx.

"You fought the archfiend," said one of them, holding out

his sword. "Take this and finish the job."

Jarlen stepped forward and took the sword from him. The second soldier also offered his weapon.

"We'll help as much as we can," he said. "The demon's coming for you."

Uryx removed the sword from his body as the fountain lowered him to the ground near Jarlen.

"You will not challenge me," said the archfiend. "Yield now or die."

"I offer you the same terms," said Jarlen, pointing both blades at him.

Uryx spun the sword between his skeletal hands but didn't advance. Either he was trying to intimidate Jarlen, or he was creating a distraction. Jarlen looked down as several tentacles extended from the river and grabbed his limbs. He severed two of them with his swords, but more took their place. Meanwhile, Uryx lunged forward for the kill. Jarlen barely had time to put up a defense, but he successfully blocked the next few swings by sprouting another two arms from his body.

"Call your army," came a shout from the south. "The traitors are just behind me."

Mammon barreled in from the forest, his white fur stained black with ichor.

"It's over," Obidicut called out, chasing after him. "Your reign and your treachery are done. Don't help him, Uryx. He planned to kill us all."

Dis followed at a slower pace, with two of his legs broken.

Uryx backed away from Jarlen and raised his hands toward the river. The tentacles retreated halfway before merging with other limbs and torsos. Mammon stopped beside the huge creature that had just formed and turned to face his pursuers.

"Uryx knew about your plan all along," said Dis.

"It doesn't matter." Every muscle in Obidicut's body had

tensed, and he stood more than a head taller than Jarlen had recalled. "They're weaker here, especially without our support. Kill them all before Mammon calls for reinforcements."

They charged forward, probably thinking Jarlen was another one of Uryx's river monsters. Either way, they'd planned to kill him, but he wanted them to know who had destroyed their plans of ruling this world.

Jarlen gazed into the forest to the south, searching for his body now that Obidicut was no longer carrying him. The archfiend must have dropped him before fighting Mammon. Jarlen concentrated but couldn't feel his body anywhere. Perhaps the sense of loss he'd felt before wasn't because of the Ferfolk. It had been from his dying body. Now he was stuck in this monstrous form. He fell to the ground, disheartened.

Nearby, Obidicut squared off against Mammon, while Dis faced the tentacled abomination. Uryx returned to his perch atop the river and called forth another hideous servant. This one appeared to be an enormous sphere covered in fang-filled mouths. Several crooked legs jutted out from the bottom to help move the creature around. It towered over Jarlen, ready to swallow him one bite at a time.

"Go ahead," he said. "My life is over anyway."

The creature extended a sharp beak toward him but was stopped by a glint of silver. Four Ferfolk soldiers, including Tyraz, had joined the battle. They carved into the spherical demon, driving it away from Jarlen and drawing Uryx's wrath. The archfiend threw his arms forward and sent a spray of limbs from the river toward the Ferfolk. The soldiers knocked a few of them out of the air, but arms and legs latched onto their bodies and dug into their skin.

Jarlen jumped up and snatched the limbs from them five at a time, slicing them up with his swords.

"It's me, Jarlen," he said. "Can you understand me, Tyraz?"

The young Ferfolk dodged more body parts coming at him while helping Jarlen free his companions. Either he couldn't hear the words, or they weren't coming out of Jarlen's mouth the way he intended. When the battle was over, he'd figure out a way to communicate with his friend. Until then, however, he had to focus on ridding this world of the archfiends.

Uryx didn't slow his attacks, sending out one wave of body parts after another, far too many to defend against. There had to be another way to protect the Ferfolk. Jarlen wondered if he had the ability to counter the archfiend's attack, perhaps by summoning his own spirits to help. He raised a pair of arms, concentrated on the Black River, and chanted, "*Fero hlifian iewan gerecednis.*"

To his surprise, spirits in the river responded to his incantation, welling up under Uryx and throwing the archfiend onto the ground several paces away. Two Ferfolk charged at the demon, shouting war cries, but he recovered from his fall and countered their swings with ease.

Jarlen glanced at the other two battles. Dis had skewered the tentacled demon with one of his legs, but his opponent had immobilized him in a vice grip. Mammon, although wounded, seemed evenly matched against Obidicut, who had gained another foot on his already tall frame. Aiax led a dozen more Ferfolk soldiers from the east, but they didn't know which side to fight for. Jarlen understood their confusion. He couldn't let any of these demons win. They all had to go, starting with Uryx.

As he made his way toward Uryx, the new Ferfolk engaged him until Tyraz turned their attention elsewhere. Perhaps he didn't belong here, either. With his body gone, this was no longer his home.

"Uryx," he called out. "As you can see, I can communicate with the creatures in this river. Return to the netherworld, or

I'll turn them all against you."

The archfiend sunk his fingers into the chests of his opponents before facing Mammon.

"This world is not under your control," he said. "You've failed your end of the bargain."

"Do not leave me," growled Mammon as he moved the fight closer to the fountain.

Uryx ignored his plea, dived into the river, and disappeared. His river monsters, however, remained behind to continue the fight.

The spherical demon advanced on Jarlen again, but without Uryx's will to keep it under control, he quickly forced it into submission.

"You're lost without your master," he said and commanded it to back up. "Go to him with a message. This world will never belong to the demons."

The creature rolled backward until it plunged into the river. Jarlen turned his attention to Dis's opponent, but the tentacled creature resisted his will for several minutes. Perhaps it was more powerful because Uryx had created it first. He focused his concentration until he took over its mind. Instead of trying to crush Dis, he instructed the creature to lift the archfiend into the air, carry him back to the fountain, and jump through the portal.

When Tyraz looked his way, Jarlen pointed at Mammon and Dis with two hands and gestured at the fountain with two others. Tyraz understood him and led the Ferfolk around the remaining archfiends. With a coordinated attack, they pushed the demons toward the portal one small step at a time.

As soon as Uryx left this world, the Black River reversed its direction. The fountain subsided into the altar, pulling back both streams much faster than they'd expanded. The archfiend might have been gathering it back into the netherworld, but it didn't matter. Only two archfiends remained.

Jarlen headed toward the battle, along with another dozen Ferfolk warriors.

"You've lost," he said. "Leave this world forever."

Obidicut stepped away from Mammon and eyed Jarlen.

"It can't be you," he said. "I didn't think you could do it."

"Forget him," said Mammon, "and join me again. We can still take this world as our own."

"What about your army in the netherworld?" asked Obidicut.

"Half of it's yours if you stand with me now."

Tyraz and the Ferfolk soldiers redoubled their efforts, slashing and lunging with their weapons.

"You'll never defeat us," he shouted and plunged his pick into Mammon's leg.

Mammon smacked him aside, but more warriors surrounded him. Obidicut went after the Ferfolk, crushing one after another while ignoring his wounds. The weapons could harm the archfiends, but not enough to kill them.

With the Black River draining away, Jarlen worried that the portal might close soon. He charged forward, grabbed the archfiends, and carried them into the river. Far stronger than he realized, he held them firmly as he hopped through the portal into the netherworld. Behind him, Uryx sealed the link between worlds, probably to ensure he didn't lose any more of his precious river.

Jarlen released the demons and backed onto the neighboring hexagonal island, wondering when they would attack. Instead, both Mammon and Obidicut laughed.

"Welcome to your new home," said Mammon. "Prince Jarlen."

Chapter XXVI

Starting Anew

Chara paced around the campsite, weaving between the tall trees. Jarlen had said he'd return soon, but it had already been more than four hours. She didn't even have a chance to speak with him before he left with Obidicut, the fiend who'd just murdered an innocent Terun. How could he trust that evil demon?

"We've given him enough time," said Aiax. "The demons started guiding the river northward again. We can't wait for Jarlen any longer."

Tyraz rose from his seat near the fire.

"Many thanks for delaying any action," he said. "Jarlen might still come back to help, but we cannot let these fiends destroy our world."

"Men," said Aiax. "Prepare for battle."

Teruns and Ferfolk jumped at his command, sharing the lot of picks and hammers. There should have been more weapons that could affect demons, but these would have to suffice. Tyraz chose a sturdy pick and stopped in front of Chara.

"I don't suppose you'll lend me that Terun dagger of yours," he said.

Chara squeezed the hilt of the small blade.

"Then try to stay near me," said Tyraz. "I don't want to worry about you throughout the fight."

She followed him to the lookout point, where Aiax surveyed the scene. It appeared that Obidicut hadn't returned either, and there were no new demons around. The Teruns might have a chance to defeat them this time, especially with help from the Ferfolk soldiers.

"Destroy them all," shouted Aiax as he led the charge toward the Black River. "They do not belong in our world."

Chara and Tyraz rushed toward one of the triangular headed demons, while the rest of the group split up against the ice demons and the frog demons.

The triangular headed demon, wielding its two pronged pole arm, screeched out a warning before pointing its weapon at Tyraz. Chara held back several paces, thinking she could sneak closer once Tyraz had distracted their opponent. The demon lunged several times, much quicker than it appeared. Tyraz barely blocked the first two attacks, but the third one clipped his shoulder.

"You'll have to do more than scratch me," he said and went on the offensive.

He took a huge swing at the demon and stepped in closer when the two weapons hooked against each other. The demon removed one hand from the pole arm and raked Tyraz's chest, cackling as it drew three lines of blood with its claws.

This might be Chara's only chance. She sneaked around the demon, tiptoed closer, and drove the dagger at its back. The demon spun around and caught her arm before the blade reached its target. It lifted her into the air and drew back its weapon, ready to skewer her. She tried kicking its face, but it held her too far from its body. Its circular mouth didn't move much, but she knew it was smiling.

With a furious roar, Tyraz plunged the pick into the creature's chest. The demon dropped Chara as it fell backward, clutching the Terun weapon. Tyraz jumped forward to wrestle the pole arm away, while Chara scrambled closer and sank the dagger into its neck. A Terun or Ferfolk would have perished already, but this demon kept fighting back. It removed the pick and flung it twenty paces away, but Tyraz finally gained control of the creature's weapon. He pulled back and threw all his weight behind the attack, sending the long blade completely through the demon's chest.

Nearby, the demons had overpowered the Teruns. With the Ferfolk soldiers already engaged against their own powerful opponents, Aiax rushed in to help. By the time Tyraz was able to join the melee, Aiax had torn through a half dozen demons, saving most of the Teruns. Unfortunately, the Ferfolk commander had sustained heavy wounds. Tyraz destroyed the last remaining pair of ice demons but couldn't save Aiax. He sat with the body as the Ferfolk soldiers joined him. They'd lost their leader and a true hero.

Without anyone to force it northward, the end of the river expanded in all directions. Each piece of vegetation in its way withered at the slightest touch, but at least the river wasn't heading straight for the Cold Ocean anymore. Hopefully, Jarlen would return from wherever he went and find a way to stop it.

The Ferfolk and Teruns mourned their losses long into the night, but Chara couldn't join them. Jarlen hadn't come back, the Black River kept expanding into this world, and several archfiends still roamed the land. Morning came and went, as did afternoon, before anyone else was ready to discuss plans.

"The river keeps growing larger," she said. "Eventually it'll reach the ocean and the cursed island. We have to stop it before it destroys our world."

"Then we have to defeat the robed demon near the altar," said Tyraz. "I'm sure that fiend is pulling that black morass through from the netherworld."

"How do you plan to destroy him?" asked Chara. "We

couldn't best Obidicut, and the robed fiend is probably much more powerful."

"Our only hope is a full assault, ignoring anything else. We focus on killing the robed demon no matter who or what else shows up. Many lives will be lost, but we will prevail."

He strolled around the campsite, stopped behind Chara, and placed his hand on her shoulder.

"I have a different mission for you, however."

"I'm fighting with you," said Chara without looking at him.

She tried to stand but he held her down.

"You will not be part of this battle," he said. "You will remain hidden from the demons. If we lose, you must recruit the rest of my people. Aiax sent them into the desert to hide, but I fear no part of this world will be safe."

Chara laughed nervously.

"They won't listen to me. It would be much better for you to recruit them."

"I certainly would have more influence among the Ferfolk." Tyraz released his grip as he maneuvered around to face her. "But you must also work with the Arboreals. Convince the two groups to join against the demons or lose their entire world."

Chara stared into his desperate eyes. He was truly concerned about everyone. No matter what happened to him against the robed archfiend, he needed to hope there would still be a chance for victory. Chara couldn't let him down.

"If the demons win tomorrow," she said, "I'll bring back an army of Ferfolk, Arboreals, and Teruns to continue the fight."

He removed a weak smile from his face as he turned away from her and ordered the group to get some sleep before their big confrontation.

Chara handed him the Terun dagger, but he closed her fingers around the hilt and pushed it back.

"You'll need it," he said, "along with any other Terun weapons you can recover from our battle."

"You're acting as if you've already lost," said Chara.

"We have to prepare for the worst." Tyraz kissed her on the cheek. "You already noted how powerful these archfiends are. Just make sure you stay well hidden."

"The robed demon will not see me." Chara gave him a quick hug and turned her face to hide a few tears. "I promise."

She wasn't sure if anyone else rested that night, but she stayed awake wondering what had happened to Jarlen and how they could find an advantage over the demon lords. It would have helped if Jarlen had written down all he knew about necromancy and the netherworld, but they'd just have to make do with what they'd already learned.

By morning, Chara felt as if she'd been awake for a week. She wanted to rest more, but a commotion from the area where the Black River gushed out of the altar drew the Ferfolk army into battle sooner than they'd planned. Chara kept back more than a hundred paces, hiding behind a dense thicket. She had difficulty watching the fight, but no demons, including flying ones, could spy on her.

It appeared that the archfiends must have had a falling out, because Obidicut and Dis were attacking Mammon and a river monster. Another one of the river monsters had turned on its robed creator. Jarlen had to be involved somehow, but Chara couldn't spot him anywhere. She drew the Terun dagger, and crawled through the forest. Having Jarlen around changed everything, possibly even turning the battle in their favor. If he needed help in any way, she'd give it to him.

Chara kept far from the fighting on her circuitous path around the altar, but she couldn't find Jarlen anywhere. After a series of unintelligible shouts between the robed demon and its opponent, the archfiend allowed the river to consume him, probably sending him back to the netherworld. Chara wanted to call out to Jarlen, but it was too dangerous. She continued the trek on her hands and knees, picking up a thick coating of mud along the way. As she nestled behind a wide trunk, the river monster that had been fighting Dis picked up the archfiend and carried him into the river. Soon after that, the robed demon's opponent scooped up both Mammon and Obidicut and jumped into the river with them as the black waters reversed their direction.

A great cheer rang out from the Ferfolk and Teruns. They'd defeated the demon lords, but Chara knew Jarlen had been the key to victory. He must have had a reason for remaining hidden during the battle, but now that it was over, he'd show himself.

Chara brushed herself off and ran toward the celebration.

"They're already planning the feasts," said Tyraz, pressing his hand against a wound, "but we've lost so much. I don't feel like celebrating."

"Nor do I," said Chara. "We have to look for Jarlen."

"I certainly was surprised that he didn't show up," said Tyraz. "Where do you think he is?"

Chara glanced around the forest, focusing on the former path of the southern stream. The Black River had destroyed all vegetation in its path, leaving a corridor several paces wide leading away from the altar.

"Let's try south," she said. "If we reach the end without any luck, then we'll follow the northern branch. We must find out what happened to him. You know he was responsible for our victory somehow."

"I have no doubt," said Tyraz with a nod. "Let's get started."

The corridor through the forest never veered from its course.

It cut through trees and shrubs in Ferfolk territory and continued its path deep into the Arboreal Forest. Chara and Tyraz followed it day and night, stopping only for brief rests when they were too tired to walk. During their hike, animals seemed to avoid the unnatural clearing. Not a single bird or squirrel crossed their path for two days, making the trip much quieter than a casual stroll through the woods outside of Kroflund.

"That looks like the end of the stream," said Tyraz as he jogged ahead a few paces.

Chara sped up to catch him, stopping within a large clearing of damaged trees. Huge limbs lay scattered about, having been violently torn off their trunks. Farther south, the Arboreal Forest appeared even denser than usual, unwilling to let anyone pass, including the Black River.

"I guess he wasn't down this way," said Chara as she sat on one of the downed logs. "We'll head back after I rest for a moment."

Tyraz joined her on the seat and stared into the sky. Even though he hadn't said anything, she knew he was hoping to find Jarlen. They hadn't known each other a long time, but they'd saved each other's lives many times. Chara only met both of them recently but felt as if they'd been friends for a lifetime.

A faint munching noise came from nearby. Chara wouldn't have investigated, but it was the only sound she'd heard other than from themselves. She hopped over a few more logs to where a body lay pinned under a heavy branch surrounded by scavengers. Chara scared the animals away as she rushed toward the body. A feeling of dread overcame her, and when the face came into view, her legs collapsed.

"It's Jarlen," she said and looked back to Tyraz with tears in her eyes. "He's dead."

"It can't be," said Tyraz, grabbing the large branch and lifting it off Jarlen. "Wake up!"

He shook the body ever more violently until Chara pulled him away and buried her face in his chest. This was no coincidence. Jarlen dying at the edge of the southern stream proved he had something to do with the demons turning on one another, and Chara wouldn't let his sacrifice remain unknown.

"Stay with him," she said. "I'll find some Arboreals to give him a proper burial."

"You're not going alone." Tyraz held her tightly. "There might still be demons around."

She tried to shrug him off, but he wouldn't let go until she relaxed.

"We weren't there to protect him when he was alive," she said, "but we will not leave him alone in death."

"Then I'll carry him," said Tyraz, "all the way back to Kroflund if necessary."

He removed his shirt to wrap part of the body before hoisting it onto his shoulder. Chara led him away from the stream's path of destruction into the dense forest, shouting every few steps. After a few hours, a group of five Arboreals surrounded them.

"It took you long enough," said Chara. "Go find Cassor. Tell him that Jarlen gave his life to send the demons back to the netherworld."

Two of the Arboreals leaped back into the trees and disappeared, while the others gathered large leaves to cover Jarlen's body. A quick incantation melded the leaves into a hard shell.

"Will this heal him?" asked Chara.

The Arboreals' somber faces destroyed her hopeful smile. She sat next to the cocoon and waited, refusing to move even as night approached.

Late the next day, Cassor arrived with Aquila and a dozen other Arboreals. He wrapped his arms around Chara and held her for several minutes.

"Join us," he whispered in her ear before accompanying Aquila in a soft chant.

Vines lowered from the treetops, looped around the cocoon, and raised it up into the branches. From there, more vines and branches passed the body from one tree to another, carrying it northward, probably toward Hillswood. Aquila led the procession through the trees, while Cassor stayed behind on the ground with Chara and Tyraz. They continued through the afternoon and into the night until Cassor stopped them somewhere outside of Hillswood. Chara couldn't tell how close they were to the hamlet, but several new Arboreals joined their group, possibly Jarlen's distant relatives.

They surrounded Cassor and Aquila and sang a mournful tune that caused vines to lower Jarlen's cocoon to the ground. Each of the Arboreals laid a flower on the cocoon before retreating to the back of the crowd. The two elders were the last to leave their offering, after which they sent the rest of the Arboreals away.

"The next portion of the ceremony is typically attended by close family members only," said Aquila. "Jarlen would have considered both of you his siblings. Please stay."

Chara and Tyraz huddled closer as the Arboreal song decreased in tempo. Roots came up from beneath the soil, wrapped around the body, and gently pulled it under. Chara took Tyraz's hand in hers for comfort. She still found it difficult to believe her friend was never coming back.

The ritual lasted several hours, but Chara wanted it to continue forever. As long as the elders kept chanting, she didn't have to say her final goodbye, but as the sunlight waned, the singing came to an end.

"Please remain here in Hillswood, at least for the next few days," said Cassor. "We will celebrate Jarlen's life and recall his amazing feats."

Chara looked at Tyraz and received a sullen nod. She didn't feel like attending a party, but this was a good start to ensuring his sacrifice didn't go unnoticed. Perhaps the Arboreals knew more than she did about his involvement with the demons. She'd make sure to write down everything she learned in Hillswood before moving on to Kroflund and Terun City. Nobody would forget Jarlen's name after she was done.

The celebration lasted a week, occasionally lifting Chara's spirits during the brief moments she forgot about their recent losses. She'd borrowed writing instruments and a stack of blank leaf paper from Aquila to document everything she learned about Jarlen and had already filled two score pages. The more she wrote about his life, the more she realized some of his troubles could have been avoided if he had the proper knowledge about necromancy. She found Cassor recounting a tale to a group of tenderlings and pulled him aside when he was done.

"There will be time for writing after the celebration," he said. "You should join us around the Gathering Tree. Even Tyraz seems to be more relaxed around us recently."

"Maybe the battle with the demons will bring the Ferfolk and Arboreals closer," said Chara with a smile, "but I'm concerned about anyone following Jarlen's path in the future. He needed a proper warning about necromancy, something nobody had given him."

"That school of magic died with him," said Cassor, "but I understand your worries. What can I do to help?"

"I'd like to learn more about Jarlen and his fascination with necromancy."

Cassor shied away from her with a look of horror on his face.

"I'm no wizard," she said. "I just want to document everything that happened. This way, any future wizards will know the risks involved."

"You are welcome to live in Hillswood as long as you wish," said Cassor. "You may speak with anyone in the hamlet and research the topic in our library."

"I can't read Arboreal."

"Then you'll learn." Cassor's tension eased. "When you're done, we can help preserve the pages so they last many springs."

Chara removed the Terun dagger from her belt.

"Do you think the Teruns would forge this into a cover for the book?" she asked. "It will protect the contents and show future generations what type of metal affects demons—in case they need it."

"I'm sure they would oblige for such a worthy cause." Cassor took her hand and led her toward the center of town. "For now, please put down the book and have some fun."

Chara joined the festivities for a few hours, but spent most of her time interviewing Arboreals about their knowledge of Jarlen. By the end of the celebration, Tyraz looked more relaxed than Chara had ever seen him.

"Are you done with your book?" he asked. "It's time to return to Kroflund."

She'd been too scared to tell him about her project, but she couldn't postpone it any longer.

"I'm not going back to Kroflund yet," she said as she averted her eyes.

"Do you need another few days?"

She gathered a few pages to show him.

"This will be a warning to future necromancers," she said. "I have to finish it."

Tyraz held her shoulders and turned her to face him.

"How long do you need?"

She wiped a few tears from her eyes.

"This could take many years," she said. "There is so much to learn."

"Then I'll stay here and help you."

Her heart jumped as she pulled him close.

"But what about Kroflund?"

"The city will be rebuilt and repopulated with or without me," he said. "Besides, I've grown accustomed to Arboreal food. I'd miss it if we moved back."

Chara handed him a few blank pages and a twig pen. Tyraz had chosen her over his own people. She gave him a broad smile. Together, they'd ensure the safety of future generations.

The End

Glossary

Aiax	Aiax is the military leader of the Ferfolk. His left hand is missing two fingers, he has a scar up the left arm, and his chin is covered in rough whiskers.
Aquila	Aquila, granddaughter of Falgoran, is one of the three Arboreal elders. She keeps her hair in a bun with three feathers and several loose strands.
Arboreal	Arboreals are a race of tree-dwellers from the tropics with pale green skin. They are polite, slow to make decisions, excellent climbers, and able to speak through nearly imperceptible facial expressions.
Arboreal Forest	The Arboreal Forest is an expansive forest covering the southern portion of the continent.
Blaeculf	A Blaeculf is an intelligent and aggressive canine, twice the size of a gray wolf, with a muscular body covered in black fur.
Cassor	Cassor, one of the three Arboreal elders, wears his long green hair in braids and has scar along entire arm.
Chara	Chara is a human female from the town of Luceton on the Cold Ocean. She remained behind when the rest of the humans left to find a new home.
Cold Ocean	The Cold Ocean is a large body of water north of the continent.
Dark Whey	Dark Whey is a sticky, black substance made from bone powder and used by Necromancers.
Dis	Dis is a demon prince and former ruler of the Lava Plains in the netherworld. He ap-

	pears as either a huge spider crab, a human with horns on his head, or a small worm with a spike on one end of its body.
Elementalism	The manipulation of air, earth, fire, and water.
Eslinor	Eslinor, one of the three Arboreal elders, is beautiful with long hair. Some of her ancestors were human.
Ferfolk	The Ferfolk are leather-skinned warriors from the desert. They are resistant to the direct effects of magic.
Forbidden Wood	The Forbidden Wood is the remains of the human city of Zairn. It is surrounded by an enchanted wall of thorns.
Fracodian	A Fracodian is a hairy, pug-faced cross between a human and a bear. Some are able to become berserk, gaining strength and speed for a limited time.
Gathering Tree	The Gathering Tree is the center of an Arboreal hamlet. It is frequently used for meetings by the village elders.
Great Library	The Great Library was formerly a monastery in fourth ring of Zairn but now holds the largest collection of books and scrolls in the land.
Great Ocean	The Great Oceans is a large body of water east of the continent.
Hillswood	Hillswood is an Arboreal hamlet located in the center of the Arboreal Forest. It is home to the three Arboreal elders.
Jarlen	Jarlen is a young Arboreal whose mother was human. He has the typical light green skin of an Arboreal but the brown hair and eyes of a human. As Zehuti's apprentice, he learned both Thaumaturgy and Necro-

Krofhaven	mancy. Krofhaven, the largest Ferfolk city, is located just south of the Pensorean Mountains.
Mammon	Mammon is a demon prince with the goal of ruling the entire netherworld. He appears as either a giant covered in white hair, an enormous golden lizard, or a humanoid with geometric shapes for his body and limbs.
Necromancy	Necromancy is the study of death and the dead.
Obidicut	Obidicut is a demon prince and former second in command to Dis. He appears as a tall human with black skin and spikes on his body.
Pensorean Mountains	The Pensorean Mountains separate the human lands from the Cold Ocean east of Terun City. They are covered by white pine forests.
Sabretooth	A Sabretooth is a powerful feline predator with long fangs. Arboreals will occasionally tame sabretooths as attack cats against large targets.
Septu	Septu, second in command to Aiax, has a deep hatred of Arboreals.
Sorcery	Sorcery is the summoning and controlling of spirits.
Tenderling	A Tenderling is a young Arboreal only a few springs from becoming an adult.
Terun	The Teruns are a race of mountain-dwellers. Short and manipulative, they are the masters of metal and stone.
Terun City	Terun City is the mountainside home of Terun traders, healers, and merchants. It is

	less prestigious than the Undercity but more impressive to outsiders.
The Black River	The Black River is composed of spirits instead of water. It runs between the different realms of the netherworld.
Tyraz	Tyraz is a young Ferfolk warrior who befriends Jarlen.
Undercity	The Undercity is the lower half of Terun City, located beneath the Tooth of the Gods.
Uryx	Uryx is a demon prince and ruler of the Black River. He appears as a skeleton in a black robe.
Wastelands	The Wastelands is a vast desert covering the central and western portion of the continent.

Legends of the Four Races

The Legacy of Ogma by E. A. Rappaport 978-0-9789393-0-4 292 Pages $12.95	The thief wants riches. The knight wants justice. The warrior wants a good battle. The sorcerer wants power. Each adventurer carries a mysterious crystal sphere that will lead to a long-hidden secret beneath the sea.
Forging Paradise by E. A. Rappaport 978-0-9789393-2-8 306 Pages $12.95	After a supposedly mythical race of desert warriors invades the human territories and destroys every city in its path, five former enemies must travel together into the netherworld and harness the unpredictable power of demons to defeat the seemingly invincible army.
Shadow from the Past by E. A. Rappaport 978-0-9789393-4-2 282 Pages $12.95	Mysterious fires fan an ancient grudge between Arboreals and Ferfolk, pushing lifelong enemies toward a devastating war. Two young strangers must overcome their mutual mistrust and uncover the real force threatening to ravage the land.
Secrets of the Undercity by E. A. Rappaport 978-0-9789393-3-5 308 Pages $12.95	Abandoned and betrayed as a child, Halia seeks revenge. Frustrated by his limited abilities, Oswynn seeks powerful magic. The paths of the thief and apprentice cross when battling an eruption of dangerous half-breed creatures that might destroy an entire kingdom.
The Lesser Evil by E. A. Rappaport 978-0-9789393-5-9 306 Pages $12.95	Villagers and animals are disappearing from the coastal towns of the Cold Sea. The only ones who can restore peace are a necromancer, obsessed with bones and death, and a cunning thief who only cares about protecting his gold.
Lyche by E. A. Rappaport 978-0-9789393-6-6 316 Pages $12.95	An evil spirit, trapped within a volcano for ages, escapes its fiery prison with a vow to destroy all life. When no one else believes such devastation is possible, a young wizard and his companions must oppose the powerful creature on their own.
Voices from Below by E. A. Rappaport 978-0-9789393-7-3 326 Pages $12.95	When Halia and Xarun hear cries for help coming from their recently deceased friend, they must find a way to open a portal to the netherworld and send aid.
Whence Chaos Born by E. A. Rappaport 978-0-9789393-8-0 308 Pages $12.95	In a world ravaged by the awesome forces of nature, where homes and families are ripped apart by the winds and water of massive tsunamis and terrible earthquakes, a hero rises over the gale.
The Black Flood by E. A. Rappaport 978-0-9789393-9-7 296 Pages $12.95	Demons have breached the void and intend to claim the world as their own. Even with the combined forces of the Arboreals, Ferfolk, and Teruns, little can stand in their way.

Legends of the Four Races
An Interlocking Matrix of Nine Fantasy Novels

Please visit **http://www.owlking.com** for information about:

The Weapons Trilogy: Books 1, 2, 3
- I – *The Legacy of Ogma*
- II – *Forging Paradise*
- III – *Shadow from the Past*

The Transmuter Trilogy: Books 4, 5, 6
- I – *Secrets of the Undercity*
- II – *The Lesser Evil*
- III – *Lyche*

The Netherworld Trilogy: Books 7, 8, 9
- I – *Voices from Below*
- II – *Whence Chaos Born*
- III – *The Black Flood*

The Betrayal Trilogy: Books 1, 4, 7
- I – *The Legacy of Ogma*
- II – *Secrets of the Undercity*
- III – *Voices from Below*

The War Trilogy: Books 2, 5, 8
- I – *Forging Paradise*
- II – *The Lesser Evil*
- III – *Whence Chaos Born*

The Necromancer Trilogy: Books 3, 6, 9
- I – *Shadow from the Past*
- II – *Lyche*
- III – *The Black Flood*

Made in the USA
Middletown, DE
13 August 2021

45967451R00166